"Don't leave me again."

"That's the last thing I want." Frustrated because he couldn't make her understand what she meant to him, Reilly said, "I won't let them hurt you, Mandy. If it means leaving, I'll leave. If it means staying, I'll do that instead. But I won't let them get you." He drew a sharp breath. "I'll kill them all before I'll let them touch you."

"You…" He'd shocked her with his brutal honesty. "You don't really mean that."

"You wanted the truth. That's the only truth I know." She didn't actually move, but her eyelids flickered, and he sensed her inner withdrawal. "I was a good cop, Mandy. I won't say I never bent the rules, but I was a good cop."

"Then how can you talk about killing, as if—"

He cut her off. "Because you're more important. If anything happens to you, I'll take them to hell with me."

Dear Reader,

It's no surprise that Intimate Moments is *the* place to go when you want the best mix of excitement and romance, and it's authors like Sharon Sala who have earned the line that reputation. Now, with *Ryder's Wife,* Sharon begins her first Intimate Moments miniseries, THE JUSTICE WAY. The three Justice brothers are men with a capital M—and they're about to fall in love with a capital L. This month join Ryder as he marries heiress Casey Ruban for reasons of convenience and stays around for love.

Popular Beverly Barton is writing in the miniseries vein, too, with *A Man Like Morgan Kane,* the latest in THE PROTECTORS. Beverly knows how to steam up a romance, that's for sure! In *Wife, Mother...Lover?* Sally Tyler Hayes spins a poignant tale of a father, a family and the woman who gives them all their second chance at happiness—and love. *Reilly's Return* also marks Amelia Autin's return. This is a wonderfully suspenseful tale about a hero who had to fake his own death to protect the woman he loved—and what happens when she suddenly finds out he's really still alive. In *Temporary Marriage,* Leann Harris takes us to the jungles of South America for a tale of a sham marriage that leads to a very real honeymoon. Finally, Dani Criss is back with *For Kaitlyn's Sake,* a reunion story with all the passion you could wish for.

Let all six of these terrific books keep you warm as the winter nights grow colder, and come back next month for even more of the most excitingly romantic reading around, right here in Silhouette Intimate Moments.

Yours,

Leslie J. Wainger
Senior Editor and Editorial Coordinator

Please address questions and book requests to:
Silhouette Reader Service
U.S.: 3010 Walden Ave., P.O. Box 1325, Buffalo, NY 14269
Canadian: P.O. Box 609, Fort Erie, Ont. L2A 5X3

REILLY'S RETURN

AMELIA AUTIN

Published by Silhouette Books

America's Publisher of Contemporary Romance

SILHOUETTE BOOKS

ISBN 0-373-07820-X

REILLY'S RETURN

This edition published by arrangement with Harlequin Books S.A.

® and TM are trademarks of Harlequin Books S.A., used under license.
Trademarks indicated with ® are registered in the United States Patent
and Trademark Office, the Canadian Trade Marks Office and in other
countries.

Printed in U.S.A.

Books by Amelia Autin

Silhouette Intimate Moments

Gideon's Bride #666
Reilly's Return #820

AMELIA AUTIN

is a voracious reader who can't bear to part with a good book—or a good movie. She owns over four thousand titles—including romance, science fiction, adventure and mystery—as well as hundreds of movies from the thirties, forties and fifties.

Amelia's first novel, *Gideon's Bride,* won the Romance Writers of America's Golden Heart Award. Like *Gideon's Bride,* the setting for *Reilly's Return*—the Bighorn Mountains of Wyoming—resulted from nine months spent in that state, where Amelia fell in love with the people, the lifestyle and the picturesque landscape.

Amelia loves to travel, and has lived in or visited thirty-seven of the fifty states in the U.S. She currently resides in Minnesota, where the long winter nights create the perfect backdrop for writing, and she just completed her second term as treasurer of Romance Writers of America.

For my bookend sisters,
Diana and Peggie, with love.
One taught me to read, the other to write…sort of.

Chapter 1

The lock was pathetically easy to pick.

Reilly O'Neill cursed under his breath as the tumblers fell into place after only a few seconds' work. What the hell was Mandy thinking of, still having such a worthless lock on her back door? Her house was so isolated, she might as well just put up a sign saying Rob Me. This thing wouldn't keep a determined child out, much less someone bent on doing her harm.

The doorknob turned and the door swung open. Reilly slipped inside. Even after almost twelve months away he remembered the simple layout of Mandy's house, so he didn't need light to guide him. Surefooted, cloaked in darkness, he made his way to her bedroom.

He'd been shadowing Mandy for the past three days, not wanting to approach her in public, and by now he knew her routine. She'd be home in a few minutes, at about a quarter to midnight. The first thing she'd do was go to her bedroom, strip out of her clothes, and take a shower. And he would be waiting.

At one time in his life, Reilly would never have been

able to wait like this, to see Mandy from a distance and not go to her. But waiting—and watching—had become second nature to him now. Amazing how your priorities change when just staying alive long enough to see tomorrow's sunrise enters the equation. Though the immediate danger was supposed to be over, his instincts said otherwise, and old habits were hard to break. Anyway, it was safer for her this way. The last thing he ever wanted to do was jeopardize Mandy.

Reilly paused for a moment just inside Mandy's bedroom, as a once-familiar scent came back to him—the lilac fragrance that Mandy always wore. Even her sheets had smelled of lilacs, he remembered now. With that thought came memories of the two of them entwined on her bed, her long, honey-blond hair streaming across his chest, the sheets pulled around them as their bodies cooled.

A sudden surge of desire hit him, and Reilly cursed again. It had been far too long since he'd held her, far too long since he'd made love to her in this room. Somehow he'd forgotten how the smell of lilacs affected him.

No, that wasn't right. Not forgotten, exactly. He just hadn't let himself remember, or he'd have gone crazy with longing during all these months away from her.

He sat on the edge of Mandy's bed, then stretched out, overwhelming his senses with her scent. If he was going to torture himself with memories, he decided, he might as well make it worth his while.

Mandy. She'd been the best thing that ever happened to him, a vivid patch of color in an otherwise black-and-white world. The months he'd spent with her were the happiest in his life. Now, lying in her bed, he could almost hear her voice, husky with passion, calling his name. No one but Mandy could say "Reilly" quite the way she could.

It wasn't his real name. It wasn't even the name on the six-month-old California driver's license in his wallet. In fact, he'd lost track of the number of different aliases he'd used in his career. But Reilly was the name Mandy knew him by, so Reilly he would be once more.

God, he was tired. Tired of running. Tired of waiting. Well, it wouldn't be long now. She'd be here soon, and he'd hold her and love her to his heart's content. And he'd never leave her again. Never.

Amanda Edwards trudged toward her back door, juggling a bag of books, her purse, keys, and a take-out container of food she'd picked up at the Lucky Horseshoe Bar and Grill. She no longer wanted it, but her concerned friends harassed her when she skipped meals, so she figured she'd at least eat a few bites before tossing the rest.

Once on the back porch, Mandy dropped the book bag beside the door and fitted her house key into the lock. She noted absently that the door was already unlocked when she turned the key, though it didn't really register. She'd always been careless about locking the doors when she left, but in the small town of Black Rock, Wyoming, it wasn't much of an issue.

Inside, she flicked on the kitchen light with her elbow, then dumped everything on the table, kicking off her shoes at the same time. Her feet, like the rest of her, ached. She headed for her bedroom, unbuttoning her blouse as she went.

You're pushing yourself too hard, she told herself for the millionth time, as she rotated her tired shoulder muscles to relieve the strain of another late night spent cataloguing her bookstore's inventory and entering it on the computer she'd recently bought. It was a tedious task, made all the more so because she'd turned down all offers of help from her friends. It wasn't so much that she wanted to do all the work herself, but rather to stretch the monumental task out as long as possible. She needed to keep busy, especially at night, so she wouldn't have time to think.

Exhausted, she pushed open her bedroom door. If she had the time, she might have stopped and wondered how her body could make it on so little sleep these days. Maybe it was just as well she didn't sleep much, though, because

the one thing she couldn't keep on a tight emotional rein
was her dreams. Or her nightmares.

Without hearing a thing, Mandy suddenly knew she
wasn't alone. A shadow moved swiftly in the darkness, and
her scream was cut short when a strong hand closed over
her mouth. Another arm encircled her waist, pulling her
backwards against a hard, male body. Terrified, she clawed
at his hand and arms to escape, her heart pounding so hard
blood drummed in her ears. Her assailant's iron grip tightened, squeezing the breath from her lungs.

"Damn it, Mandy, stop it. It's me." The low rumble, a
voice once as familiar to her ears as her own, shocked
Mandy into stillness. Emotions long pent up burst into life,
and she sagged against the muscled arm imprisoning her.

"Reilly." She moaned the name against the muffling
hand, then suddenly her mouth was freed as both arms
turned her around and enveloped her. Lips sought hers—
warm, alive, passionate. And for a wild moment Mandy let
herself believe, kissing him back with equal ardor. Though
a moment ago she'd been desperate to escape, she now
sought to get closer. Her hands clutched at his shoulders,
as if she could pull him into herself and keep him there,
safe, forever.

Then reality crashed in and she tore herself away. Sur-
prisingly, the man let her go. Mandy's eyes strained to see
in the darkness as she fumbled behind her for the light
switch. The sudden glare of light blinded her for a second,
and she blinked. Then gasped. A stranger stood across from
her. A tall, dark-haired stranger with Reilly's voice.

"You're not Reilly." She couldn't quite disguise her
fear, but went on the attack nevertheless. "Who are you?"

A harsh laugh was surprised out of him, followed by a
soft curse as he touched his face. "Damn! I forgot...."

Pain stabbed through Mandy's chest like a knife thrust.
The tone, the inflection, everything about this man's voice
poignantly reminded her of Reilly. *It can't be Reilly,* she
thought frantically. *Reilly is dead.*

A queer, set expression settled over the stranger's face

as he stared at her. "Have I changed so much, Mandy? My face, yes. But when you kissed me, I thought..."

She shook her head. "You're dead," she whispered. "Reilly's dead."

"No." His lips tightened into a thin line beneath his mustache. "I've been to hell and back, but I'm alive. And I plan to stay that way."

Spots danced at the edges of Mandy's vision, darkness closing in. Then her knees buckled, and for the first time in her thirty-one years she fainted.

Reilly caught her as she fell, sweeping her into his arms and carrying her to the bed. He laid her down on top of the pale blue comforter, then took both of her hands in his much larger ones, rubbing them with a surprising gentleness.

He whispered her name once, and then again. All the while his senses were drinking in the sight, scent and feel of her. She smelled of warm woman and lilacs, and her lightly tanned skin was petal-soft beneath his scarred fingertips. She was even more lovely than he remembered, yet different somehow, as if suffering had refined the all-American-girl prettiness into womanly beauty. The signs of suffering were obvious: mauve shadows beneath her eyes that had never been there before, tiny lines bracketing her down-curved lips. She was thinner, too, than she'd been twelve months ago, although her breasts, cupped in the lace-trimmed bra revealed by her unbuttoned blouse, had lost none of their fullness.

But it didn't matter how she looked. She was his Mandy, and that said it all. The only thing that mattered to him right now was that the woman he loved had stared at him as if he were a stranger. Maybe to her he was.

Damn it, he wouldn't think like that. He'd come back as soon as he could, as soon as it was safe for her. The only reason he'd left her behind in the first place was that he hadn't wanted to put her in harm's way. If she thought she could forget what they'd once had, she'd better think again.

Just because my face has changed doesn't mean I've

changed, Mandy. I'm still the same man inside, the same man you fell in love with before. And I'm the man you'll love again.

Aloud, he said, "Mandy, wake up!"

She stirred, her head tossing on the pillow as if she were denying something. But Reilly wasn't about to let her deny *him.* "Come on, Mandy," he said softly, urgently. "I know you can hear me. Wake up now."

Mandy's eyelids flickered, but she resisted, not wanting the dream to end. How many times had she dreamed she heard Reilly calling her name, then surfaced to face harsh reality with tears streaming down her face? It seemed so real this time. If she could only keep from waking, maybe, just maybe...

"Damn it Mandy! I said wake up!"

Her eyes flew open, her hand instinctively touching the old-fashioned gold locket she wore around her neck, her talisman against the nightmares. But this wasn't a dream. It was frighteningly real.

"Reilly?" Her brain said no, it couldn't be. Yet her heart, which she'd thought was dead inside her, said yes. *Yes!*

How *could* it be him? Mandy blinked, her gaze focusing on the stranger's face, moving from feature to feature, searching for proof that her mind could accept. His eyes. Yes, those were Reilly's eyes, tawny-brown like a cat's, with tiny flecks of green. But nothing else was recognizable until he smiled at her. She caught her breath when the smile beneath the dark mustache revealed gleaming white teeth, perfect except for the slight overlapping of the front two. Just like Reilly's.

"Hey, lady." He relaxed a little, and his smile deepened. "When you fall for a man, you really *fall,* don't you?"

Her eyes slid closed for an instant at the memory of another man saying those same teasing words to her so many heartbreaking months ago. Her lashes were damp when her eyes opened again.

In wonder and disbelief she reached for him. Then doubt

seized her a split second before she touched his cheek, and she pulled her hand back abruptly. "No," she said, shaking her head. "No."

The stranger's smile faded, his lips settling into a grim line. Suddenly Mandy realized how vulnerable she was. Her pulse kicked into overdrive and she panicked, scrambling from the bed. To her surprise, he made no move to stop her, not even when she put the length of the room between them.

Mandy blushed when she noticed that her blouse was gaping open. She rebuttoned it as fast as her trembling fingers allowed, then confronted the stranger her heart kept insisting was Reilly.

"I don't understand," she said, as much to herself as to him, her voice shaking slightly. She took a deep, calming breath and let it out slowly. "I *saw* it." And for a brief moment she let herself remember the horror of seeing Reilly's Blazer burst into flames, with him trapped inside. Her voice shook again as she whispered, "I saw you *die*."

His brows snapped together and he frowned as if perplexed. He started toward her, his hand outstretched. Then something crashed through the bedroom window, shattering the glass and the silence. "Get down!" he yelled, diving for her, knocking her off her feet. He rolled her into the corner, shielding her with his body.

There was the smell of gasoline followed by a whooshing sound, and the whole room ignited. Mandy watched in horror as rivulets of fire streaked in all directions, following the gasoline's path across the hardwood floors. Flames lapped everywhere—her great-grandmother's braided rag rug and white lace curtains, the hem of Mandy's chenille robe hanging from a hook on the closet door. Just that quickly, smoke began swirling around them.

The stranger slid to one side. "Come on," he yelled above the crackling roar. "We've got to get out of here!"

He crawled toward the door, dragging Mandy beside him. Too shocked by everything that had happened, and with no time to think clearly, she followed him blindly.

They avoided the grasping edges of the fire and rapidly made their way toward the kitchen, but when Mandy would have stood up to open the back door, he dragged her back down.

"No. It's not safe. They're probably waiting out there." He coughed to clear his lungs. "We'll have to use the trapdoor," he rasped, heading for that corner of the room.

Mandy blinked at him, baffled by the first part of his speech. The last part she clearly understood. She didn't know how he knew, though. She'd never told anyone, not even Reilly, about the trapdoor leading to the root cellar her great-grandfather had dug into the side of the mountain behind the cabin. But now wasn't the time to ask. She'd have to add it to her list of unanswered questions, which was growing longer with each passing minute.

He had the trapdoor open now, and was beckoning to her. Mandy hesitated for only a second, but it was one second too long. Glass exploded inward as the window over the kitchen sink shattered, followed by the now terrifyingly familiar whooshing sound. She screamed. A searing wall of flame sprang up almost instantly, dividing the room, and Mandy scuttled backward to escape. She wasn't quick enough. A tongue of fire raced toward her with horrifying speed, and caught her.

"No!" The man who called himself Reilly was there before Mandy knew it, passing through the inferno as if impervious to its touch. He smothered the flames licking at her clothes with his bare hands, ignoring the pain he must be feeling, ignoring his own clothes' smoldering edges. But even though she was nearly in shock, Mandy had the presence of mind to do what she could to help him by slapping at the glowing embers.

He didn't seem to need her help. He dragged his shirt off, crushing it between his powerful hands to finish the job she started. Crouching beside her, he reached over and jerked open the refrigerator door, letting it swing wide. Jars and containers scattered, falling helter-skelter as he pulled out a half-full water jug. He uncapped it and soaked his shirt, then splashed the rest of the water over Mandy's hair and clothes. The sudden coldness surprised a gasp out of her, but he didn't stop there. He draped his wet shirt over her head, then swept her into his arms.

"Hang on."

She couldn't see a thing, could only trust him. She clung tightly as she felt him duck down, gather his strength, then leap through the flames again.

This time when he passed through the fire he grunted in pain, a sound that reverberated in Mandy's soul. It seemed like an eternity, but it was actually only seconds later that he set her down and stripped the shirt off her head. She barely had time to recover her balance before he began pushing her through the trapdoor.

The fire raged on, the intense heat and smoke pressing against them like a mighty hand. Mandy glanced upward, saw paint shriveling on the walls beside them, and knew they had only a few seconds left. She grasped the sides of the ladder, refusing to acknowledge the blisters that had formed on her palms, praying that the wood hadn't rotted in the years since the last time she'd gone down this ladder.

The rungs held, and she descended quickly into darkness, counting each rung automatically, just as she'd done in childhood. Above her, the stranger with Reilly's voice began his own descent, blocking out most of the light with his body. Then he pulled the trapdoor shut, cutting off the last of the light.

The acrid smells of singed hair, wood smoke and musty, damp earth closed around Mandy in the dark, and a disorienting wave of queasiness washed over her. She swayed, then swallowed hard, telling herself she had only two rungs left to go, but it took her last bit of courage and strength to take those last steps. When she finally made contact, the solid earth beneath her questing foot had never felt so good.

Light-headed, coughing and wheezing, she collapsed to her knees and put her head down between them, hoping she wouldn't faint again. Then a strong arm came around her, calming and steadying her, and she knew she was going to make it. When she felt and heard the sudden, wracking coughs shaking his body, her first-aid training came to the fore.

"Breathe deeply," she said, trying to take her own advice. She strained to see him in the stygian darkness as she reversed their positions, but she didn't need to see to know that he tried his best to follow her instructions. She could hear each tortured breath he drew into his smoke-filled lungs as a counterpoint to her own.

"We can't...stay...here," he managed between wheezes, and Mandy knew he was right. Any minute now, the planks above could burn through and collapse on top of them. There was only one place for them to go.

Her eyes were finally adjusting. Enough light seeped through the minute cracks above that she could make out shapes. She thought about standing up, but quickly discarded that idea. Without light to guide them through the tunnel, they were better off crawling, especially since the dirt floor was rough and uneven.

Mandy wrapped an arm around his bare shoulders. "Come on," she urged. "Follow me."

She couldn't have carried him. She couldn't even have dragged him very far, although she would have tried, if necessary. He had saved her life upstairs, twice, and she owed him. Even if he hadn't, she wouldn't have left him behind to fend for himself—it would have been unthinkable. But it was a good thing that he was able to make it without much help from her.

Mandy pushed up the crossbar that guarded the door at the entrance to the tunnel and it thudded to the ground. The door swung open, hinges creaking ominously. She tried not to think about spiders, poisonous snakes, or any of the other creepy crawlers they might encounter in the passageway. As a child she'd been fearless in her explorations of the cellar and the connecting cave, but that had been years ago. Most children have no sense of their own mortality, and Mandy had been no different. Now she was all too aware that life could be snuffed out in a heartbreaking instant.

Never again would she take chances she didn't have to take. But she didn't have a choice right now.

They moved out of the cellar and into the tunnel. The surrounding air felt cooler almost immediately; away from the smoke it was easier to breathe. Mandy scoured her memory as she moved awkwardly through the tunnel on hands and knees, with one hand groping the wall, feeling her way, and tried to remember how far it was from the cellar to the cave. But she'd never traversed the passageway in total darkness before, and her memory played her false. The wall ended without warning. Off balance, she pitched forward on her left side, scraping her elbow and bruising her shoulder.

Strong hands pulled her to her knees. "You okay?" The rough, smoke-damaged voice held deep concern. Mandy nodded before realizing he couldn't see her.

"I'll be fine," she said quickly, rubbing her damaged arm to relieve the sting.

He coughed, then asked, "Can you go on?"

A loud explosion rocked the earth before she could answer, and Mandy found herself knocked flat, once again shielded by the body of the man who claimed to be Reilly. Small rocks and clods of earth rained down on them, jarred loose by the explosion. They waited for endless minutes while a fine powder of dirt sifted down from the cave's ceiling, but no other explosions were forthcoming.

"Must have been the propane tank," he said at last, so matter-of-factly that Mandy's anger flared momentarily.

Who did this man think he was, taking the destruction of her home in his stride?

Her home.

She'd been born and raised in that house, had lived there most of her life. Every possession she owned, every memento lovingly created or collected by four generations of her family was burning to ashes even as they spoke, and she could do nothing to stop it.

Sudden grief rose in her, pushing aside the anger, and she blinked back unexpected tears. She'd lost so much a year ago that the loss of her house should have paled in comparison, but it didn't. Maybe it was *because* she'd lost so much already that this latest blow assumed even greater significance.

Mandy scarcely noticed when the body almost crushing hers against the hard cave floor moved away, but when warm arms closed comfortingly around her and lifted her up, she reacted instinctively.

"No," she said, struggling out of his embrace.

"Are you okay?"

That husky voice in the darkness, so reminiscent of Reilly's, sent shivers of elemental awareness through Mandy, and without thinking she sought the locket at her throat. The delicate, filigreed gold, warmed by her skin, comforted her as it always did. *I haven't lost everything,* she reminded herself. *I still have this.*

"I'm fine," she answered, dashing her tears away, smearing the gritty silt on her skin into a muddy paste. *Wonderful,* she thought wryly, gathering strength as she took stock of her situation. No shoes, nylons in shreds, burned clothes and now filthy to boot. She wanted to laugh, but was afraid she'd turn hysterical once she started. And she had no idea how the man beside her would react if she did.

"Are you sure you're okay?" He sounded doubtful.

She forced conviction into her tone. "I'm sure."

"Then we'd better get moving." He shifted, and Mandy thought she heard a muffled grunt of pain.

"What is it?"

"Nothing. Let's go."

He was lying. She didn't know how she knew, but she did. It was pointless to pursue the matter now, though, because she couldn't see to prove it. When they got out of the cave she'd check him out thoroughly, no matter what he said.

She started off, crawling along the left outside wall of the cave, hoping she wouldn't disturb a sleeping rattler or something equally dangerous, only to find herself unexpectedly held back.

"I'll go first this time."

He didn't wait for her consent. His big body just brushed past her in the passageway and took the lead. She followed close behind, hands and knees protesting at the rough surface under them. As they felt their way, Mandy wondered how he seemed to know exactly where to go. Like his knowledge of the trapdoor into the cellar, his knowledge of this cave was unexpected and alarming. She made a mental note to ask him about it when they got out.

She no longer trusted her memory to tell her how far they had to go to reach the outside entrance, so she wasn't surprised when he stopped abruptly. He stood, then pulled her to her feet. "Wait here," he ordered.

Mandy was startled enough by his air of command that for a moment she obeyed him. Then she whispered, "The hell with that. I'm not staying behind in the dark," and turned the corner just as he had done. Moonlight glimmered beyond the entrance, silhouetting his powerful frame, and she headed for the light, and him.

He swung around. "Damn it, I said to wait in the cave!" His words came out in an angry hiss, and Mandy drew back sharply.

"Why?"

"Because whoever firebombed your house could be waiting to blow our heads off. That's why!"

Faced with that, all Mandy could think of to say was, "Oh," then felt extremely foolish. This time when he told her to wait, she did, her heart pounding fiercely as she counted the seconds until his return. She had no idea what was going on, but she wasn't stupid. There was danger out there, danger that threatened both of them.

She didn't know what she'd do if she heard gunfire. Go after him, she supposed, although what she thought she could accomplish against armed men was beyond her. Still they, whoever *they* were, had destroyed her home and almost killed her. Maybe it was better to go down fighting than to cower in the dark, waiting for death to find her.

The gunfire never came, but he did. Mandy heard a faint sound, and then he was there beside her.

"All clear," he said softly. "You can come out now." He took her hand in his much larger one and led her to the opening.

The cave entrance was some distance from her house, and faced away from it. When Mandy clambered out, she knew she shouldn't turn around to see the destruction of her family home, but something inside her made her look.

Chapter 2

Crackling orange flames, stark against the night sky, leapt around the skeletal frame of Mandy's home in a macabre dance of destruction. A swirling wind fed the fire and dispersed the smoke in all directions. Mandy watched in horrified fascination for just a few seconds before she had to turn away, shaken and trembling, but it was long enough for the picture to be forever etched in her memory. She'd known in the cave that her home was gone, but there was knowing, and then there was *knowing*.

Sirens split the night, and from her vantage point Mandy saw headlights making their frantic way up the mountain road from town. Small though it was, Black Rock boasted a volunteer fire department with the most modern firefighting equipment available. *Someone must have seen the flames or heard the explosion of the propane tank and called it in,* she thought. Too late, of course, but somehow the realization comforted her. She'd lived here all her life, had helped her neighbors through their disasters. Now it was her turn, and they were quick to respond. Out of everything she'd lost, that, at least, was something salvaged.

She steeled herself, then resolutely turned back toward the fire and started down the incline. She had plenty of questions that needed answers, the foremost being who had done this, and why. But that could wait. Her friends and neighbors couldn't. Even though it was too late to save her home, they could still keep the fire from spreading.

"Come on," she said over shoulder as she started down the hill.

A strong hand grabbed her before she'd taken three steps, and swung her around. "Where the hell do you think you're going?"

"I'm going to help."

"No way."

Mandy tried to shake free of his grasp, but to no avail. "I can't just do nothing! You said it was all clear." She gestured toward the people spilling out of the trucks and cars that had pulled up a safe distance from her house. "I have to at least let them know I'm okay."

He shook his head emphatically, keeping a firm grip on her arm. "No. It's better if people think you're dead. For now, anyway."

She stared at the stranger as if he were crazy. "I can't do that!"

"I can't let you do anything else." His tone was implacable, and Mandy suddenly realized that he'd stop her any way he could.

"What if someone's injured trying to rescue me?"

The man who claimed to be Reilly hunched one shoulder and grimaced ruefully. "Someone was."

For the first time Mandy saw the blood oozing down his arm. "Oh, my God! You *are* hurt!" She reached up, turning him a little so she could see how bad it was. The wound was jagged and ugly, and still bled sluggishly, but thankfully didn't appear to be too deep. It would need stitches, she guessed, and would probably leave one heck of a scar, but she didn't think it was deep enough to cause any permanent muscle damage.

"How did this happen?"

He shrugged, and Mandy cast her mind back. He'd shielded her with his body when the propane tank blew. Was that it? Everything had happened so fast, and she'd been so shook up she could hardly remember.

"Sit down," she said, and to her surprise he obeyed, settling his large frame onto a convenient boulder. Without stopping to think, she reached for the half-slip she wore beneath her skirt and slid it off. She tried to rip it, then caught her breath when her blistered hands protested in pain. Impatiently she set her teeth in one corner of the stubborn material and worked at it until she was rewarded with a tearing sound.

Reilly submitted to Mandy's gentle ministrations, welcoming the few minutes it gave him to come up with some kind of justification for why she couldn't let anyone know she was alive. How much should he tell her? How much *could* he tell her? His plans were all shot to hell now.

Damn it! I should never have gone to her house tonight, should never have taken the chance. I should have listened to my instincts in the first place.

He knew why he'd ignored his sixth sense. He'd never needed anyone before Mandy, hadn't even believed that kind of need existed. But from the first time he'd seen her, from the moment she'd literally tumbled, laughing, into his arms, he'd known she was trouble.

Even now, with dirt and tears smearing her face and her long, golden hair tangled and filthy, she was the most beautiful woman he'd ever seen. Not every man would agree with him, but then, they'd never lain naked with her in the moonlight.

His woman. Then. Now. Forever. It was that simple. He'd returned because he couldn't stay away. Now Mandy had paid the price of his weakness.

How do I tell her that this is all my fault? And after destroying her home, how do I tell her that to protect her I may have to leave her again, this time for good?

"There. That should stop the bleeding for now." Satisfaction colored Mandy's voice as she tied the last knot.

"But it needs to be disinfected, and you're going to need stitches. Black Rock doesn't have a doctor, but—"

"No. No doctor." Reilly shrugged his left shoulder, testing its mobility in the makeshift bandage.

"What about Cody Walker, then?" she said, and Reilly recognized the name. Mandy's friend was the sheriff of Black Rock. "Cody's had paramedic training, and—"

"*No.* No doctors and no cops. There isn't time and it isn't safe. We've got to get out of here. They'll be back."

"What do you mean, they'll be back? Who are *they* anyway? And why did they firebomb my house?" She shook her head, scowling. "I don't understand any of this."

"I know you don't," he said softly. "I wish I had an explanation for you, Mandy. You'll just have to trust me for now."

"Trust you?" She lifted her chin in an all-too-familiar gesture that Reilly knew meant she was about to dig her heels in. "I don't even know who you are!"

"You know me." He deliberately used his bedroom voice, and her eyes flickered away, then back, as if unsure. "You were perched on a ladder, trying to dust the tops of your bookshelves the first day I walked into your bookstore," he continued. "I startled you, and you fell off the ladder, right into my arms. I said, 'Hey, lady, when you fall for a man…'"

"'…you really *fall*, don't you?'" Mandy finished for him in a voice scarcely above a whisper. "I thought I'd imagined it before." She swallowed visibly and squeezed her eyes closed, then wrapped her arms around herself against the cool night air and the memories that he sensed were swamping her. The same memories that had tortured him for so long.

When Mandy finally looked at him again she was trembling, and once again Reilly cursed himself for putting her through this. It was too late to change things, though. All he could do now was make sure nothing else happened to her.

He grasped her arm and pulled gently. "Come on," he said. "My truck's beyond that ridge over there."

Afterward, Mandy would blame her state of shock and confusion. That was the reason she went with him without further protest. The emotional and physical battering she'd taken in the last hour had left her numb, and she scarcely remembered the trip from the mouth of the cave to his pickup truck. At one point she stumbled. Reilly—and it *was* Reilly, she now acknowledged, although she shied away from everything that meant—Reilly glanced at her bare feet, then swept her into his arms over her feeble protests. He cradled her against his bare chest and carried her the last hundred yards. She almost felt as if it were happening to someone else, that it wasn't she who laid her cheek against his shoulder, that it wasn't she whose heart pounded in rhythm with his.

Reilly set her down a short distance from his truck, which was parked off the shoulder of a little-used dirt road. "Hold on a second," he said. He circled the vehicle, obviously searching for something, then returned to pick her up again.

He placed her inside the truck's cab, then reached for the leather jacket slung over the back of the seat and wrapped it around her. "Buckle up," he said, and she obediently did so while he fished behind the seat and dragged out a worn duffel bag. He pulled out a rumpled flannel shirt, which he shrugged on and buttoned, then a clean pair of socks. He slipped the socks on Mandy's bruised feet. The socks were much too big, of course, but the thick cotton was soft, warm and welcome.

Reilly's truck looked the worse for wear inside and out, but the engine roared to life with a throaty growl when he turned the key. It reminded her of his old Blazer. The Blazer had looked just as battered and disreputable, but he'd babied that engine like nothing she'd ever seen, and it had responded for him just as this one did.

Mandy blinked. Thinking about the Blazer reminded her

of the last time she'd seen it. Engulfed in flames, with Reilly inside.

They drove for several minutes in silence. The numbness was wearing off now, and with its departure came a host of questions. She blurted out the first one that occurred to her. "What were you looking for back there?"

"Footprints."

"Did you find any?"

"Yeah."

She shook her head. "I guess I don't understand. If you found footprints, then I would think—"

"I found *my* footprints. That's all. If they had tampered with the truck and then tried to erase any sign that they were there, they'd have erased my footprints, too."

"I see." She digested Reilly's answer, then grabbed another question from the top of the list. "Who are these people you keep referring to as 'They'?"

Reilly spared her a glance before turning his attention back to the road. "I'm not sure."

Was he telling the truth? She couldn't be certain. The truck ate up another half mile of road before she asked, "Why did they burn my house?"

He slowed and downshifted as the truck rounded a curve. "I don't know."

Now she knew he was lying, and anger surged inside her. If he thought she was going to let him get away with it after all she'd been through, he'd better think again. "Where are we going?"

"I don't know that, either."

Anger bubbled over. "That's not good enough," she said. "I want some answers, and I want them now." He ignored her, and her anger grew. "Stop this truck and let me out!" she demanded, unbuckling her seat belt and twisting in her seat. "I'm not going another inch with you unless I get some honest answers!"

He cursed under his breath and hit the steering wheel in frustration, then winced. He braked suddenly and swerved onto the shoulder, but left the engine running.

"Damn it, Mandy," he said, "I'm trying to keep both of us alive long enough to *give* you some answers." His gaze pinned her in the dark. "You're not making it easy."

"I just want to know what's going on here," she continued gamely. "I haven't even started asking questions."

"Like what?"

"Like where have you been all this time? What happened to your face? Who's after us? Why can't we go to the police?" She paused for breath, then added, "I think I deserve to know that much, at least. Don't you?"

Silence stretched between them, and after a minute he ran his hand over his face and sighed. "Yeah, I guess so. But it's a long story, and I don't know all of it yet. Just trust me a little, okay? I promise you, I'll answer your questions as best as I can when I'm sure we're safe."

She believed him. There were a million reasons why she shouldn't, and only one reason why she should. But that one reason carried more weight than all the others combined.

She glanced at his hands resting lightly on the steering wheel, remembering his wince when he pounded the steering wheel, remembering those same hands slapping at the flames that had threatened her less than an hour ago. Impulsively she reached across and slipped her fingers beneath his, turning his palm over. She felt the blisters even before she saw them, angry red even in the pale moonlight.

Blisters notwithstanding, a shock of recognition jolted her when she fitted her palm against his much larger one, and without thinking she entwined her fingers with his as memories came flooding back....

Reilly's hands fascinated her almost as much as he did. Between customers she'd covertly watched him work for the last two hours as he put together the new bookshelves she'd hired him to build for her bookstore, and something about the methodical way his hands flexed and moved mesmerized her. She wondered what those large, square hands would feel like on her skin, and she shivered.

This is crazy, she told herself. *You scarcely know this man.*

She didn't understand this fascination he held for her, but she was powerless to stop it. And she had a sneaking suspicion that even if she could, she wouldn't. He was her mystery man. Unlike the other single men in town, she hadn't grown up with him, hadn't hiked through the woods or played softball or raced horses with him. But it was more than that. Colors seemed brighter when he was around, emotions sharper. Sometimes when she watched him she got the eerie feeling that she was only seeing the surface that he wanted her to see, that there were layers to him that could take a lifetime to reveal.

The attraction wasn't only on her side. She knew instinctively that his feelings for her went beyond the casual flirting he indulged in. She'd surprised a certain look in his eyes more than once, a sort of hunger—no, more like a...yearning expression, although there was a strong element of frank male appraisal in it.

So why hadn't he asked her out? She'd given him all the encouragement she could, had let him know as delicately as possible that she was unattached and would welcome his attentions. But so far he'd ignored every opening she'd given him.

True, Black Rock didn't offer much in the way of nightlife. Aside from one movie theater and two bars, only one of which had a live band and then only on Friday and Saturday nights, the town's residents had to drive to Sheridan or Buffalo for entertainment. But she didn't think that was the reason he'd held back.

She tore her gaze away from him when another customer walked up to the register. She rang up the sale and made change with a smile, then stole another glance at Reilly.

This time he caught her at it and their eyes met and held. For once he wasn't hiding behind a quip and a grin, and Mandy's smile faded as her heartbeat picked up. This man, with his powerful hands and smiling yet lonely eyes, tugged at her heart as no man had ever done, and set her nerve ends tingling in ways she'd never believed possible.

She wanted those hands on her body, moving over her bare skin with the same patient strength with which he worked the wood, bringing her body to life. But even more, she wanted to erase that loneliness from his eyes.

I can do it, Reilly, she pleaded silently. *If you'll trust me.*

The memory receded, leaving Mandy shaken. "All right," she whispered finally. "I'll wait for an explanation. For now, just tell me where you're taking me."

His harsh bark of laughter startled her. "I wish I knew," he said, drawing his hand away.

"If you don't know where we're headed, how will you know when it's safe?" He didn't have an answer for her, and she said, "I know a place."

His brows drew together in a skeptical frown. "Where?"

"Cody has a cabin up by Granite Pass that's less than an hour from here. I know he wouldn't mind if I used it."

"How secluded is it?"

"Very. No neighbors for miles. There's only one way in, and you can see and hear anyone coming long before they get there."

"Okay," he nodded. "Sounds good. Which way do I go?"

Mandy peered through the windshield at the surrounding blackness. "Turn here."

Reilly braked. Rocks and dirt spurted behind them as he turned onto a road that was little more than a two-wheeled wagon track. The truck jounced over several bone-jarring ruts before Reilly said, "Are you sure this is it?"

"I'm sure."

He shrugged and concentrated on keeping the truck on the road, which wound up and around the mountain. The bouncing headlights didn't help matters, making it hard to see more than a few feet ahead, and Reilly slowed even more. The road ended abruptly in a small clearing.

"This is it," Mandy said.

He looked around the clearing. "Where?"

She opened the door and slid out. "We walk from here."

He rubbed his bandaged shoulder. "I was afraid of that."

She chuckled at his laconic tone. "It's not that far," she reassured him. "Through those trees, fifty, maybe sixty yards."

"Great."

"You don't happen to have a flashlight, do you?"

For an answer Reilly leaned over and opened the glove compartment, pulled out a large, chrome-plated flashlight, and flicked it on. He handed it to her.

"Thanks."

He grunted, a response that could have meant anything, grabbed his duffel bag from the floor, then reached under the seat. When he straightened, Mandy's eyes widened. No one who lived in Wyoming as long as she had could be a stranger to guns, but she'd never seen Reilly with one before. And it wasn't just an ordinary gun, either. This thing was a Smith & Wesson semiautomatic cannon.

"Since when do you pack a gun?"

Reilly checked the clip, then set the gun down on the seat beside him while he strapped on the shoulder harness. "I've always carried one," he said finally. "I just never let you see it before."

He holstered the .45 with a professional air that told Mandy more plainly than words just how familiar he was with it. She shivered and wrapped his jacket around her more securely. *What else don't I know about you, Reilly?* she wondered. *And do I really want to know?*

He locked the truck's doors and pocketed the keys. "Let's go."

They followed the path, Mandy leading the way and limping a little with only his socks protecting her feet, Reilly bringing up the rear. Without the truck's headlights, and with the moon and stars partly shielded by a ghostly bank of clouds, there wasn't much light to guide them through the inky darkness other than the wavering beam of the flashlight Mandy carried.

The strong scents of pine and sage enveloped them, carried by a chilly north wind that rustled leaves and set the underbrush swaying. Night birds called to each other in the darkness. Reilly listened intently, his gaze darting back and forth at each cracking twig, each soft rustle.

He hated it. Hated being out of his element. Put him down inside the city limits of any metropolitan area, and in no time at all he'd find his way. But out here he was little more than a novice, and he didn't care for the way it made him feel. It wouldn't be so bad in the normal course of things, but in their current situation it could be deadly.

Their current situation. What a feeble phrase to describe this nightmare. How the hell had they tracked him to Mandy's? And how had they known just when to strike? Somebody was going to answer for this, Reilly promised himself. Never mind that they'd tried to kill him a year ago. Never mind that they'd tried again tonight. That was business. He'd known what he was up against from the beginning. But they'd involved Mandy now, and *that* he wouldn't forgive. Whoever had betrayed him—and betrayal was the only thing that made sense—whoever it was, Reilly was going to make him pay. In spades.

Cody's cabin materialized out of the shadows. Roughhewn and built of native materials—unfinished split logs and what looked in the poor light like mud—it blended in with its surroundings. Reilly noted with grudging approval that the cabin was situated so as to be easily defensible.

Mandy marched up the porch steps to the front door, grasped the old-fashioned latch, and lifted. The door swung open easily.

"Doesn't Walker believe in locks?"

She paused on the threshold and turned toward Reilly. "He doesn't keep anything worth stealing here. And anyway, Cody says that if someone really wanted to break in, a locked door wouldn't keep them out. This way he doesn't have to worry about a busted window. Besides,'' she added, with just a hint of impatience, ''we look out for each other out here. If someone happened upon this place, chances are they'd be either lost or in trouble of some kind. Cody keeps the cabin stocked with non-perishables, just in case.''

''Lucky for us.''

Was that sarcasm in his voice? Mandy's level gaze bored into him, but she didn't call him on it. ''Yes,'' she said evenly. ''Lucky for us.''

Reilly knew he was being unreasonable, but suddenly he was sick of hearing about Cody Walker's virtues. He'd met the man back when he'd first moved to Black Rock a year and a half ago. He knew Mandy and Walker were good friends, growing up together in the small town, and she had told him once that she and Walker had even dated in high school. But something in the way she talked about him now set Reilly's sixth sense humming.

He opened his mouth to question her, then closed it again. If he started asking now, Mandy would counter with questions of her own. And he still hadn't made up his mind what, if anything, he was going to tell her. He'd promised her some answers, but until he knew what was going on, it might be safer for her if he stonewalled.

''Come on,'' she said, interrupting his thoughts. ''It's cold out here. The sooner we get the generator going, the sooner we'll have electricity and heat.''

Reilly followed her inside, through what appeared to be one large, high-ceilinged room, and out the back door. Baffled, he finally asked, ''Where are you going?''

''The generator's outside,'' she explained patiently, ''in that little shed over there.'' The flashlight beam picked out the solid structure ahead of them.

''Why didn't we just walk around?''

''Because it's dark out, the path is rough, and in case you forgot, I don't have any shoes.''

That silenced him. Guilt was becoming a constant companion, he thought wryly, as he considered the discomfort she must have suffered on the way up here. She hadn't said a word, though. Hadn't complained. An unexpected flicker of pride in her took him by surprise. His Mandy was tough when the chips were down. How many men could say that about their women?

Feeling somewhat superfluous, Reilly watched as Mandy checked everything over, then quickly started up the gas-fueled generator. "Ta-da!" she said triumphantly over the loud, thrumming sound produced by the generator. "Now we have power!"

She started back toward the cabin, but before she had taken two steps he caught her arm. "Wait," he said. He leaned over and swung her into his arms, then strode up the path.

"You shouldn't be carrying me with that bad shoulder," she protested.

"I want to. It's my fault you don't have any shoes."

"But—"

"Just let me do it, okay? Let me at least pretend that you need me."

She didn't say anything until they were back inside the cabin. As he set her gently on her feet, she whispered something under her breath that Reilly didn't catch.

"What did you say?"

At first he thought she wasn't going to tell him. Then she said slowly, "I needed you, once." She fumbled for the circuit breaker, pushed it into place, then clicked on the light switch. The sudden brightness was blinding. He blinked, saw the emotionally raw expression on Mandy's face, and closed his eyes in pain.

"Mandy, I..."

"I needed you," she continued. "Even though I thought you were dead, I still needed you. I called your name when I—" She caught her breath, cutting off the rest of what she'd started to say.

"Mandy..." He reached for her, but she backed away.

"No," she said, her voice breaking. "No. It's too late. I don't need you anymore."

Chapter 3

It's too late. I don't need you anymore.

Mandy's words and the unspoken accusation buried in them sliced through Reilly. It was like the switchblade a cornered and desperate young street tough had used on the rookie cop he'd once been, cutting him to the bone. He flinched, then touched his chest and brought away his hand, staring at it as if he actually thought he'd see his own blood there.

He swallowed hard, then looked from his hand to Mandy's face, searching for an explanation in her eyes, but finding none. Didn't she know him at all? Didn't she know he'd have done anything, *anything*, to keep her safe, even if it meant tearing out his heart? Did she really think it had been easy to leave her, the only woman who'd ever bothered to look beyond his hard exterior to the vulnerable man inside?

Curling tendrils of anger started in the pit of his stomach, then quickly spread. All his life he'd fought against injustice. How many times had he been falsely accused by his various foster parents of one misdeed or another, innocent but unable to prove it? How many times had he protested his innocence, then suffered in burning silence the harsh punishment meted out, knowing that further protest only brought more punishment? That was why, when he'd reached manhood, he'd joined the marines and then the police force, not out of a sense of civic duty, but out of a hunger to see justice served.

Disillusionment joined his anger at Mandy. A year ago he'd been closer to her than he'd ever been to anyone in his life, had let her inside his emotional defenses in ways he'd never thought possible. For the first time he'd loved without reserve, and look where it had led him. Mandy had claimed to love him, but love hadn't mattered after all. She was no different from the others, jumping to conclusions, putting the worst possible connotation on his actions without giving him the benefit of the doubt.

"Damn you," he said tightly, the words rasping in his throat. "Damn you." Wounded, he swung around and walked out into the night.

When Reilly hadn't returned fifteen minutes later, Mandy went looking for him. She wasn't bitter or mean by nature, and she'd never deliberately hurt anyone before. But she'd known as the words left her mouth that they'd been designed to hurt Reilly, and they had. The look he'd thrown her just before he walked out was burned into her mind, and now her conscience was nudging her.

"I'm too tired for this," she muttered crossly to herself. Nevertheless, she pulled on an old pair of Cody's boots, stopping for only a second to think about the laughable picture she made in her torn blouse, bedraggled skirt, and too-large cowboy boots. She wrapped Reilly's jacket around herself against the cold, then went after him.

He hadn't gone far. Mandy found him leaning against the shed housing the generator, staring out into the impenetrable darkness. He turned at the sound of her approach, and she stopped several feet away from him. Bitterness was etched on his face, and his defiant stance poignantly re-

minded her of something. She couldn't place the memory—
her sleep-deprived mind refused to work properly. But her
own bitterness melted a little in the face of Reilly's.

Her voice was gentle when she said, "Come back inside,
Reilly."

"Why?" The word came at her like a bullet.

"Why?" Mandy considered it, then said, "Because it's
very late. Because it's cold out here, and will only get
colder before the night's over." An owl hooted in the distance, a lonely sound, made even lonelier by the wind
soughing in the trees. She shivered and snuggled into Reilly's leather jacket, remembering a time when it had been
his arms, not his jacket, that had warmed her. Then she
raised her chin and added, "And because I'm not going in
until you do."

Something reached him. Whether it was her stubborn-
ness, or the pathetic sight she made, she didn't know, but
something reached him. He relaxed noticeably, and one
corner of his mouth twitched. Mandy could have sworn he
was fighting the urge to smile.

"Tough guy, aren't you?" he drawled at last.

Mandy's heart jolted, as it did every time familiar
phrases came from the stranger she now acknowledged was
Reilly. How many times had he teased her with just those
words, in that same fake Western drawl?

"Tougher than you'll ever be," she answered in kind,
with only a slight wobble in her voice that betrayed how
emotionally his words had affected her.

Incredibly, his face softened even more, a strangely vulnerable expression replacing the bitterness she'd hated,
knowing she'd put it there. He stepped toward her, his hand
outstretched. "Mandy?"

A thousand questions were embodied in that one word,
questions she wasn't ready to deal with just yet. But she
could no more have refused to take his hand than she could
have voluntarily stopped breathing. Her hand slid into his,
and his fingers tightened around hers as if they were closing

on a lifeline. His grip was almost painful, but not quite. Not quite.

She resisted the temptation to walk into his embrace and have him hold her with that same desperate strength, but it wasn't easy. Lord knew it wasn't easy at all. Her voice husky with emotion, she said softly, "Let's go inside."

Back in the cabin, Mandy built a fire in the fireplace to supplement the meager warmth put out by the electric space heater, then placed the fireguard in front of it. She turned to find Reilly perusing the one-room cabin's sparse interior furnishings, especially the one unmade double bed in the corner.

"I'll bunk down in front of the fire," he said firmly, before Mandy had a chance to say anything.

"That's silly," she exclaimed, moving to the closet by the front door. "There's a foldaway cot in here." She dived inside and was already struggling to get the unwieldy cot out when she added, "You're bigger than me, so I'll take this and you can have the bed."

He took the cot from her and set it up easily in front of the fireplace, then tested it with his weight. "I'll take this," he said, and from his tone Mandy knew there'd be no arguing with him.

Men, she thought, a flicker of amusement finding its way through waves of tiredness. *They're so predictable.* Without another word she took folded sheets, blankets and pillows from the closet, laid some on his cot, then set the rest on the double bed.

She straightened, then looked up at Reilly. "I don't know about you, but even as tired as I am, I don't think I can crawl into bed smelling like this. While you were taking your walk, I turned on the water heater." She gestured toward the bathroom. "I doubt there's enough hot water for both of us to take a shower, but if I run the water in the tub we can share it."

His tawny eyes gleamed unexpectedly, wickedly, and Mandy suddenly realized she'd been too careless in wording that statement. Heat crept into her cheeks. "We can

take *turns*," she amended primly, then felt foolish. Once
upon a time she'd gloried in sharing everything, including
her body, with this man. Once upon a time taking a bath
with him wouldn't have occasioned even a second thought.
But everything was different now.

The wicked gleam in his eyes faded. "Take your bath,"
Reilly said softly, turning her around and giving her a slight
push in the direction of the bathroom. "I don't mind going
second."

Mandy closed the bathroom door behind her, then for the
first time caught sight of her reflection in the mirror over
the utilitarian sink. A tiny shriek lodged in her throat, but
she remembered the man on the other side of the door and
stopped herself just in time.

Her hair had taken the worst punishment, she decided
after careful deliberation. Smoke and dirt had matted it
down, but it was the singed areas that made her cringe—
they gave her a lopsided look.

She took a moment to put the stopper in the old-fashioned tub and turn on the faucet. Water gushed into the tub,
and she checked the temperature with one hand, wincing
as the heat stung the blisters on her palms. She adjusted
the hot-water flow, then returned to the mirror and contemplated her reflection.

She didn't have scissors handy, or she'd have hacked
away at her hair to even it up. She borrowed Cody's hair-
brush instead, ignored her sore palms, and ruthlessly
brushed out as much of the mess as she could.

The tub was full now. Mandy turned off the water and
quickly stripped to the buff, shooting a glance at the bathroom door to make sure it was shut. There wasn't a lock
on the door, and it concerned her for a moment. Then she
was ashamed for even thinking it necessary. Reilly would
never invade her privacy. She knew that as surely as she
knew anything.

She stopped just long enough to wash out her bra and
panties and hang them on the towel rack to dry, then
grabbed a clean, but well-worn, washcloth from the small

stack on a shelf above the tub, and slid into the water. Her hands throbbed a bit, so she lifted them out of the water, and laid them on the cool porcelain sides of the large, claw-footed tub. Then she immersed the rest of herself, hair and all, and just lay back, soaking her aching body, letting the warm water ease away the pain. When she caught herself dozing off, she sat up with a sudden splash and began scrubbing.

A small pang of guilt reminded her that Reilly was waiting to use the water after her, and if she didn't hurry, his bath would be stone-cold. She quickly washed her hair and rinsed off by immersing herself again, then got out and dried off as fast as she could, wrapping the towel around her hair as she considered what to wear.

There was no way she could put her filthy clothes back on, against her clean skin—she shuddered at the thought. She spotted a dark blue terry-cloth bathrobe hanging behind the door and debated with herself for a moment. She really should leave it for Reilly, her better side argued, but her better side lost.

"He must have other clothes in his duffel bag," she rationalized, as she shrugged the bathrobe on and tied the belt loosely around her waist.

The robe was way too big for her, of course, but it was clean, soft and comfortable. She kicked her scorched and dirty clothes into the corner, figuring she'd worry about them tomorrow.

She rubbed her hair until it was no more than damp, then combed it out as best she could. Her arms were so heavy she could scarcely lift them, and she finally gave up and put the comb back on the sink.

She emerged from the bathroom feeling human once more, but more tired than ever, and found that Reilly had made up both the cot and the bed. Guilt poked its sleepy head up again, and she mumbled her thanks, then crawled gratefully between the sheets. She was asleep almost before her head hit the pillow.

Reilly turned off the overhead light, so that the only illumination in the room came from the fireplace, which cast dancing shadows along the walls. He stared down at Mandy for a long time. Her freshly washed hair hadn't had time to dry, and the damp golden strands lay in loose disarray upon her pillow. One strand clung to her cheek, and without thinking he moved it, tucking it behind her ear.

She stirred slightly, and the bathrobe gaped open at the neck. He told himself not to look, but it was a futile resolution at best. Her sweet-smelling skin beckoned, the shadowy hollow between her breasts a torment he couldn't resist.

His body reacted in typical fashion, sweeping away his fatigue.

She shifted in her sleep and the loosely tied belt gave way, exposing even more of Mandy's body to his hungry gaze. He told himself not to touch, but already his fingers were sliding from the gentle pulse in her throat toward the creamy curve of her breast. She sighed, a helpless little sound, and an unexpected wave of tenderness washed over him.

Then, and only then, did he realize what he'd almost done. *Only a bastard would take advantage of a woman when she's defenseless,* he told himself.

He tugged the blankets up, covering her completely, and ignored the little voice in his head that urged him to ease under the covers beside her, and take what he'd done without for almost a year. Denying himself was harder, much harder than he'd ever thought possible.

In the bathroom he shucked his clothes in record time, peeling off the bandage on his shoulder with a careless disregard that would have appalled Mandy.

Bathing in the now tepid bathwater helped a little, but not much. His heavy arousal refused to be assuaged. His body knew what it wanted, and wasn't about to let him forget it, especially since he could vividly imagine her in this very tub only a few minutes ago, the same water lapping at her slick skin just as it was lapping at his. And the sight of Mandy's delicate bra and panties hanging on the towel rack did absolutely nothing to help.

He soaped his body roughly, hoping to rein in his imagination, but to no avail. His mind wandered along a familiar path, one it had taken so often in the last twelve months that he knew it by heart.

He'd never intended to become Mandy's lover. No matter that his good intentions had swiftly fallen by the wayside under her gentle onslaught, at least his conscience was clear on that point. He'd never intended to become involved with her. He just hadn't counted on Mandy's determination.

Reilly smiled a little to himself. A determined Mandy was not someone to tangle with. She'd single-mindedly lured him to her bed with the most potent aphrodisiac known to man—love. She'd turned those loving blue eyes on him and he'd fallen with a thud that still reverberated in his ears. It had baffled him at first, this control she held over him, but eventually he'd succumbed to temptation, and found that being loved by Mandy was the next best thing in the world.

Loving her was the best.

Loving her. The washcloth faltered as Reilly remembered, and for a moment he could have sworn he smelled lilacs.

Blood pounded throughout his body, pooling, as usual, between his legs. He cursed long and low. *I don't need this,* he reminded himself savagely. *I really don't. And neither does Mandy.* But he had no control left.

He splashed water on his face and scrubbed ruthlessly, ignoring the tight pain in his palms, then rinsed off and climbed out of the tub. There were only two towels—a clean one on the shelf, and the damp one Mandy had used and then hung beside her underclothes. Reilly chose Mandy's towel, briskly rubbing himself off, picturing her doing the same thing.

He was most definitely aroused now.

With his foot he pushed his dirty clothes into a heap beside Mandy's smaller pile, then stood in front of the mirror, finger-combing his damp hair. There was a comb on the sink, but Reilly drew the line at using Cody Walker's comb. The shelf of shaving items caught his eye, and he rubbed his chin, fingers rasping against his unshaven jaw. He'd shave tomorrow, he decided. And he'd use his own razor, not Walker's.

He padded naked into the main room and fished around in his duffel bag until he came up with a clean pair of underwear. He normally slept in the nude, but he figured he should spare Mandy any embarrassment he could, especially after his shameful behavior earlier.

This wasn't how he'd envisioned spending the night when he'd broken into her house earlier. He laughed under his breath. Now *that* was the understatement of the year.

He touched a hand to his injured shoulder and brought it away clean. No blood. Good. He hadn't reopened the wound. He'd hate to bleed all over the sheets. Not that he cared if he ruined Walker's sheets, but he didn't want Mandy to worry.

The cot creaked beneath his weight when he settled on it, and the canvas wasn't very comfortable or forgiving for a man who'd gone through what he'd gone through tonight.

Reilly's thoughts moved from the hard cot on which he lay to the incredible softness of Mandy's skin, and the scent of warm woman that rose from her body as he'd caressed her earlier. If nothing else, he'd have that to add to his small hoard of precious memories when he left again.

If he lived long enough, he'd take those memories out someday, and they'd make the sacrifice worthwhile, knowing that Mandy was safe.

If he lived long enough.

Mandy woke slowly, painfully, her body protesting and her mind rebelling. She snuggled deeper under the covers, but someone was moving stealthily about the sunlit room, and she couldn't get back to sleep. For some strange reason, though, she wasn't alarmed that she wasn't alone. Instead, she smiled drowsily to herself.

"Good morning."

The familiar, masculine voice brought her wide awake. For one disoriented moment she forgot where she was, and she sat up suddenly in bed, her heart pounding. She blinked, then all at once everything came back to her—Reilly, the fire, their flight to Cody's cabin.

"I didn't mean to wake you." The deep voice sounded closer. Mandy glanced up to find Reilly looming beside the bed, looking tall, dangerous and very male in jeans and a black T-shirt. He was wearing the shoulder holster, too, and there was a gun in it. She'd almost forgotten about that part.

The direction of his gaze made her realize with a start that the robe she was wearing had come loose during the night and was hanging open. She snatched the lapels closed and fumbled to retie the belt as faint color mounted her cheekbones.

He held a steaming cup of coffee in his hand, and he offered it to her. "Black, no sugar, just the way you like it."

She shook her head in refusal. "No, I...not just yet." She pushed her sleep-tangled hair away from her face, swallowed, and blinked again.

She'd never been a morning person. Her bookstore didn't open until ten because she needed to potter around for an hour or so in the mornings before she even started getting dressed—"easing into the day," she liked to call it.

But Reilly *was* a morning person. She'd forgotten that about him. And it was obvious he'd already been up for some time. He couldn't have been very comfortable on the cot last night, but he looked as if he'd had ten hours of uninterrupted sleep. His chin was shaved with military precision, and not a hair was out of place. Even his clothes, which should have been wrinkled from packing, looked as if they'd come straight from the dryer.

A flash of memory reminded her that once upon a time this man had almost convinced her that waking up with the sunrise wasn't such a bad idea after all. Not when your lover "eased" you into the day the way Reilly loved to do.

Mandy mentally slammed the door shut on those memories when she realized shivers of sensual awareness were darting through her. She stole a glance at Reilly, and was disconcerted to find him leaning against the wall, watching her. He was still holding the cup of coffee she'd rejected earlier and was sipping from it. His eyes queried hers over the top of the cup.

"What is it?" she asked, surreptitiously peeking down to make sure her robe wasn't gaping open.

A laconic smile touched his lips. "Isn't that my question?"

"What do you mean?"

He took another swallow of coffee as he considered his reply. "Let's just say I don't remember you ever waking up that abruptly." His knowing eyes reminded her that he knew her matutinal habits all too well, just as she'd known his, and warmth crept into her cheeks at the reminder.

Reilly moved suddenly and she started, but he was only heading for the coffeepot on the stove. He refilled his cup, then pulled another mug down from the cabinet and half turned toward her. "Are you sure you don't want some?"

She tossed back the covers and clambered out of bed. "I do, actually, but first..." She tightened the belt on the robe, then headed for the bathroom.

Reilly watched her movements with male enjoyment. There was something sexy about a woman, warm and rumpled from bed, he decided, even if the bed she'd risen from wasn't his. And of course, he'd seen her rising in golden glory from *his* bed often enough to remember the lazy, possessive pleasure it evoked.

The door closed behind Mandy, and Reilly turned back to the coffeepot. He filled her mug and set it on the counter, then lifted his own and carried it to the front door, and outside.

The morning was well advanced, the sun already high above the trees. Last night's wind had died down, leaving only a slight passing breeze to ruffle the leaves and the sparse vegetation.

Reilly had already checked the perimeter once this morning, but he checked it again now. Satisfied that they were safe, at least for the moment, he sat down on the steps, drinking his coffee, and thinking.

He didn't have a clue what he was going to tell Mandy about everything that had happened. Any minute now she was going to join him, and the questions he'd postponed answering last night were going to come tumbling out of her. He doubted she'd let him put her off any longer.

You've got two choices. You can tell the truth. Or you can lie. Which is it going to be?

He hated like hell the thought of lying to her. That had never been his intention. Oh, he'd deceived her when they'd first met, of course, by not telling her the truth about who he really was and why he was there, but that had been as much for her own protection as for his. In the past he'd evaded uncomfortable questions he had no answers for, rather than look into those clear blue eyes and outright lie. He didn't know if he had it in him to do so now.

"But how can I tell her?" His words were tinged with despair.

How can you not? his inner voice chided him. *You know what she thinks. She thinks you deserted her, that you never loved her at all. Can you leave her again, this time for good, without telling her what really happened?*

"It would be better for her," he reasoned out loud.

"Don't you think *I* should be allowed to decide what's best for me?"

Reilly jumped, spilling hot coffee all over his left hand while his right hand reached for the gun in his shoulder holster. He froze with it pulled halfway out, and swore. He shoved the gun back in place, transferred the cup to his other hand, then shook drops of coffee off the first one and wiped it on his jeans. Then he turned around.

Mandy stood in the open doorway, eyes flashing, golden curls tossed impatiently back over her shoulder, hands on her hips in confrontation. Part of him marvelled that she could look so feminine wearing a man's checkered flannel shirt with the sleeves rolled up, and worn but clean jeans that were obviously too big for her, while another part of him wondered where she'd found the clothes. Then his eyes narrowed and a muscle twitched in his cheek. They were Walker's. Had to be.

An unreasoning jealousy swept through Reilly, as unwelcome as it was unexpected. It didn't make sense, but there it was—he didn't want Mandy wearing clothes that belonged to another man, especially Walker. It galled him that they had to impose on Walker's unknowing hospitality by using the man's cabin, but Reilly could deal with that. What set his teeth on edge was seeing *his* woman wearing the other man's clothes.

Then he remembered her question.

Chapter 4

"I said," Mandy repeated with exaggerated emphasis, "don't you think I should decide what's best for me?"

All at once Reilly knew he couldn't tell her everything. As much as he hated lying to her, until he knew what he was going to do, he couldn't take the chance of hurting her again.

She's had a year to get over you, he told himself. *If you explain, if you tell her you came back to ask her to go with you because you've always loved her, what would that accomplish? You may not be able to take her with you this time, any more than you could before, no matter how much you might want to.*

And he wanted. *How* he wanted. Mandy was even more entrenched in his heart now than she'd been before he'd left her. There were times in the past twelve months that he'd wished it were different. That *he* was different. It would have been better for everyone concerned if he could have forgotten her, forgotten the way she looked, the way she smelled, the way her smile pierced his heart. But he couldn't forget. No other woman would do for him, because she was the woman he loved. If he couldn't have *her,* he didn't want anyone else.

Reilly allowed nothing of what he was feeling to show on his face. Not even the slightest twitch of a muscle betrayed him, as he said coolly, "I guess you're right, Mandy. You're old enough to make your own choices."

Her hands dropped to her sides, and she looked like a woman who'd just had the wind taken out of her sails. Then a puzzled expression crept into her eyes, and he waited for the inevitable questions with a patience he'd learned the hard way.

"What's going on, Reilly? I think I have the right to know that, at least."

He nodded. "I'll tell you what I can." He glanced one more time around the clearing, his eyes and ears alert, then trod up the wooden steps. Mandy moved aside to let him enter, then followed him inside.

He'd already scoped out the cabin's interior this morning before Mandy had woken. Other than the bed and the cot he'd put away earlier, there weren't a lot of choices for sitting. He didn't trust himself anywhere near the bed with her, so he pulled one of the two paddle-back wooden chairs away from the small kitchen table and seated Mandy in it. Then he pulled the other one out for himself, turned it around and straddled it, resting his arms over the back.

Several openings occurred to him, but he discarded them all, until at last she said, "Well?"

He ran his hand through his hair, then took a deep breath and let it out in a huff. "There's a lot I can't tell you. No, wait," he said as she started to interrupt. "First let me explain why."

"Okay."

"There are men out there who want to kill me. Why is not important. The less you know, the safer it is for you. Suffice it to say that these men traced me to you. They didn't follow me. There's a difference. But the fact that they know about you means your life is in danger, too. That's why I don't want anyone to know you're still alive.

As long as they think we're both dead, we've bought a little time.''

"Who are 'They'?''

"I can't tell you that.''

"Why do they want to kill you?''

"I can't tell you that, either.''

"So much for those questions.'' A touch of sarcasm laced her words. "You're not telling me any more than you told me last night, and that was nothing.'' She folded her arms across her chest and her foot began to tap the floor. "Are you in trouble?'' At his ironic laugh, she shook her head impatiently and clarified, "I mean with the law. Have you done something illegal?''

"No.''

Her exasperated expression turned puzzled. "Then why can't we go to the sheriff? Cody would help us. I know he would.''

Reilly considered how best to put it. "It's a risk, Mandy. One I don't choose to take until I've had a chance to think it through.''

After a moment she said, "That's not good enough.'' She jumped to her feet and began pacing the room. "First you tell me there are men after you who want to kill you, and me, too, but you won't say who they are or why. Then you say you're not in trouble with the law, but you won't go to the sheriff.'' A short bark of sarcastic laughter escaped her, and she turned to confront him. "Can you give me a single reason why I should believe you?''

Emotions roiled within him, and he gazed at her for several seconds, willing her to remember a time when he had given her every reason in the world to believe him.

She breathed sharply and her eyes widened, as if his message had somehow gotten through to her, then she shook her head in angry denial. "It's not going to be that easy.''

"What do you want me to say?'' He stood and kicked his chair aside. "I know it sounds crazy, put like that, but you're forgetting one thing. Last night happened. It wasn't a dream, it wasn't something I made up. It was real, damn it!'' His eyes pinned hers, forcing her to remember that, too. ''I would have thought by now you'd realize this isn't a game they're playing.''

Pictures from last night rose in Mandy's mind, pictures she'd subconsciously repressed because she wasn't emotionally ready to deal with them. Then for a searing moment she was back in the blazing inferno, smoke filling her lungs, flames scorching her skin, as everything she cherished burned down around her. ''No,'' she whispered, suffering the loss of her home all over again. ''I know it's not a game.'' Silence stretched taut between them, until she raised a stricken face to his. ''So what happens now?''

Reilly hesitated, wondering how much he should volunteer. He hated having to remind her of what she'd lost last night, of how close they'd come to dying, but at the same time it seemed to have diverted her mind from the fact that there were things he hadn't explained yet. Like why he'd been in her house in the first place.

''The first priority,'' he said, ''is to make sure you're safe. Now that they've traced me to you...'' He shook his head. ''I don't know. I don't dare let you go back to Black Rock. If you turn up alive, they'll know I'm alive, too. They've already proved they're willing to take you out to get to me. They wouldn't scruple to kidnap and torture you to find out what you know. And if they have any smarts at all, they'd hold you for ransom.''

''But I don't have any mon—''

''Not money. Me. They'd offer to release you in exchange for me.'' He watched as that registered with her.

''What...would make them think that would work?''

His lips thinned as he fought his instinctive response. *Didn't she know?* he thought. *Hadn't she already figured out that's why he'd left her twelve months ago?*

Obviously not. ''If they found me in Black Rock—and we know they did,'' he said aloud, ''—then they know it would work.'' Let Mandy make what she would out of that statement.

"So what are we going to do?"

"*We're* not going to do anything."

"What do you mean? I'm involved in this, too."

"I'm uninvolving you."

"That's not your choice to make!"

He gave her a deliberately cool look. "Isn't it?"

"No! I was in that fire, too, you know. I could have died. Doesn't that count?" She was getting angry again. "That was *my* home they destroyed. Maybe you don't understand what that means. Maybe…" Her voice trembling, she struggled for the right words. "Maybe home doesn't mean anything to you." He flinched, but in her anger she didn't see it. "I grew up in that house. My whole life was there." She was shaking all over. "Not just *things*. Memories. Photos. Little reminders of—" Her hands covered her face and she sobbed once. Then she furiously scrubbed the tears from her eyes with the heels of her hands. "All of it gone. Do you think I can just walk away from that as if it never happened?"

Heat surged through his body. As long as he lived he'd remember her like this, her head thrown defiantly back, her body in her borrowed clothes radiating energy that had no outlet but her tearstained eyes, her voice. If things were different, she'd be in his arms so fast it would make her head spin. He'd have her on that double bed in the corner before she knew it, and he'd give her a constructive use for all that fire.

But he couldn't change the past, and the reminder of the sacrifices he'd made, and would make again, roused his temper. He took a step toward her, quivering with anger spawned by fear for her. "Listen to me, Mandy, and listen good. These are killers we're talking about. They don't play by the rules. They've killed before. They'll kill again. But it's not going to be you. Do you understand? I won't let it be you!"

They stared at each other for stunned seconds, then Reilly slammed out of the cabin.

He didn't have a destination in mind; he just knew he

had to get away before he revealed anything more. Once he was outside, however, his old training took over, and he circled the cabin, checking the mantraps he'd set early that morning.

He'd made the trip to the truck just as dawn was breaking. He'd automatically searched for signs of tampering and had satisfied himself that it was still safe. Then he'd retrieved several coils of rope and wire, and some other innocuous-looking odds and ends he always carried in the back of the truck, and had rigged his own version of an early-warning system all along the outskirts of the cabin clearing.

The methodical routine of checking their perimeter calmed Reilly down and let him regain his perspective. He made a mental note to warn Mandy about the traps before she accidentally stumbled into one. Then he took himself to task.

Don't let it get to you, he reminded himself sternly. *An emotional man gets careless. And a careless man gets dead real quick.*

It was hard to be emotionless around Mandy, though. He had few defenses against her, and the ones he had didn't amount to much. "That's no excuse," he muttered to himself. "Do you want Mandy to pay the price of your carelessness?"

There was only one answer to that.

Inside the cabin, Mandy wondered half-hysterically what had ever happened to her ordinary, peaceful life. Ever since she'd first met Reilly a year and a half ago, her life had been an emotional roller coaster. She'd gone from a placid existence to intense happiness to intense grief in less than six months. She'd survived, barely. She'd just begun rebuilding her life, and now this. She didn't know how much more she could take.

Something was going on here that she hadn't quite figured out. The bare-bones story Reilly had told her rang true—the charred wreckage of her home proved much of it—but he'd only touched the surface. She wanted to know what he was holding back, and why.

Now that her system was no longer reeling from last night's emotional and physical shocks, there were other questions she wanted to ask. Questions of a more personal nature. Questions whose answers could tear her apart.

Had he been using her all along? That one hurt, striking where she was most vulnerable. She didn't want to believe it, but it would explain why he'd left her a year ago and why he'd come back now that he was in trouble again.

But if that's true, why did he pretend he loved me? Why did he go so far with the charade? she asked herself. *That's what I can't understand.*

It was easy to see why he'd slept with her. She'd all but thrown herself at him eighteen months ago, and he was a man, after all. But the rest—the tender looks, the shared confidences, the way he held her after making love—those were the things that had seduced her into believing herself loved. Those were the things that made no sense now.

Then again, nothing made sense right now.

Her stomach growled, reminding her that she hadn't eaten much in the last twenty-four hours. Lunch yesterday had been a sandwich and an apple at the bookstore, munched on in snatches between waiting on customers and restocking the bookshelves. As for her late-night supper, it had gone up in flames with the house.

She sighed and tucked her hair behind her ear, pushing her unanswered questions to the back of her mind along with thoughts of her house, just as she'd done last night. She couldn't dwell on them now, she knew, because if she did she'd either fall apart or drive herself crazy.

Food, she thought, pulling a pot out of the kitchen cabinet. *The universal panacea. That's what I need right now.* Nothing ever looked quite so bleak on a full stomach.

As Mandy studied the well-stocked pantry, it occurred to her that for the first time in almost a year she was actually looking forward to a meal. Eating had become a necessity, something you did at regular intervals—like combing your hair or brushing your teeth—but not something you gave a lot of thought to. Now she found herself seriously debating the merits of beef stew from a can versus oatmeal with evaporated milk. She chuckled at the absurdity, but deep inside, a tiny corner of her heart acknowledged the source.

Suddenly impatient with the direction her thoughts were taking, she told herself to make up her mind. She checked her watch, and when she saw it was only midmorning she decided on the oatmeal.

She would have cooked enough for Reilly, too, despite their argument and his stormy exit, if she hadn't seen that he'd already eaten breakfast. A pot and spoon had been used and washed, then left on the draining board to dry.

She started making up the bed while waiting for the water to boil, wincing when she accidentally ruptured one of the blisters on her hands. She stopped and fetched a Band-Aid from the bathroom, then continued where she'd left off.

As she tucked in the last corner and fluffed the pillow, she wondered how long she and Reilly would have to stay at Cody's cabin. Not that Cody would mind, she knew, even if they cleaned out the pantry and ran the fuel tank dry. She and Cody had known each other ever since they were toddlers, and they'd been friends all the way through high school.

Of course, they'd grown apart somewhat in the intervening years, she mused, sitting down on the newly made bed. Cody had joined the marines out of high school and she'd gone away to college, but when he'd returned to Black Rock a few years ago, they'd picked up the threads of easy friendship again.

She grimaced. Friendship on her part, she admitted. Cody's emotions had run deeper. There'd never been anything more between them, though. At least there hadn't been until—

A hissing, spattering sound broke her train of thought, and Mandy dashed for the stove, where the water was boiling over. She quickly removed the pot from the burner and turned down the heat, then stirred in the oatmeal. As she did so she couldn't help thinking about the mistake she'd made in not recognizing the truth where Cody was concerned.

Things aren't always what they seem, she reminded herself, spooning oatmeal into a bowl. *You have to look below the surface, and that's what you didn't do because you'd labeled Cody a friend. It was different with Reilly, remember? It was hard getting past his emotional defenses, at first, but you kept at it until—*

She gasped. The spoon dropped from her suddenly nerveless fingers and she sank into the nearest chair to consider the idea that had just occurred to her.

"What if he *wasn't* pretending back then," she whispered. "What if he did love me?"

Mandy had just finished washing up her breakfast dishes when Reilly walked through the back door. She turned toward him, and he paused in the entryway, his searching gaze gauging her mood.

"We have to talk," he said slowly.

She folded the dishcloth and draped it over the faucet to dry, then leaned one hip against the counter and said, "I know."

He surprised her. "Can you handle a gun?"

She blinked and straightened. "Yes. Why?"

"I mean really handle a gun."

She nodded. "I was target-shooting with a pistol by the time I was ten. It's been awhile, so I'm probably rusty, but yes. I can handle a gun."

"Good." He bent down and tugged up his jeans leg, then straightened with a gun in his right hand. Her eyes widened. He checked the safety and opened the slide, then reversed the gun and held it out to her grip first. When she took it, he said, "That's a Smith & Wesson semiautomatic, nine millimeter. There's a round chambered, and eight in the clip."

Mandy closed the slide and cradled the gun in both hands, careful not to point it in his direction. The metal was still warm from its proximity to his body. "What do you expect me to do with this?"

He ignored her question and strode to his duffel bag beside the fireplace. He dug inside and brought out a box of ammunition and a spare clip, both of which he carried back and placed on the counter beside her. "If I wasn't afraid of attracting attention, I'd have you shoot a few rounds to get the feel of it," he said. "But we can't chance that now. That gun has been my backup gun for a long time, and it's never let me down," he continued, "but it's got a kick and it pulls slightly upward. Aim low, just above belt high, if you're not sure." He paused, then added, "I've set traps around the clearing's perimeter for your protection. If nothing else they'll at least give you enough warning time to be prepared. I'd prefer it if you stayed in the cabin, but if you have to go outside for some reason, don't wander far. I don't want to come back and find you in one of my traps."

"Come back? Where are you going?"

"I have some business I have to take care of. It might take some time, but I should be back before dark."

"I see." Mandy carefully placed the gun Reilly had given her on the counter next to the clip and the box of ammunition, then thrust her suddenly shaking hands into her pockets to hide them. "You're just leaving me here, then?"

His face was grim. "There's no phone in this cabin, Mandy, and even if there were, I wouldn't use it. I have to make some calls, get some information, set some things in motion, but I don't want anything traced back here. You should be safe enough here, safer than being out there with me."

She gestured toward the counter. "Then why the gun?"

"Because I'm not taking any chances. Not with you."

Her eyes darted to his shoulder holster. "What about you? If it's not safe for me out there, it's not safe for you."

She swallowed hard and her voice was scarcely more than a whisper when she asked, "Who'll watch your back?"

"I can take care of myself," he said, and when Mandy started to argue, he added, "It's not open for discussion."

She stared at his set expression for a full minute, trying but failing to read something, *anything* of what he was feeling in his face. Then, in a flat tone carefully wiped clean of emotion, she said, "You're not coming back, are you." It wasn't a question. Bitterness welled up inside her, crept into her eyes, edged her voice. "You're just going to walk away, leaving me to put my life back together. Again." She swung around and stared unseeingly out the window over the kitchen sink. Her fingers closed on the edge of the countertop, needing desperately to hold on to something. "Go, then."

Let it go, he told himself, fighting the urge to justify, to explain. *Maybe it's better if she believes it. Maybe it'll be easier for her down the road if she thinks I'm the kind of man who'd desert her when she needs me the most.*

He couldn't do it.

"Mandy." Her whole body stiffened when his hands descended on her shoulders, and she resisted his efforts to turn her around. "I'm coming back. You have to trust me on this. I'm coming back," he insisted, then added the silent rider, *unless I'm dead.*

The thought terrified him. Not that he might die, but that by dying he would leave Mandy stranded, alone and helpless. But it was too dangerous to take her with him out in the open, exposed, where the killers who were after him could get to her.

"Just go," she said tightly, and Reilly knew she didn't believe him. He searched for a way to explain without involving her further in the mess he was in. The right words wouldn't come. Words had never been easy for him where his emotions were concerned.

His hands dropped to his sides and he took a step back. He stood there a moment more, cataloging in his mind the way her blond curls grazed her shoulders and tumbled down her back, the way her waist curved softly inward above the flare of her hips in the ill-fitting jeans, the way her small bare feet betrayed her vulnerability.

Buried deep in his aching soul was the impossible wish that she would turn around and smile once more in the way that had captured his heart so long ago. He wouldn't ask, though. It had to come from her.

She never turned, not even when his footsteps sounded like a death knell across the cabin's plank floor as he made his way to the front door. He paused with his hand on the doorknob for one final backward glance, hoping against hope that she would soften and look his way. If this was his last sight of her, if death prevented him from returning as promised, then he wanted her picture vividly imprinted in his mind so that his last dying thought would be of her.

"Mandy?"

"What?" The gruff sound held echoes of past pain, and Reilly realized anew how much she'd suffered the first time he'd left her. Was that why she wouldn't, *couldn't*, watch him walk away again? Maybe, but the knowledge didn't help.

He swallowed the lump in his throat and steeled himself for rejection, before saying, "Wish me luck?" It was the only thing he could ask of her.

She drew a deep, shuddering breath, visible even across the room. Then she let it out in a rush and her hands tightened their grip on the counter. "Good luck."

For the first half hour after Reilly left, Mandy refused to let herself think about him, about the danger he was walking into. Just as she refused to let herself speculate on whether or not he would really return this time.

At first she remained where he'd left her, staring out of the window, her ears straining to hear something other than the echoing silence that had enfolded her when the door had clicked shut behind him.

Then she gave herself a mental shake and set about putting the cabin to rights. The place was filthy, she decided.

As far as she could tell, no one had really cleaned the cabin in a long time. Dust coated every surface, so thick she could write her name in it. Her name, then Reilly's. When she realized what she'd done, Mandy hurriedly brushed both names into oblivion, then dragged out what few cleaning supplies she could find and set to with a vengeance.

Eradicating months of grime was hard work, but it wasn't enough to keep her thoughts from straying to Reilly. Her mind followed him fearfully through the woods to his truck, then down the winding mountain road to the highway, and beyond. Each time she caught herself doing it, though, she forced her thoughts to something else.

As she wielded the broom around the room, careful of her tender hands, she wondered what would happen to her bookstore. Alice and Judy, her longtime friends and part-time helpers, thought she was dead most likely, as did everyone else in town. Alice worked mornings, when her twin daughters were in kindergarten, while Judy, who split the duties of caring for their ailing mother with her married sister, worked afternoons and Saturdays. Would they be able to keep the Book Nook open for business? Black Rock was really much too small to support a bookstore of its own, but Mandy's store drew customers from other small towns in the area and from the surrounding ranches. She operated on a shoestring budget, as did most small stores these days, but since she'd inherited her house from her parents debt-free, the income from the store had always covered her simple needs, and she'd been happy enough.

Until Reilly.

Reilly. Was he okay? Had they tracked him down, the mysterious and deadly *They* who were after him? What were those phone calls he had to make, and to whom?

Reilly again. "Don't think about him," she told herself firmly as she opened the back door and swept out the pile of dirt her broom had accumulated. Why should she worry herself sick over him, when he'd left her without a backward glance, just as he'd done before? Why should she care about him when he didn't give a damn about her?

That's not true, and you know it, her conscience chided her. *Don't forget he saved your life last night. Twice. That must mean something.*

Last night. Was it only last night? Mandy glanced at her watch for confirmation. So much had happened in the past twelve hours that it somehow seemed much longer since she'd walked into her bedroom and found Reilly waiting for her.

Against her will she remembered Reilly's crushing embrace in the dark, the desperate hunger in his kisses, as if he'd been as starved for her as she'd been for him. The shock of his appearance when she'd believed him dead, followed by the terrifying ordeal of their narrow escape, had pushed that memory to the furthest recesses of her mind until this moment. Now she dragged it out and considered it.

Why had he even been there? That was what she should have asked him when she had the chance. It didn't make sense for a man on the run from killers to turn up in her house in the dead of night. What had he thought she could do for him? Help him? Hide him?

No, that didn't seem like the Reilly she knew.

But then, you never really knew him, did you? her bruised heart cried.

She'd always known that there was a strong inner reserve in Reilly, a part of him he'd kept to himself despite all her efforts. She'd once teased that he had No Trespassing signs posted all over him. But there'd been a time when she'd thought she was making progress in tearing down those fences he used to keep people at a distance, a time when she'd believed he loved her.

She leaned her weight against the broom and stared out into the distance. Spring in these mountains was always late in coming, but by now the trees were painted with variegated shades of green. A light breeze played through the flourishing undergrowth and tickled the leaves, setting them dancing against the vivid blue Wyoming sky. The beauty of the scene didn't really register, though; her mind was occupied with something far more important.

You do know him, she told herself, striving for a dispassionate assessment. *You loved him as much as any woman ever loved a man, slept in his arms, gave him your trust. You weren't a gullible, love-starved spinster, believing a slick con man's lies. You* loved *him, so much so that you—* She cut off the last thought, shying away from even thinking it because she knew she still wasn't able to deal with those memories.

After a couple of calming breaths, she returned to her original train of thought. Her heart was wrong this time, she decided instinctively. There had to be more to his story. There *had* to be.

His face haunted her. When she'd said those hurtful things to him last night, he hadn't defended himself. He'd looked at her as if she'd mortally wounded him with her accusations, but he hadn't rushed to his own defense as most men would have done.

No, she thought, *he hasn't really told you anything yet. And why is that?*

"He's protecting me," she whispered, answering her own question. "That's the only thing it can be. If he doesn't give a damn, why would he care what happens to me?"

Her eyes narrowed, and her normally gentle mouth firmed. She had a host of unanswered questions, and whether Reilly liked it or not, he was going to answer them when he came back.

If he came back.

Chapter 5

Reilly barreled down I-90 in his truck—"letting the horses run", as some of the locals colorfully called it, although he was careful not to exceed the posted speed limit. He wasn't chancing some local cop or state trooper stopping him for speeding.

He fiddled with the radio's Seek/Scan button, but other than a couple of country-and-western stations and a man reading what sounded like a farm report in French, all he found was static. He turned the radio off in disgust. He didn't understand Basque French, so that station was worthless, and as for the others, how anyone could listen to country music for more than ten minutes at a time was beyond him. All that cryin', lovin' and leavin' got old real quick.

Mandy loved it, though. Country music had been playing in the background when they met in her bookstore, some song about standing outside the fire. He hadn't really been paying attention—his first sight of Mandy had taken all of that—but later on she had insisted it was "their" song and had played it often. Reilly had been forced to admit that for a country-and-western singer, Garth what's-his-name wasn't half-bad.

He checked his rearview mirror again. Other than a few eighteen-wheelers, there'd been little or no traffic around since he'd pulled onto the interstate fifteen minutes ago. Still, he couldn't be too careful.

Satisfied no one was on his tail, Reilly turned his mind back to the job ahead of him. The first thing he needed was information. Unfortunately, the only way to get it was to let someone know he was still alive, and right now that was chancy at best. Someone had betrayed him, someone he trusted. Other than his former partner on the police force and a handful of high-ranking federal agents, no one had known what he'd set out to accomplish five years ago. Most of those men were dead now, murdered in cold blood or killed in the line of duty. Of the men who were still alive, only two knew about Mandy. And one or both of those men had betrayed him.

His thoughts were grim as he considered his limited options.

One, he could turn around, head north for the Montana border, and keep driving until he hit Canada. It wouldn't solve anything, but it would buy some time. He had enough money to get by for several months, and he could always fall back on carpentry if things got desperate.

He considered and discarded that option in less than a minute. There was no way in hell he was leaving Mandy, not until he was damn sure she was safe. If he was going to Canada, she was coming with him. And the way things now stood between them, he doubted he could convince her to go anywhere with him.

A second possibility was getting in touch with Trace McKinnon, his contact in the witness-protection program, or McKinnon's highly respected superior, Nick D'Arcy. That option went the way of the first. McKinnon and D'Arcy were the only men who knew that Reilly had intended to return to Black Rock for Mandy. One or the other was a traitor, but he didn't know which one. He wasn't risking Mandy's life on guessing wrong.

His third and last choice was the least palatable personally: he could contact Sheriff Cody Walker, as Mandy had suggested last night. Reilly respected him professionally, had seen him in operation a few times in the months Reilly had lived in Black Rock. They'd even worked together toward the end. He knew nothing against Walker, and since Mandy trusted the man implicitly, Reilly didn't know why he hesitated.

Maybe it was just that he kept getting these vibes from her whenever Walker's name was mentioned. Nothing *bad*, exactly. Just the uneasy feeling that there was something he didn't know, something he *should* know. Something between the two of them, from which Reilly was excluded.

He couldn't afford to let his personal animosity toward Walker affect his decision, though. Not with Mandy's life at stake. Now that he'd had time to consider it, taking Walker into his confidence was the only logical, the only *safe* choice, however much he hated to admit it.

If only Josh was alive, Reilly thought, not for the first time, *none of this would be necessary.*

For a moment Reilly once again mourned the death of his partner. Josh Thurman had been the older brother he'd never had, the one man he'd trusted with his life, a man who'd trusted Reilly with his own. He'd lost track of the number of times he and Josh had been there for each other in tight corners. It wasn't something he'd been conscious of. It just *was*, and he'd taken it for granted. If Josh were alive...

But Josh had been dead for more than a year, along with his wife and infant son. Reilly's grief over their deaths had surprised him with its intensity. He hadn't realized how deep his feelings had run. Rage at the injustice of it all, an emotion he was much more familiar with, had joined grief and guilt, swiftly building to explosive proportions.

He was used to burying his emotions beneath a cool facade, though, metamorphosising them into unyielding determination. Denied the emotional outlet that attendance at Josh's funeral would have given him, he'd held his own private wake over a bottle of Irish whiskey instead. As he'd said goodbye to the man he'd loved like a brother, he'd sworn that no one else would ever die because of him.

He'd kept that promise so far, even though the price had been impossibly high: it had cost him the woman he loved.

Now Mandy's life was threatened again, and he had only himself to blame.

Curled up in a blanket in front of the fireplace, Mandy sleepily checked her watch for the umpteenth time. She sighed tiredly. It was only nine o'clock, but she'd already showered and changed back into Cody's robe in preparation for bed, where she longed to be. Last night's traumatic activities and today's strenuous workout cleaning up the cabin had worn her out, but she couldn't go to sleep yet. She was waiting for Reilly.

Suppertime had come and gone with no sign of him, and the sun had long since set in a fiery ball behind the mountains. She'd sat on the front step and watched night fall like a starry black curtain, leaving her cold inside and out. And alone. More alone than she'd felt in months.

Now it was almost bedtime, and Reilly still hadn't returned. So much for his promises.

She glanced at the gun he'd given her, resting within easy reach on the floor behind her, and wondered whether Reilly's leaving it with her meant she was on her own from here on out.

Guns didn't scare her. She respected them, but she'd grown up around men and women who used them regularly and had used them herself, so she wasn't intimidated by them. She'd kept the pistol with her all day, even when she went to the bathroom. Although Reilly had refused to explain exactly what was going on, he had made it clear that she was in danger, and she wasn't stupid enough to take chances with her life. Despite everything she'd lost, at least the fire last night had proved beyond a shadow of a doubt that she wasn't ready to give up on life just yet.

Mandy chuckled humorlessly. *Funny. Not so long ago you wanted to die,* would *have died if you'd had your way.*

Every day since then had been a constant struggle to forget. Her friends had worried about her, especially Alice and Judy. Sometimes their loving concern had made her feel smothered, but mostly she'd been grateful for their support. They'd helped just by being there. Not pushing her to talk about it, but not shying away from the subject, either.

The pain was still there, would always be there, but time *had* softened it a little, just as people said it would. She hadn't believed it at the time. She'd been inconsolable then, when she'd just lost Reilly and the—

No, she wouldn't think about that time in her life. She'd start crying for sure, and she'd be an emotional wreck when Reilly returned.

Reilly.

Mandy checked her watch again. Nine-fifteen. She wrapped the blanket tighter around her, inched closer to the fire, and wondered how long she could cling to the pitiful hope that Reilly was ever coming back.

Reilly crouched in the shadows behind the detached garage, which was connected to Cody Walker's house by a covered walkway. He'd debated picking the lock on the side door and waiting inside the house, as he'd done at Mandy's, but had decided against it for one very good reason. He wasn't familiar with the interior layout of Walker's house as he had been with Mandy's, and since he didn't dare turn on a light, it wasn't possible to scope it out before the sheriff came home. One of the things he'd learned the hard way as an undercover cop was always to leave himself an escape route. That way, if things didn't go down as planned, he wouldn't be trapped.

When he'd become involved with Mandy all those months ago, the first thing he'd done was check out her house from top to bottom. Not snooping, because he respected her privacy, but merely to familiarize himself with his surroundings. That's how he'd known about the hidden cellar. He hadn't been looking for it, really, but it hadn't been hard to find. The house's foundation had made him curious, and the interior measurements hadn't added up in his mind, so he'd suspected an old root cellar or something along those lines. Discovering the cave had been an unexpected bonus.

His precautions at Mandy's house so long ago had paid off last night. He wasn't about to go against his training now.

Night pressed in all around him, and Reilly checked the luminous dial on his watch, wondering where the hell Walker was. If he didn't come home soon, Reilly was going to have to leave to retrieve his truck. He'd walked here after parking several blocks away in the Black Rock Cinema's parking lot, knowing that his truck stood the best chance of going unnoticed there. Small-town residents were notoriously nosy, he'd learned. If he'd left the truck on any residential street in town, the odds were that it would have attracted undue attention, something to be avoided at all costs, since the truck and its contents wouldn't stand up to more than a cursory inspection. But the last movie would be letting out shortly, and unless he wanted to chance it, he'd have to move his truck soon.

Come on, Walker, he thought, his patience wearing thin.

He flexed his hands, working out the stiffness and the slight swelling caused by the small blisters on his palms. Thank God they weren't as bad as he'd first thought. He could easily ignore the pain but he couldn't afford to have his reaction time decrease. Not when there was so much at stake. Not when Mandy's life depended on him.

He wondered what she was doing right now, what she was thinking. He'd told her he should be back before dark, and it was long past that now. Was she afraid, all alone out there in the middle of nowhere? Did she think something had happened to him? Or did she think he'd deserted her?

The last one was probably on target, he thought bleakly,

especially since she'd already shown him how little she believed anything he said. He had no way to contact her, though, since the cabin had no phone.

He sighed soundlessly, and shifted his position, then froze when a car chugged down the otherwise quiet street. But it went on past without stopping, and Reilly relaxed a little.

Tiredness swept through him as the adrenaline surge drained away, but he ignored it. He hadn't had a lot of sleep last night, but that wasn't anything new to him, and he refused to give in to the momentary weakness. He'd been on worse stakeouts than this, and there were too many things left to do before he could let his guard down in sleep.

Although he'd decided to wait for the enveloping cloak of darkness before contacting Walker, he hadn't been idle this afternoon. He'd visited hardware and feed stores in Sheridan and Buffalo, picking up the items he needed, but in such a way as to avoid suspicion, he hoped. Both cities were so relatively small by New York standards that New Yorkers would have scoffed at calling them cities, but they were large enough for him to escape notice, something that wouldn't have happened in Black Rock.

He'd also bought some clothes for Mandy, spreading his purchases around so that no one would particularly remember him buying them: a couple of simple cotton tops in one store, two pairs of jeans in another, undies and a bra in a third. He'd bought what he knew Mandy liked, disregarding the cost. He owed her, he'd reasoned. It was his fault that the only clothes she had left were the ones she'd been wearing at the time of the fire. It wasn't until he was picking out a warm zippered jacket in a discount store on the edge of town that he'd realized he had another motive. He didn't want Mandy wearing Cody Walker's borrowed clothes a minute longer than she had to.

While he was at it, he'd also stocked up on nonperishables at a grocery store in Sheridan, enough to last them a couple of weeks. It didn't make a lot of sense, since he was bringing Walker in on the operation, but Reilly was reluctant to eat the man's food. He didn't want to be indebted to Walker any more than absolutely necessary.

The low purr of a well-tuned engine alerted him only a few seconds before two strong headlight beams swung into Walker's driveway. Reilly stayed right where he was. The garage door clattered and hummed as it rolled upward in response to a garage-door opener's radio signal, and the sheriff's 4x4 drove forward into the unlit garage. Reilly had already taken care of the overhead light by unscrewing it a couple of turns in the socket; he'd have the shield of darkness when he made his move.

He pulled his .45 out of its holster, then waited. He heard the car door slam shut, followed by a muffled curse. Walker must have tripped over something in the dark. The garage door rattled closed, and the firm tread of footsteps made their way toward the covered walkway. Reilly slipped silently around the corner of the garage. Cody Walker had just unlocked the back door, and Reilly had his gun cocked behind the sheriff's right ear before Walker even knew he was there.

"Not a sound," Reilly ordered, his voice pitched to carry no further than Walker's ears. "No, don't turn around." He grasped the collar of Walker's uniform shirt for additional control. "Use two fingers to pull that gun out real slow," he said, referring to the revolver in the sheriff's gun belt, "and hold it out at your side." When Walker silently complied, Reilly said, "Now drop it. Carefully." Walker did that, too, and the gun landed on the dead grass beside the steps with a small thud. Then Reilly gave him a slight push. "Inside."

Walker entered the house with Reilly right behind him, the .45 still cocked and threatening. The kitchen was dark, with only faint traces of moonlight gleaming through one window. Reilly was waiting patiently for his eyes to adjust, when the sheriff said coolly, "I don't have more than twenty dollars on me. There's a fifty stashed behind a photo in the living room, but other than that, pal, you're out of luck."

Reilly had to admire the other man's coolness under pressure. Walker had tensed when he'd first felt the gun pressed against his skull, but otherwise his big, lean body had betrayed no sign of fear or trepidation.

"I don't want money," Reilly said. "I want information." He waited for that to sink in, then added, "And I need your help."

"If it's help you want, you couldn't come to the office like normal folks?"

The acerbic statement surprised a laugh out of Reilly. "Ice water in your veins, huh?" he approved. "A man after my own heart." His tone sharpened. "If it was just me, Walker, I wouldn't have come to you in the first place. But it's not just me. It's Mandy Edwards."

Walker stiffened. "Mandy's dead." His gravelly voice sounded as if it hurt him just to say the words, much less know them for the truth, and Reilly relaxed his grip on the man's shirt just a fraction.

"No, she's not. She's very much alive, and if I have anything to say about it, she's going to stay that way. I'm betting my life you feel the same."

Mandy could scarcely keep her eyes open. It was late, she was exhausted, and the warmth of the fire was making her drowsy. But she stubbornly refused to surrender to the welcoming arms of sleep. If that meant she stayed up all night, then she'd do it. And when morning came without Reilly's return, she'd *know*, and then her heart could stop its foolish wishing.

Her eyes drifted shut. *I'm so tired,* she thought. *Tired of pretending I'm strong. Tired of fighting off the memories.*

She hadn't voluntarily opened the door to where her memories of Reilly were stored in so long that it was almost second nature to keep them locked up, but last night Reilly had forced her to remember. He'd picked the lock on her memory just as he must have picked the lock to break into her house. Now the unlocked door stood ajar, beckoning her to peer inside.

Don't do it, part of her warned. *You'll only hurt yourself if you do.*

Her heart refused to listen. *I'll just look at the good memories,* she reasoned. *The safe ones. It doesn't have to hurt.*

The bookstore, she decided. That was safe enough. There was nothing about the memories of Reilly and the bookstore that could hurt her.

Reilly had come in for a book just after she'd opened that morning, had rescued her from the ladder, and had stayed. And stayed. And stayed. Thinking back, she couldn't remember exactly what they'd talked about all that time. Books, of course, at first. They'd found they shared similar tastes in some areas, and laughingly agreed to differ on others. She adored John Grisham and found his books fascinating. He preferred the gritty realism of Lawrence Sanders. Neither cared for the depressing pretension of what passed for "literature" these days, but when he diffidently confessed that he'd once accidentally picked up a Linda Howard book and hadn't been able to put it down, she'd fallen in love.

Oh, not really. Love had actually taken a little longer, but she'd certainly formed a serious crush on him that morning. He was so different from the other men she knew. Even now she didn't know what it was about him that had attracted her so strongly, but whatever it was—sex appeal, charm, personality—it had thrown her for a loop. She was a small-town girl, born and raised, and she'd liked it that way. She'd been happy enough with her life before he'd come along. Maybe it hadn't been exciting, but there'd been a genuine satisfaction in the comfortable sameness of her days.

Reilly changed all that. Changed *her.* His smile made her feel young and giddy, while his eyes told her she was sexy and exciting. He'd seemed to find her as fascinating, as irresistible, as she found him.

She hadn't wanted him to leave that day, had kept him leisurely talking about this and that while her brain feverishly worked to think of some excuse to see him again.

When he'd let slip that he'd just moved to Black Rock and was looking for a likely location to establish his carpentry business, she'd eagerly volunteered to help, and even offered him his first job—building new bookshelves for her store.

She smiled dreamily. Reilly's work had been first-rate, but it wouldn't have mattered to her if the bookshelves had fallen apart as soon as she stacked books on them. She would have done anything at that point to keep Reilly in her life.

Only two short months later they'd become lovers.

"It's late. I should get going," Reilly had told her, making a halfhearted attempt to rise from where they both reclined on large pillows in front of her fireplace, but Mandy wasn't about to let him go now. She'd waited so long already, all her life, it seemed, to make love with this man. She'd set the stage for tonight: a candlelit dinner, coffee afterward in front of the roaring fire, soft music playing in the background. And she was wearing the blue silk blouse she'd bought for the occasion with, daringly for her, no bra beneath it. No, he wasn't leaving tonight if she could help it.

"Don't go." She put a hand on his arm and felt the corded muscles tighten beneath her light touch. "Please."

He looked down at her, an expression she couldn't fathom on his face. Desire was there—she couldn't mistake that—he wanted her as much as she wanted him. But…pain? How had she hurt him?

"Mandy, this isn't a good idea. I—"

"Don't leave me." She scarcely recognized her own voice, a husky plea with a little catch in the middle that slipped past his defenses. Everything he felt for her was reflected in his face in that moment, and what she saw there gave her the courage to continue. Her fingers slid down his arm and captured his hand, then she lifted it and drew it to her breast.

She saw it in his eyes, the moment when he succumbed.

A flash of intense longing sparked between them and his head came down, his lips finding hers. In between kisses that stole her breath and set her body on fire he told her—warned her, really—that he wasn't a gentle man. But he was. He *was*. Gentle, and fierce, and loving...

Mandy woke as she was gently lifted into a strong pair of arms. Her eyelids fluttered open, but it was too much work to keep them that way, so she let them slide back down, a satisfied smile touching her lips.

Reilly had returned. She'd known deep down that he would. She'd pretended that she hadn't believed him, because she'd been afraid of being hurt again, but her heart had known all along. Explanations could wait. They weren't important now. He was back, and that was all that mattered.

A minute later she was lowered to the bed. Still in that dream state, she clung to the arms that held her, afraid that if she let go she'd awaken from the dream and find he'd never been there at all.

"Let me go, Mandy." The deep growl was real, but it held reluctance, and she knew he didn't really want her to let go, no matter what he said.

"No," she protested in a throaty voice, tugging until he came down beside her on the bed. The line between reality and dreams blurred, and she curled up against him, one arm thrown across his chest as if she could hold him captive that way. "Don't leave me." His chest moved up and down beneath her arm, a strangely hypnotic motion, and she murmured a request her heart had secretly been longing for since last night.

"What did you say?" The voice rumbled in her ears.

She sighed and snuggled closer. "Hold me," she pleaded, and sighed again—a contented sound this time—when his arms slid around her body. Then, for the first time in a year, she went to sleep in Reilly's arms.

Reilly lay awake holding his love, his body hard and aching with unslaked desire. It hadn't taken much to arouse him—the sight of Mandy wrapped in a blanket, with her head pillowed on her arm, fast asleep in front of the fireplace had accomplished that. Picking her up and carrying her across the room had been bad enough. Adding Mandy's delicate fragrance, which no expensive perfume could rival, had swelled his arousal to painful proportions.

This was subtle torture, worse than last night, worse than anything he'd ever imagined. Mandy's body was warm, soft, and oh, so inviting to the man who'd been denied access to it for so long. Her rounded breasts, covered by dark blue terry cloth, rested enticingly against his chest, and every shallow breath she took pressed them closer.

Sweat broke out across his brow. Lovemaking with Mandy had always been explosive, he remembered, shaking with the strain. Holding her like this reminded him vividly of the two of them lying naked and sated in each other's arms, their bodies damp, their frantic breathing slowing in the aftermath.

"Damn it!" The whispered words were softly but vehemently spoken, and his hand slid down to ease the restricting denim between his legs.

This would never do. He'd never last the night like this. It would kill him. *Better think of something else, Reilly, pretty damn quick.*

With an effort that cost him, he forced his thoughts away from the woman in his arms, and back to his earlier conversation with Cody Walker.

He'd gotten what he went there for—Walker's help. And if it had been any other man, Reilly wouldn't have had such a hard time accepting it.

He laughed soundlessly. What an understatement that was. His instincts had begun humming again as he'd talked with Walker about Mandy, the conviction growing that there was *something* neither of them was telling him.

He reached across and arranged the blanket more securely over Mandy, making sure it covered her. Then he thought, what the hell, and tugged it over himself as well.

He shifted positions and tucked her body closer to his while he was at it.

Staking a claim, Reilly?

He ground his teeth together. Damn straight, he was staking a claim. Mandy was *his*, at least until he was forced to let her go. She had started this by pulling him down on the bed with her. He'd tried to stop her, but he was only human, and there was a limit to how much he could take.

She murmured in her sleep, words too faint for him to catch, then snuggled her face against his shoulder before subsiding again. Reilly's breathing quickened, along with his heartbeat and a few other parts of his body. Then something occurred to him, pushing his physical awareness of her to the back burner as he considered it.

Maybe Mandy thought she didn't believe him, maybe when she was awake she'd argue again that she no longer needed him. That didn't matter anymore. What mattered was that subconsciously she still trusted him. She could deny it all she wanted to, but she couldn't sleep so peacefully in his arms like this if she didn't.

For the first time since his return, tension relaxed its iron grip on Reilly. It made absolutely no sense to feel this good about his discovery, because there was a strong possibility he'd eventually have to give her up again. But he loved her, and always would. At least now he knew she still loved him, too.

Chapter 6

"What do you think you're doing?"

Reilly was jolted awake from an erotic dream by the indignant question. He cracked one eye open, then the other, and found Mandy leaning over him in the predawn light, clutching the blanket to her chest like an outraged virgin. He sighed and closed his eyes. He wasn't ready for this. Judging by the gray shadows in the room, he'd had four, maybe five, hours of sleep. Not enough after the events of the last few days. His body, semiaroused by the dream and the proximity of the woman who had warmed the bed at his side until a moment ago, now felt cold and abandoned. As a result he was tired, edgy and hungry, though not for food. And he definitely wasn't in the mood for the confrontation looming before him.

An insistent hand pushed against him. "Get out of my bed."

"No," he said, his eyes flicking open to stubbornly meet hers. He was damned if he would. He wasn't a yo-yo she could bob up and down on a string as the mood took her. She'd dragged him into bed with her last night, and he wasn't getting up until he was good and ready. He'd had far too little sleep the last few nights, and she was the primary cause, so unless danger threatened them, he was staying right where he was.

His curt refusal astonished her. "What do you mean, 'no'?"

"Just that. You invited me here last night, and I'm staying."

She clearly hadn't been expecting that response. For a moment she stared at him as if she didn't quite know what to say. Then with a muttered imprecation, she threw the blanket down and scrambled off the end of the bed, flounced into the bathroom, and slammed the door.

Reilly closed his eyes again and rolled over onto the spot Mandy had just vacated, then groaned. The down pillow, the sheets, *everything* smelled of her, reminding him of his recent dream, and his body responded with predictable results.

"Damn," he mumbled against the pillow, but without heat.

What did you expect? his inner voice taunted him. *She was half-asleep last night. She probably doesn't even remember what did or didn't happen.*

"I do," he said to the empty room. "I remember." He wished his body didn't. When Mandy got out of the bathroom, he was going to need a long, cold shower, or he'd never make it past breakfast.

He lay there, face down, breathing in her scent. His arousal pressed against the mattress in bittersweet torture, and he tried to will himself back to sleep. It didn't work. He kept imagining Mandy in the bathroom, going through those peculiar female rituals of getting dressed, and his pulse speeded up until he groaned again. There wasn't a snowball's chance in hell he was getting any more sleep this morning.

A few minutes later he heard Mandy stomp barefooted out of the bathroom. The sound of banging cupboards, slamming drawers and rattling pans got his attention, too, and Reilly rolled onto his side. He propped his head on one arm and looked toward the tiny kitchen area. Mandy was making breakfast—for one or two?—and obviously didn't care that he was trying to sleep.

She was wearing Walker's shirt and jeans again, and he cursed under his breath. He hadn't had a chance to tell her about the clothes he'd bought for her yesterday. Given her mood, he doubted she'd be interested in hearing about them right now.

He jackknifed into a sitting position, then dropped his legs over the side of the bed and stood up. He adjusted the fit of his jeans—denim was never meant to expand that much—yawned and stretched. His muscles protested, and he imagined he could hear his joints creaking. He was getting too old for this, he thought, as he rotated his left shoulder to see how the wound there was healing. Running around like James Bond was a game for younger men.

Hold on there, O'Neill. Thirty-nine isn't exactly decrepit. You're in better physical shape than a lot of men half your age.

Yeah, but it still didn't make him feel any better. He could keep up, all right, could still push himself to the limit, and beyond, without his body failing him. But there was a price to pay. Time was, he could go all day and night without feeling it in his bones. Nowadays it took him a few minutes to work out the kinks before his body was ready to face the morning.

He sank back on the edge of the bed. He'd be forty years old soon, he mused—if he lived through the next month. The older he got, the faster the years passed. He would be fifty before he knew it, then sixty, seventy. And what would he have to show for his life?

No wife. No children. Nothing to prove that the man who'd been born Ryan Callahan had lived on this planet. Nothing of himself to leave for future generations.

A strange, wistful yearning filled him as he watched Mandy bustle around in the kitchen. A long-forgotten memory came back to him—he couldn't have been more than three or four—and he saw his mother moving in the kitchen of their Brooklyn brownstone, making breakfast for his father. She'd been miffed about something, and his dad had been trying to tease her out of it, but she'd refused to break down and smile at his humorous efforts. Eventually his dad, a construction foreman, had gone off to work. The moment the door closed behind his dad, however, his mother had been at the window, peering out through the curtains, her lips moving in her oft-repeated prayer that God would bring her husband home safely again.

God had been inclined to listen that day. Patrick Callahan had returned that night as usual. But before the year was out, little Ryan Callahan was an orphan, his father killed in a fall from a high-rise under construction, his mother dead of a broken heart. Pneumonia was what the doctor told the parish priest and what the priest explained to four-year-old Ryan, but Ryan knew better. His mother had wasted away until death was a welcome relief from a life made unbearable by grief.

Reilly shook his head, wondering what had revived those ancient memories. He wasn't a man normally given to deep introspection, but the last eighteen months had wrought profound changes in his life, in him. Falling in love did that to a man. It gave him ideas. Made him think about settling down, making a home. Maybe having a couple of rug rats of his own to dandle on his knee or toss gleefully in the air the way he dimly remembered his dad doing with him.

He'd give anything to have that chance now. Now, when it was too late.

"Breakfast is ready." The clipped sentence broke in on his thoughts, and although the edge to Mandy's voice told him she was still upset, Reilly welcomed the interruption. His thoughts made bad company this morning.

He glanced at the table, where Mandy had set two places. Obviously she wasn't upset enough to deny him something as basic as food. He caught her eye. "Thanks," he said, and meant it.

She shrugged, a noncommittal gesture, and turned her back to him again as she fetched the coffeepot. He allowed himself one more lingering look at the woman he'd once hoped to make the mother of his children. Then he shut down his emotions, as he'd first learned to do thirty-five years ago.

He picked up the shoulder holster he'd slipped off last night and had slung over the headboard within easy reach. By long-standing habit, he checked the .45 before sliding it back into the holster, then made for the bathroom. "Give me a minute," he said, "and I'll be right with you."

Breakfast was canned corned-beef hash and powdered scrambled eggs—neither of which did much for the taste buds. But at least the coffee was hot, strong, and delicious. Reilly had two quick cups, needing the reviving kick of caffeine.

Mandy was giving him the silent treatment, speaking only when spoken to, asking no questions, and answering his questions with terse sentences that killed any chance at conversation. Finally he gave up.

He scratched his unshaven cheek absently, fingering the stubble, and made a mental note to shave later. He hadn't had time before breakfast. He needed a shower, too, but that would have to wait until after he checked the perimeter traps. He'd checked them when he returned last night, tired as he was. They'd been undisturbed then, and he was pretty sure they still were, but he didn't like leaving things to chance.

He rose and poured himself a third cup of coffee. "Do you want any more?" he asked, holding out the pot.

"No thank you."

He sipped his coffee standing at the stove, while he made a decision. When he sat back down, he took a breath, leaned his elbows against the table and said, "I talked to Walker last night."

Mandy had been pushing her food around her plate uneaten. Now she glanced up in surprise. "Cody? I thought you said you didn't trust him."

"That's not exactly what I said. What I said was that I needed to think about it first." He gave her a steady look. "I decided you were right."

"Oh." She thought about it for a minute. "How much did you tell him?"

"Everything."

"Everything?" Her chin came up, and he didn't like the glint in her eyes. "I see. You told Cody, but you won't tell me." Her chair scraped backwards as she stood up, strong emotions controlling her movements. She cleared the table with haste, almost throwing the plates and utensils into the sink.

She stood there a moment, then swung around. "It's my life." She thumped her chest in frustration. "*My* life. I have a right to know what's going on, damn it! You have no right to keep me in the dark. This isn't the eighteen-hundreds. We don't equate women with chil—" Her voice faltered, a stricken expression on her face, but she rallied. "We don't equate women with children anymore."

Silence followed her outburst. Reilly studied her in the early-morning light coming through the window over the sink, really studied her for the first time since the night of the fire. As haunted as she'd appeared that night, she was even worse now. There was a pinched look about her, lines of strain pulling her lovely face into a sad reflection of the woman he'd fallen in love with, and he realized she was at the end of her rope. She couldn't take much more.

"Sit down," he ordered abruptly, pulling a chair out for her. She didn't comply right away—it was plain she didn't much care for his ordering her around, especially in the middle of an argument—but he just waited patiently until she seated herself. Then he asked, "Have you ever heard of a man named David Pennington?"

Her brows knitted as she thought for a moment. Then she shook her head. "No, I don't think so. Should I have?"

"No reason for you to, I guess, although his name was

in the news a while back." He hesitated. "David Penning-ton is...*was* the leader of an anarchist paramilitary orga-nization, the New World Militia. They, the group, that is, believed that any government—federal, state, or local—is inherently bad, and should be overthrown. They were fa-natically dedicated to bringing that about in this country."

The questioning expression in her eyes encouraged him to continue. "Pennington is an ex-marine who served in Vietnam back in the early seventies. He was drummed out of the service—dishonorable discharge—for insubordina-tion. At the time there was a host of other possible charges pending against him, including drug dealing, gunrunning and black-market profiteering, but none that the military could make stick."

Mandy looked confused, but he pressed on. "After his release from Leavenworth, Pennington disappeared. He sur-faced a few years later with a sizeable fortune—no one's sure from where—and began recruiting his own private army."

She gasped, and Reilly paused for a moment. "Yeah," he said finally. "His own army. He started off with ex-soldiers nursing grudges against authority, like himself, and a few ex-cops who disliked what they saw as the govern-ment's 'soft' attitude toward the criminal element. By the time he was done, though, he'd recruited men from just about every walk of life."

"But...what does that have to do with you?"

He silenced her with a waving motion of his hand. "I'm getting to that." He mulled things over for a moment, strip-ping the story to its barest essentials. "The Feds had been watching Pennington for years, of course. FBI. ATF. DEA. But they couldn't pin anything on him. The Bureau of Al-cohol, Tobacco and Firearms *knew* he was stockpiling weapons, but all they could trace were legal purchases. They suspected he was behind several major thefts of mil-itary weapons, including antitank and antiaircraft missiles, but again, they had no proof. The few informers the Feds found who were willing to talk all turned up dead."

"I can't believe it!" She was stunned. "This is the United States. Not some terrorist-occupied country."

"Believe it." Reilly's eyes narrowed. "Pennington's New World Militia isn't the only one out there, but they were the biggest, the strongest, and the best paid. And of course, Pennington was one smart son of a bitch. The Drug Enforcement Administration had long suspected him of belonging to one of the most powerful drug cartels in this country, mainly to support his expensive 'hobby.' They just couldn't prove it."

Mandy shook her head in disbelief. "But someone must have known. I mean—"

He chuckled, but it wasn't a humorous sound. "Yeah, someone knew, all right. A lot of someones, actually. But Pennington was good at spreading his wealth around, if you know what I mean. Money can buy a lot of 'friends' in high places, especially in uncertain times."

He paused for a moment, gauging her reaction, then continued. "In any case, nothing could be proved against him. The FBI and DEA both tried to infiltrate Pennington's organization, but with no success. The Militia was a tight-knit bunch, a 'brotherhood,' as it were, especially in the upper ranks. Membership was by invitation only." He smiled coldly. "And once you joined, membership was for life. No one ever left the brotherhood alive. Those who tried, died. That's when the Feds approached me."

She caught her breath and covered her mouth with one hand, then shook her head. "No!" she said, dropping her hand to the table. He watched her fingers clench, her knuckles turning white. "I don't believe it."

Reilly knew she wasn't talking about the brotherhood's membership criteria, but still he asked, "What don't you believe?"

"I don't believe you were a member of the New World Militia." Her lips trembled, and she clutched her hands together as if they'd tremble, too, if she let them. "You *couldn't* be."

He studied her in silence, then said, "Oh, but I was, Mandy. I was. I was Pennington's right-hand man."

For all of five seconds Mandy believed him. Ice water seemed to trickle through her veins, leaving her dazed and speechless. Then sanity returned, accompanied by a surge of burning anger. Her chair grated along the wooden floor as she jumped to her feet. "I don't know what kind of game you're playing," she said hotly. "But you're not playing it with me!"

She almost made it to the door before he caught her. "Mandy, wait!"

But she was too angry to listen. When he swung her around to face him, her palm cracked across his cheek with such force that it left her hand numb. "Damn you!" she cried, struggling for freedom. "Damn you!"

He pressed her against the wall, using his body to hold her, but she'd had enough. "Let me *go!*" Desperation lent her strength, and she twisted out of his arms and ran out the door.

She didn't know why she was running, or where. She just knew she couldn't stay there any longer listening to Reilly make up stories that mocked the love she'd once felt for him, that mocked the ordinary life she'd once hoped to share with him.

She was barefoot, but he was too, and she knew her way through these woods. He didn't. If she could just make it past the clearing, she thought, she could lose him in the trees. She heard his thudding footsteps behind her and realized he was closing on her fast. She evaded his grasp and feinted left, then broke right, skimming over the rough terrain.

He tackled her at the clearing's edge. It knocked the breath out of her for a second, but she wasn't giving up that easily. He scissored her legs with his, and she fought back, scratching and squirming, breath rasping in her throat until he finally manacled her wrists and pinned her arms above her head.

His body was crushing hers and he was breathing hard, his muscled chest pressing against her breasts with every breath he took. "You little fool!" he ground out. "What the hell did you think you were doing?" He raised his head in the direction she'd been heading. "I told you I have traps out here. You almost got yourself killed!"

"I don't care!" She arched her back to try and throw him off that way, but all she accomplished was bringing her body into even closer contact with his. She squirmed beneath him. *"Let me go!"*

He gazed down at her, his face a tormented mask. As she watched, his expression changed from anger to something else. "Mandy," he groaned. "Oh, God. Mandy."

He kissed her, and she tasted despair and desperate need. She didn't want to respond, had never liked being handled roughly, but his kisses seared her, starting a conflagration that she only now realized had been simmering below the surface ever since the night of the fire. He devoured her mouth, his tongue pushing past her lips to find hers, and forcing a sob of mingled pleasure and pain from her.

His strong hands released her wrists and crept down the bare skin of her arms, stroking from wrist to elbow with unexpected gentleness. His tactile exploration left her whimpering, and he redoubled his caresses, as if her complete surrender was his goal.

Desire exploded between them, fueled by twelve months of loneliness. She moaned aloud under the onslaught and arched up, only this time it was because she couldn't bear to wait a second longer. Reilly was muttering her name repeatedly, raining kisses wherever he could reach, then returning time and again to savagely possess her mouth as if he could never get enough. He was out of control, but she no longer cared. Her legs came up around his hips, and he quickly took advantage, grinding his pelvis against hers with a familiar rhythm she strained to match.

She was trembling, but so was he, as if in the throes of a fever. His strong body was iron-hard all along the length of her softness, and bent on a single goal. It was her goal, too. It had been so long since she'd felt like this—on fire, yet never wanting it to end.

He had too many clothes on. She wanted his taut skin beneath her hands, wanted to fill her senses with the sight, the smell, the taste of him. Memories of their naked bodies entwined together flooded her with sensual heat.

"Let go of my arms," she panted, pleading, and when he did, she brought them to his waist. Her hands burrowed beneath the waistband of his jeans, and she sighed her pleasure into his ravaging mouth. She was the aggressor now. Her nails dug into his skin, tugging at his hips to bring him closer still. He responded by pulling her legs up higher, until her knees clasped his waist, and another surge of heat rolled through her.

At some point he'd removed the barrier of her flannel shirt by the simple expedient of ripping it open, and now his hands pushed her flimsy bra out of the way so his mouth could have access to her aching breasts. She sobbed for breath when his lips closed on one turgid nipple, sucking it into the cavern of his warm mouth and laving it with his tongue. Then he rubbed his bristled cheek against her breast, rasping it unbearably, forcing a cry of pleasure from her. His lips left a trail of fire as they moved to her other breast, subjecting it to the same teasing torment, and Mandy sobbed again.

His thrusts increased in intensity. Even through both their jeans she could feel him at the juncture of her thighs, huge and throbbing, and growing impossibly harder. It was too much, yet not enough. Never enough.

He whispered something in a passion-deep voice, but she was too distracted to understand, too far gone to care. Needing something to hold on to, her hands climbed his back, only to stop cold when they made contact with his shoulder holster.

The leather holster and the gun it contained doused her passion better than a bucket of cold water. Everything that had led up to this moment came back to her, and she froze. She couldn't help it. The man lying between her legs carried a gun, and she had no doubt he'd used it at some point in his life. Whether or not his story was true, the gun was real, and the fact that he wore it everywhere scared the hell out of her. The man she'd fallen in love with hadn't worn one. This was the same man, yes, but he was different, too, and the difference was as tangible as the gun he carried.

Reilly didn't notice her withdrawal at first, but eventually her stillness reached him. "Mandy?" The husky sound twisted inside her, tearing at her heart, but she wouldn't, *couldn't* let herself respond.

"Let me go." She didn't think he'd heard the flat little whisper, but he must have, because after one final thrust his hips stilled. Then, with a blistering curse, he rolled off her, and away. His body was hunched as if in terrible pain, and Mandy covered her face with her hands and turned away so she couldn't see him.

It seemed like forever before her breathing slowed, and even longer before her throbbing body forgave her for denying it the release it craved. She tugged her bra back into place, the sensation reminding her just how far they'd gone. Then the guilt hit her.

What had she been thinking of? Yes, Reilly had started it by kissing her, but she knew in her heart that it would never have gone beyond that if she hadn't responded, if she hadn't allowed herself to be pulled down into the passionate maelstrom they'd created. She'd let him think—no, *encouraged* him to think she wanted it as much as he did. Any man might be forgiven for refusing to stop on the brink of release, but Reilly hadn't. He'd been as far gone as a man could be, but he'd somehow found the strength to stop at a word from her.

What if she hadn't touched the shoulder harness and remembered the gun? She'd been a breath away from unzipping his jeans and hers, desperate for the fulfillment only he could give her. And if she hadn't stopped him, he'd be inside her now, driving for release with no protection, nothing to prevent a pregnancy neither of them was prepared for.

Oh, God, I must have been mad. How could I have forgotten, even for a minute?

How long she lay there, one arm thrown across her eyes, she didn't know. She knew she was going to have to get up sometime, and unless a miracle occurred she was going to have to face Reilly eventually. She just wanted to postpone it as long as possible.

A faint rustling in the grass nearby alerted her to his movement. She removed her arm and opened her eyes to find him crouching beside her, but the accusation she expected to see on his face was absent.

He reached for her and she flinched, but all he did was gently draw the edges of her flannel shirt together and tuck them closed. His gaze met hers, contrition darkening his tawny brown eyes.

"I'm sorry, Mandy."

She shook her head, wanting to tell him that it wasn't his fault, it was hers, but the words stuck in her throat.

"I had no business touching you," he continued. "I knew that, but I..." He fumbled for words, a wounded warrior shouldering the blame for both of them. "It's been a long time for me, Mandy. That's not an excuse, but it's the only explanation I have."

She finally found her voice. "Don't apologize, please, I...led you on and I..."

"Don't make excuses for me."

"Not excuses." She squeezed her eyes shut, then opened them again. "It's been a long time since I felt that way too," she said honestly. "I'd almost forgotten...."

His jaw hardened as a harsh expression covered his face. He stood up abruptly. "I wish I could forget. God in heaven, Mandy, I wish the hell I could forget."

Chapter 7

As Mandy watched, Reilly ran a hand over his face and breathed deeply. It seemed to help him regain control. He stood there for a moment, his legs slightly parted, still visibly aroused. She couldn't tear her eyes away.

Then he leaned over her, his hand extended, and when she took it, he pulled her to her feet. Her shirt fluttered open, and Reilly averted his gaze. Embarrassed more by his gallant gesture than anything else, Mandy captured the ends of her shirt and tied them in a knot. The soft flannel rubbed against her skin, reminding her of his earlier caresses. Inside her bra, her breasts still ached from his mouth's assault. She could hardly bear it, or the knowledge that deep down, part of her still wanted him.

She couldn't tell him that, of course, but she couldn't think of anything else to say, so she brushed past him, heading for the beckoning shelter of the cabin.

He caught her arm. "Wait." She refused to turn around, but that didn't stop him. "I owe you another apology."

"What for?"

"For before, in the cabin," he said. "For what I led you

to believe.'' After a couple of seconds Mandy figured out he was referring to his statement that he'd been Pennington's right-hand man, the statement that had triggered her flight.

''I don't know why I said it that way,'' he continued doggedly. ''Maybe I was testing you. I don't know. But I was wrong, all the way down the line, and I'm sorry.''

''Apology accepted,'' she whispered, then slipped out of his grasp. She picked her way carefully across the rough ground, conscious of his eyes on her, and went inside.

After a minute he followed her.

Reilly waited until Mandy took a seat at the table. After a short, awkward silence he picked up the story again. ''The FBI was getting desperate.'' He leaned against the counter. He couldn't tell what she was thinking, or even if she believed him, but her eyes never left his face.

''Small bombs had been set off in courtrooms where some New World Militia members were on trial. There'd been death threats before that against federal prosecutors, federal judges, even a U.S. senator, and still they couldn't tie anything to Pennington or his people. That's when the Feds came to me.''

''But why you? What could a carpenter do?''

''I wasn't a carpenter, Mandy. I was an ex-marine, like Pennington. And an undercover cop. One of the best.'' Her slight indrawn breath betrayed her shock, and Reilly met her eyes squarely. ''Woodworking was a hobby of mine, but until I moved to Wyoming I never made my living from it.''

''Oh.'' She blinked at him and Reilly wondered what she was thinking behind those wide blue eyes.

''It was an 'unofficial' operation all the way,'' he continued. ''The law says the FBI can't infiltrate an organization without evidence of a crime, but they couldn't get the evidence without getting inside. It was a vicious circle.''

He sighed. ''I'm not saying the law is wrong. It was

passed for very good reasons, and the Feds brought it on themselves by abusing their power in the past. But while Pennington sat safely inside his multimillion-dollar compound on Long Island, the militia kept spreading their doctrine of hate and violence. That's where I came in. The Feds had their hands tied, but I could infiltrate the organization on my own.''

''One man against an army?''

His eyes slid away from hers and stared into the distance for a moment, remembering. ''It only takes one man sometimes,'' he said slowly. ''One man *can* make a difference.'' His gaze returned to her face. ''I wasn't alone, though. I had my partner, Josh Thurman. And others.''

''Anyway,'' he said, ''the FBI set me up to be recruited by Pennington's bunch. A guy I'd gone through the police academy with was already a member of the New World Militia, so I had an in. The story we put out was that I was a renegade cop, fed up with the system and all too willing to take justice into my own hands. My partner and I set it up for me to be brought up on charges of police brutality, with him testifying against me. To make it convincing, I spent time on Riker's Island awaiting trial before the charges were 'dropped,' and I was allowed to resign in disgrace.''

''I...see.''

He wondered exactly what she did see, but didn't ask. If she didn't already know, he wasn't going to explain that prison was hell for an ex-cop, that he could all too easily have ended up with his throat slit or a shiv in his gut. He wasn't going to tell her about sleeping with one eye open and a hand on a makeshift knife the whole time he was there. Nor would he tell her how he'd made his rep his first day there, so that the other prisoners left him pretty much alone after that. There were some things a man just didn't tell his woman, especially if he loved her.

Too restless to sit still any longer, he stood and strode about the confines of the small room. ''I was recruited by the militia almost before the ink was dry on my resignation.

I have to admit, they talked a good line, and I could see how convincing they could have been if my situation had been real.

"Josh was still my partner in this. He took a leave of absence from the force, supposedly for medical reasons, in case anyone was curious. We worked as a team—me on the inside, him on the outside. I started as a grunt—" Her eyebrows raised a fraction and he explained, "That's military talk for a foot soldier, a private. Anyway, I started at the bottom, feeding Josh what little information I had access to, and Josh turned over what I found out to the Feds."

Reilly picked up his now cold cup of coffee, stared unseeingly at it for a minute, then tossed the dregs in the sink and refilled the cup from the pot on the stove. "I worked my way up through the ranks over the next two years—"

"Two *years!*"

He nodded. "I knew going in that it wasn't a short-term commitment. It took me two years to reach the inner circle, where the decisions were made. You see, we were gunning for more than just a slap on the wrist for Pennington. We wanted to put him away for a good long time and smash the organization in the process. For that, we needed irrefutable evidence against Pennington, a direct order for an illegal act made to a witness who could testify against him. Me."

She absorbed all that in thoughtful silence, then asked, "And did it work?"

"Yeah." He swallowed some coffee and grimaced at the bitter taste. The coffeepot had been sitting on the back burner for quite some time. He put the cup down. "Along with the upper echelon of the New World Militia, Pennington was arrested, tried and convicted. Conspiracy to commit murder, among other things. My testimony got him twenty years to life. Afterward, I entered the federal witness protection program."

Her delicately arched brows drew together in a frown of confusion. "But I don't understand. If he and the others were in jail, why did you need protection?"

Had he ever been that naive? If so, it was so long ago that he couldn't remember. "Revenge, Mandy. The Mafia has a saying, 'Revenge is a dish that tastes best cold.' And like the Mafia, the New World Militia has a long memory. I broke the code of the brotherhood, remember. I talked. Even worse, I put the grunts out of work, stopped the gravy train."

His thoughts winged to a federal courtroom two years ago, and a confrontation with an enraged Pennington after the verdict had been read. "You're a dead man, Callahan!" David Pennington had screamed at him, his normally cold eyes wild with fury. "I'll see you in hell!" Pennington's own lawyers had had to physically restrain their client before the bailiffs closed in on Pennington and escorted him from the courtroom.

But that was another thing he couldn't tell Mandy, that Pennington had put a price on Ryan Callahan's head and had raised it every time he eluded the militia's grasp. Last Reilly had heard, the going rate was half a million dollars.

"Reilly O'Neill isn't your real name, is it?"

He shook his head. "No. It isn't even the name I go by now."

"What—" She paused, undecided, then asked, "What *was* your name?"

He hesitated, then realized he had no reason not to tell her. "I was christened Ryan Patrick Callahan. Patrick was my dad's name. He died when I was four."

Mandy's eyes softened momentarily, and Reilly regretted that last sentence. He didn't want Mandy feeling sorry for him. He forced himself to look away from the sympathy reflected in her eyes, and focus on finishing the story. There wasn't much of it left, and he wanted to get it over with.

"I was a marked man," he said gruffly, "so the Feds gave me a new identity—Reilly O'Neill—and a new life. Any kind of police work was out of the question, of course, but I'd known that before I started. It was a choice I made."

And like other choices he'd been forced to make, the price was high. He'd always loved his work, loved bringing justice to his little corner of the world. It hadn't been easy, making the decision to give up years of his life to catching Pennington and then sacrificing the rest of his career. He'd talked it over with Josh, his partner on the force since his rookie year, knowing it would affect the other man's life, too.

"It comes down to this, Ry," Josh had said. "Is it worth it to put Pennington out of business for good?" Put like that, Reilly knew he'd only had one choice.

Mandy's voice interrupted his contemplation of the past. "What made you choose Black Rock, Wyoming? I mean, if you were trying to hide, why pick such a small town? Wouldn't you have been better off somewhere where you could blend into a crowd?"

He nodded. "Maybe. But small towns have one advantage. Strangers stick out like a sore thumb, just like I did when I moved here. If someone's tracking me, I prefer to know about it. At least then I have a fighting chance." There was another reason he'd chosen Black Rock, but he couldn't tell Mandy. It wasn't his secret to tell.

She was silent for a moment, then said in a small voice, "Is that what happened? Did someone track you to Black Rock?" Her arms were crossed over each other, and she was rubbing them as if she were cold. "Is that why you left?" Her soft blue eyes pleaded for an explanation. "Is that why you pretended to be dead?"

"Something like that."

"Something like that? *Something* like that?" Mandy jumped to her feet, as riled now as she'd been before. "You walked out of my life without a word, without even a backward glance, and that's all the explanation you have?" Her hands clenched into fists, but she didn't seem to know what to do with them. "Or didn't I matter to you?" Her voice broke on the last word. "Is that it? Was I just an...an easy lay while you were passing through?"

"No!" He strode toward her, grabbed her arms and shook her hard. "Don't say that. Don't *ever* say that!"

Words poured out of him unchecked. "You mattered to me! You still do, more than you'll ever know."

She was biting her lip to keep from crying. He knew her well enough to know that. "Then why did you leave me?" she asked, bewildered. "Why?"

"It's not that easy, Mandy."

"It was easy enough for you to leave me."

"No, it wasn't!" He shook her again. "It was the hardest thing I've ever done."

"Then *why?*"

"To protect you, damn it!" He hadn't meant to say it, but he couldn't bear for her to think he'd deserted her, couldn't stand the thought of adding to her pain by letting her think he hadn't cared.

"To protect *me?*" Her head moved slowly from side to side in denial, and she whispered, "That doesn't make any sense. No one was after me."

He let her go so suddenly that she teetered before regaining her balance. "Maybe not then," he said, "but the way things were going it was only a matter of time before they found out about you. I couldn't take that chance."

Anger kindled in her face, and if he hadn't been so caught up in his own turbulent emotions, he would have wondered why. "*You* couldn't take that chance? Who made it your choice?"

"I did." She swung on him, just as she had earlier, but this time he parried the blow before it could land. When her other arm came at him, he captured both arms and held tight. "Stop it, Mandy!" She struggled, her breathing shallow and hoarse, and his anger grew to match hers. "I said stop it! I left because they'd already tracked down my partner. And after they'd tortured what little information they could out of him, they killed him!"

"Oh, my God." Mandy was stunned. Things like that just didn't *happen* in real life. Not in this country. She didn't realize she'd said the words out loud until Reilly answered her.

"Yeah, they do, Mandy." Grief flickered over his face.

"The militia tried to use Josh to get to me." He let her go and took a step backwards, his arms dropping to his sides. "They kidnapped his wife and baby son. Josh knew how the militia operated. He *knew*. He managed to get word to me, warning that we'd been betrayed. Then he went after his family, knowing he was a dead man. But what else could he do?" He brushed a hand across his eyes, as if he could shield his emotions from her that way.

"They didn't just kill him, though." Reilly's internal struggle was reflected on his face, as reluctance to tell her the rest weighed against the need to convince her. "The militia wouldn't believe Josh didn't know where I was, so they threatened to kill little Jeremy and Dara, Josh's wife, unless he told them. But Josh couldn't tell them what he didn't know. So they killed Jeremy and Dara in front of Josh, then slit his throat and cut out his tongue as a warning to others."

Her breath caught and she gave a small moan of denial. "How could they?"

"Easy. Haven't you figured it out yet? They want me dead. And they don't give a damn who else dies in the process."

She didn't want to believe him. It was like something that belonged between the covers of a book. Grisham, maybe, or Ludlum. This callous disregard for the sanctity of human life that he was talking about didn't belong in her safe little world.

But her world hadn't been safe for a long time, a tiny voice whispered in her mind. Not since Reilly, or Ryan, or whatever he called himself now, had entered it.

He had to be telling the truth. You couldn't fake the kind of grief and guilt that emanated from him. Besides, even if he could make up a story like that, why would he? What did he have to gain?

"So what happens now?" Her voice surprised her. She didn't feel anywhere near as calm as she sounded. She must have taken Reilly by surprise, too, because he didn't answer at first.

"Now we set a trap," he said finally.

"With us as bait?"

He nodded reluctantly. "If I could, I'd stash you some-place safe until this is all over. But the safest place for you right now is wherever I am."

"What about Cody? Does he know where we are?"

"Only if he guessed. I didn't tell him."

"Why—"

"I don't trust *anyone* that much. I told him I'd be in touch."

"Is he going to help us?"

"Yeah. We mapped out a plan, but he's checking a few things for me to start with. We'll go from there."

Mandy glanced down at her hands, then back up at Reilly. Ryan. Whoever he was. No, she couldn't think of him as anyone but Reilly, even if he no longer resembled the man she'd fallen in love with.

He did, though. His features were different, his hair was darker, and the mustache gave him a dangerous, rakish look that hadn't been there before. But his eyes hadn't changed. They still gazed at her with the same intensity as they used to, the same...longing?

She shivered inside. It wasn't wise to remember too much about the past. The longing was there in her, too, the desire simmering just under the surface. She'd just had a potent reminder of how easy it would be to let herself fall under his spell again, to lose herself in his arms, and she wasn't going to let it happen. Not if she could help it.

"I want to know what your plans are," she said as firmly as she could. "Don't think I'm going to let you leave me in the dark again."

His eyes narrowed. "It will get ugly," he warned.

"I know."

"People could die."

He wasn't sugarcoating anything anymore, and Mandy was grateful. "I know that, too."

"Your friend, Walker, might be one of them. If he screws up..."

"I'm not a child, Reilly."

"No, but have you ever seen a man die?" He knew the moment the words left his mouth that he'd made a mistake, but it was too late to stop the damage.

White-faced, shaking, Mandy said, "Yes. I've seen a man die. I saw *you* die." He took a step toward her, but she backed away. Her voice trembled. "I know now that you didn't, but at the time..." She swallowed and fought for control. "I didn't even know if I could go on without you."

"Mandy..." Reilly reached for her, and this time she let his arms encircle her shaking body. He didn't say anything more, just pressed her head against his chest and held her until the shivering stopped.

"You weren't supposed to be there," he said at last. "You were supposed to be at work."

"I came to see you." The words were muffled against his shirt.

"Why?"

She stiffened. One moment she was soft and pliant in his arms, and the next she was taut and unyielding. It was the scene outside all over again.

She pulled away, then turned and put the distance of the room between them before facing him again.

"What's wrong, darlin'?" The endearment slipped out unnoticed by Reilly, but if anything it made Mandy stiffen even further.

"Nothing." The hard, little pellet of a word shot across the room at him. She wrapped her arms around herself, closing him out. "Nothing's wrong."

"Something *is* wrong, and I want to know what it is." He spread his hands wide. "All I asked was why you weren't at work that day, why you came to see me, and all of a sudden you freeze up as if I said something terrible." The cornered expression on Mandy's face knifed through him. God almighty, what had he done that she would look like that?

"I don't remember why I went to see you," she said

desperately. She was lying, and Reilly knew it, but he also knew that there was no point in confronting her, no reason to try and force the truth out of her when she didn't want to tell him.

"Okay," he reassured her, backing off. "It's not really important," he added, even though he knew in his gut that it was. She'd tell him in her own time, though, or not at all. "Come on," he said in a different tone of voice, heading for the back door. He stopped in the tiny hallway and turned to look at her. "If you want to know what I've got planned, I'd better show you our first line of defense before I go any further."

Too bad she didn't drink, Mandy thought later, as she paced the cabin's confines, waiting impatiently for Reilly's return. After their brief tour of the perimeter traps, he'd gone off to retrieve some things from his truck, declining her offer of assistance. That left her alone with her thoughts. Her thoughts, and her memories, neither of which made pleasant company.

Yes, she thought bitterly, it was too bad she didn't drink. Cody kept his cabin stocked with everything, even a well-hidden bottle of Jack Daniel's, which she'd discovered tucked inside a galvanized tin bucket during her orgy of cleaning yesterday. If she'd been the drinking kind, she could have numbed the dormant pain Reilly's innocent question had reawakened. If she'd been the drinking kind, she'd be able to forget, at least for a little while, what else she'd lost when she'd lost Reilly a year ago.

Oblivion. She'd sought that in a bottle of booze once before, last New Year's Eve. It hadn't helped. It hadn't really blotted out the memories, only dulled them. When she'd sobered up the next morning, the grief had returned stronger than before, leaving her heartbreakingly vulnerable to Cody's brand of sympathy.

Best not to think about that, Mandy decided, as she left the bottle of Jack Daniel's undisturbed.

Her pacing took her past the tousled bed in the corner

for the fourth time, and finally she couldn't stand it one more minute. "Can I help it if I wasn't raised to leave a bed unmade?" she muttered to herself as she briskly tugged the top sheet and blanket into place. When she picked up the pillow to fluff it, she caught a faint lingering scent. Reilly.

She pressed the pillow to her face and breathed deeply, closing her eyes as memories surged to the fore. Memories of waking in Reilly's arms all those months ago, snuggling, cuddling together in the early morning hours. She'd been shy that first morning, after her wanton behavior the night before, but he'd made it seem so natural that her shyness soon evaporated.

He was a sprawler, she remembered, his big body taking up more than his half of the bed as he slept, but she hadn't really minded. Her bed had been cold and lonely before his entrance into her life. Books had kept her company at night, but *books* couldn't hold her in the dark, couldn't warm the sheets, couldn't lull her to sleep like the sound of his breathing did.

Making love with Reilly had always been intensely exciting, better than her fantasies, and her body still craved him. Their encounter earlier proved it. But it was other things she'd missed the most after he was gone. Little things. The touch of his hand. The way his eyes tilted up at the corners just before he smiled. The scent of him on her pillows.

A sound at the front door made her drop the pillow on the bed as if it burned her. Reilly was back.

"Could you give me a hand here?"

"Sure." A furtive swipe at her damp eyes, a quickly expelled breath, and she was ready to face him. She hurried to his side and relieved him of the box of groceries tucked under his left arm. His eyes searched her face, but she kept it averted from him. She couldn't handle any more of his questions right now.

She set the box on the kitchen counter, and he dumped

the other box he carried right beside it, then caught her arm as she turned away. "You've been crying."

"No, I..." She swallowed the lump in her throat. "No."

"Mandy..." The unexpected helplessness in his voice was that of a man who hadn't had a lot of experience dealing with tearful women, especially ones who denied it. "I know this has been a lot for you to take in. I wish I could have spared you, but—"

"That wasn't why I was..."

"Then why?"

She shook her head. She couldn't possibly explain it to him, no matter how hard she tried. Some things you just couldn't put into words. And there were some things she wasn't ready to tell him, things she might never be ready to tell him. Things like—

Her thoughts shied away from that subject like a frightened colt. She couldn't even *think* about it, much less discuss it. She tore her gaze from his and snatched at another topic. "You certainly bought enough food." She began unpacking the box of groceries. "How long were you planning to stay here?"

He didn't answer her. When she glanced at him, questioningly, a can of pork and beans in one hand, and a box of Minute Rice in the other, he said abruptly, "I don't know." He reached and took both the can and the box out of her hands and set them aside. "Don't change the subject, Mandy. Why were you crying?"

Out of the maelstrom of emotions still surging within her, bitterness crept to the top. "Don't demand answers from me," she said in a tight, little voice that sounded harsh and unforgiving to her ears. "You don't have that right."

Chapter 8

Mandy's bitterness set off an explosive reaction in Reilly. "Damn you," he growled, then swung away and strode around the room. He faced her again, the emotional tightness in his chest making breathing difficult. "Maybe I deserve that," he said through the pain. "But did you ever think maybe I don't?" He raked a hand through his hair and fought for control. "I didn't desert you. I left to protect you. But Mandy—" he made sure she didn't look away "—you have to know one thing. I'd do it again if I had to."

She stared at him with accusing eyes. "Then why did you bother coming back?"

The arrow found its mark, slipping through his defenses, and he lashed out in pain. "Because I love you, damn it! Because I couldn't stay away!" His chest heaved as emotions roiled inside him. "And because I thought you loved me."

"I did love you!" Her response was a hoarse whisper.

"Did?" It hurt more than he thought possible. "Is that why you look for every chance you can to turn the knife?"

"It's not like that!"

"Then explain it to me."

She shook her head as she wiped her tear-swollen eyes. "Like you said, it's not that easy."

He took the three steps he needed to reach her, and clasped his hands around her arms. "I know it's not. Needing someone..." He swallowed, hard. "Mandy, Pennington swore he'd see me in hell for betraying him. But he doesn't have to kill me to accomplish that. If anything happened to you..."

"Would you care?"

It was a cry from a wounded and desperate heart, and Reilly squeezed his eyes shut for a second, as if he could block out her pain along with the sight of her ravaged face.

"Yes, I'd care," he whispered huskily. "I should have stayed the hell away from you in the first place, but I couldn't." He raised one hand to cup her cheek, almost surprised when she didn't flinch away. He searched for the right words and found them in his heart. "I was thirty-eight years old when I came to Black Rock, Mandy, and I'd lived most of my life alone. I thought that's the way it would always be. But I fell for you the moment I saw you, and I'm still falling."

"Please don't say things like that," she said, but her tone lacked conviction.

Hope stirred within him despite the hopelessness of their situation, and he had no defense against it. He bent his head, hesitating just long enough for her to escape if she wanted to, but she never moved. He brushed her lips with his, then pulled her closer and deepened the kiss when she made a small sound of surrender.

When he finally lifted his head they were both trembling. He let her go and stepped back, afraid that if he didn't his control would shatter. A flicker of hurt showed in her eyes before she masked it, and he knew she had no idea how close to the edge he already was.

"Did you mean it?" she asked, surprising him yet again.

"That I love you? Yeah. I meant it."

"Then don't leave me again."

"Do you think I want to?" She didn't answer and he stated, "That's the last thing I want." Frustrated because he couldn't make her understand what she meant to him, he said, "I won't let them hurt you, Mandy. If it means leaving, I'll leave. If it means staying, I'll do that instead. But I won't let them hurt you." He drew a sharp breath. "I'll kill them all before I'll let them touch you."

"You..." He'd shocked her with his brutal honesty. "You don't really mean that."

"You wanted the truth. That's the only truth I know." She didn't actually move, but her eyelids flickered, and he sensed her inner withdrawal. "I was a good cop, Mandy. I won't say I never bent the rules, but I was a good cop."

"Then how can you talk about killing, as if—"

He cut her off. "Because you're more important." He shook his head impatiently, and his jaw hardened. "If anything happens to you, Pennington's a walking dead man. I'll take him to hell with me."

Reilly had gone to stand by the front window, leaving Mandy stunned and unsure of what to say. It was too much to absorb all at once, she thought. Reilly had been right about that. She needed time, time to assimilate everything he'd told her, time to sort through her emotions. Her life had changed drastically in the last two—was it only two?—days. How could she be expected to deal with everything that had happened since?

The day before yesterday she'd still been mourning the man by the window, now miraculously returned from the grave. She'd lost her home, and almost died in the process. She'd gone to sleep last night feeling abandoned once again, only to wake in her ex-lover's arms this morning. She'd learned that passion wasn't dead in her, and that the man who'd once held the key to her heart could, by his own words, kill in cold blood.

She latched on to that last thought and amended it. No

in cold blood. No, if Reilly killed, it would only be because he cared passionately.

That was another thing she had to rethink. How could she reconcile his statement that he loved her with the fact that he'd let her think he was dead all this time? If he truly loved her, how could he have done that?

Nothing made sense any more, least of all this well of bitterness she'd discovered in herself. If someone had asked her two days ago, she'd have said that she'd give anything, *anything,* to bring Reilly back to life. Now that it was true, it was almost as if she resented him for being alive after all.

Was she really that selfish?

She looked over at Reilly's bleak profile, and realized she'd hurt him more than she'd known he could be hurt. Remorse urged her toward him, then she winced and caught her breath as a sharp pain pierced her instep.

"What is it?" Reilly swung around, concern etched on his face.

"I think I have a splinter or something in my foot."

"Let me see." He dragged a chair over for her to sit on, then knelt in front of her. "Which foot?" She raised her left one slightly, and he picked it up, propping her foot against his muscled thigh as he examined it thoroughly. "There it is." His large hands were gentle as he removed the quarter-inch splinter from her flesh, then he glanced up. "When was your last tetanus shot?"

She thought about it. "Three years ago, I think. Somewhere around there."

"Good," he said, then added, "Stay there," as he left her briefly, returning with a bottle of rubbing alcohol, a wad of tissue, and a Band-Aid from the bathroom. He doused the tissue with alcohol and dabbed it on her insole. "This might sting a bit."

Mandy flinched. It stung like crazy, but all she said was "A bit?"

A rueful grin tugged at Reilly's lips, then he blew on her foot to dry it. The unexpected sensation sent shivers of awareness up her spine. She controlled her reaction as best she could, and watched as he fitted the bandage in place.

"You know," he teased, glancing up, "if you wore shoes more often, you wouldn't have these problems."

All at once memories of other times came back to her with a warm rush. She'd always enjoyed going barefoot, the freedom of it, putting her shoes on last thing before she left the house and kicking them off the minute she came home. Reilly had teased her about all the extra work she had to go through to keep her feet from becoming too callused because of going barefoot so much. But he'd made a sensual game out of rubbing her feet with lotion after she'd soaked them, working his way up her ankles, calves, thighs....

He was remembering, too, she saw. His tawny brown eyes darkened as his chest began to rise and fall. He slowly lowered her foot to the floor, then stood up, pulling her with him. "Mandy, I..."

She knew she should move away, do something to avoid the kiss she saw in his eyes. Instead, she reached up and touched his face with a wondering hand, as longing shook her. Then their arms swept around each other. The kiss, when it came, was like nothing they'd ever shared. It spoke of the loneliness that only those who've loved and lost can know. It spoke of the longing of two people to escape a past too painful to bear yet too beautiful to erase. But above all it spoke of a passion that had never died, passion tempered by the knowledge that this was a moment stolen out of time that might never come again.

When he would have released her, Mandy clung to him. *Not yet*, her heart cried. *Not yet*. She rested her face against the warmth of his shoulder, indulging her senses, her memories, and the part of her heart that still loved him unconditionally.

It felt so natural, so *right* to be in his arms like this, to have his lips pressed against her hair, to hear his heart beating in cadence with hers. No one had ever held her as Reilly had, as if she were the only woman in the world.

Was it wrong to pretend, only for a moment, that there was no past, no future? Was it wrong to let herself be vulnerable just once more?

Eventually, though, she had to let him go. She sighed and loosened her arms, then drew back a little, and he whispered something she didn't catch.

"What did you say?" she murmured.

A chuckle escaped him. "I said, maybe I shouldn't complain about your bare feet, if that's the way you react to a splinter."

Mandy laughed, too, more from nervous relief than anything else. "I'm not always such a wimp."

Something—was it pride?—flashed across his face. "I know you're not," he said, his deep voice warm with admiration. "I don't know any woman who could have done even half as well in this situation as you have."

She was already melting inside, but his words of praise finished the job. "Thanks," she said shyly. There was an awkward pause, during which they stared longingly at each other and tried not to show it. Then Mandy said, "You know, I never thanked you for saving my life the other night. I guess I got so caught up in what was happening, that I—"

Reilly made a dismissive motion with his hand. "It was my fault you were in danger in the first place."

"Why do you do that?"

"Do what?"

"Play down the things you've done. Act as if they don't mean anything. This isn't the first time, either."

He seemed at a loss for words, his thoughts turned inward. "Maybe—" he said slowly "—maybe because when I was growing up I was taught that anything I did was suspect. So I...I guess I learned not to look for affirmation from anyone but myself."

"I don't think that's the same thing."

Reilly's smile was crooked. "It is where I come from, Mandy."

She opened her mouth to ask him to explain, but he cut

her off. "Speaking of shoes," he said, although they'd been doing nothing of the kind, "I bought some for you yesterday." He went to a large paper bag stashed in the corner by his duffel bag. She'd noticed it earlier, in passing, but hadn't really had a chance to ask him about it.

He handed her the bag unopened. "I think you'll find everything you need in there." He nodded toward the bag. "There's a couple changes of clothes for you—jeans, shirts, things like that—so you won't need to borrow Walker's clothes anymore. I also bought you shoes, socks, undies and a jacket. I think they'll fit."

She glanced into the bag, then raised puzzled eyes to his. "Weren't you afraid someone might get...I don't know... suspicious, with a man buying all of this?"

"I didn't buy them all in one place. That's partly why I was so late getting back last night. It took me longer than I thought it would, because I had to go to both Sheridan and Buffalo. I must have visited at least a half-dozen stores yesterday, not counting grocery and hardware stores."

Shame scorched her cheeks. All the while she'd been thinking he'd deserted her, he'd been shopping for her instead. She couldn't apologize without telling him what she was apologizing for, but she could thank him, if she could swallow the lump in her throat.

"Thanks." She barely managed to get the word out.

As usual, Reilly shrugged it off. "It was nothing."

Mandy wanted to insist that it wasn't "nothing," but realized she'd never convince him, so she turned away, opening the bag as she went. She dumped everything out on the bed, and discovered Reilly had even bought her a comb and a pair of scissors—presumably so she could trim her hair, which she'd been longing to do ever since the fire had damaged it—as well as a toothbrush and several other feminine necessities. She picked up a bar of lilac-scented soap that had tumbled out along with everything else. It was the brand she always used, and she sniffed it delicately, smiling a little. It was a small thing, but it touched her that he'd remembered.

Still smiling, she went to store her new clothes in the little chest of drawers by the bed. When she was finished she slid her hands into her pockets and casually leaned against the bureau. She looked over at Reilly and asked, "So what are your plans now?"

Over two thousand miles away, David Pennington sat in the war room of his Long Island compound, surrounded by the best legal task force money could buy.

He held a snifter of fine cognac in one hand, and he rolled the liqueur around and around, warming it, as he listened absently to the spirited discussion taking place among his attorneys. He took a sip from the glass, holding it on his tongue, savoring the bouquet. Savoring his freedom.

He tipped the glass in a silent, mocking toast to a dead man. To Ryan Callahan, whose death he savored even more.

A telephone shrilled insistently, bringing the conversation around the table to a temporary halt. Pennington signalled his new second-in-command, Carl Walsh, to answer it on the other side of the room, and took this opportunity to bring the discussion to a close.

"Bottom line, gentlemen," he said in a cool, emotionless voice, his gaze wandering from one man to the next. "What you're saying is that I can expect an acquittal in the new trial."

Pennington's chief counsel glanced around the table at his fellow attorneys, then cleared his throat. "Not exactly," he demurred. "Juries are notoriously unpredictable. But given the evidence the prosecution has left..."

Another man spoke up. "It was Callahan's testimony more than anything else that convicted you in the first trial. We couldn't discredit him with the jury. Now, without the tapes the appellate court excluded, and without Callahan's testimony..." The lawyer shrugged. "The prosecution doesn't have much of a case. It might not even go to trial."

David Pennington swallowed the last of his cognac,

placed the snifter on the table, and allowed himself a small, private smile. "Then it's fortunate for me that Ryan Callahan is no longer available, isn't it?"

No one answered that question, though silent looks were passed back and forth among the lawyers, and in the sudden quiet Carl Walsh's muttered curse echoed through the room. Walsh held his hand over the mouthpiece, his gaze darting across the room to his superior. "You'd better take this call, David."

Pennington's eyes narrowed at the urgent tone and the look of concern on Walsh's face, but he never lost his cool demeanor. He glanced back at his attorneys. "If you'll excuse me, gentlemen?"

Chairs were pushed back, papers were gathered up and shoved into briefcases, and less than a minute later the half-dozen lawyers had vacated the room, leaving Pennington and Walsh alone.

"Who is it?" Pennington demanded, watching as the door closed with a solid click behind the last attorney.

Walsh put the caller on hold. "Centurion," he said.

Pennington's cold gaze moved from the door back to Walsh. "Is the line secure?"

Walsh nodded. "We did an electronic sweep this morning. No bugs." The New World Militia had learned their lesson the hard way. Some of the evidence presented at Pennington's trial had been obtained through wiretaps and listening devices. That evidence had helped convict him and, ironically, had also provided him with the grounds needed to overturn that conviction and win a new trial.

"How about at the other end?"

"Pay phone. And he gave the proper code-word sequence. The line's secure," Walsh reassured him.

Pennington picked up the receiver in front of him and stabbed at the Hold button. "Yes?" he said, deliberately not identifying himself. He wasn't taking any unnecessary chances.

"Callahan's still alive." Pennington recognized the voice, confirming identification of the man known as Centurion. "When you said he was heading for Black Rock, I told you I'd take care of it," the voice continued. "But no. You wanted your boys to handle it." There was a pregnant pause. "They handled it, all right. Now the place is crawling with federal agents, sifting through the ashes, asking questions of everyone in town. And folks are cooperating with the Feds, big-time, because it's one of their own who's missing. Your boys made a big mistake, involving Amanda Edwards. You know how it is in towns like Black Rock. Now that people are stirred up and talking to the Feds, it's going to be twice as hard to get to Callahan."

"What makes you think Callahan's alive?" Pennington asked coolly, forcing down a surge of rage.

Centurion laughed harshly. "I saw him yesterday."

Pennington's nostrils flared, the only outward sign of fury he allowed himself to display. "I see." He thought a moment, then asked, "Do the Feds know he's alive?"

"No bodies were found in the house. You can't keep something like that a secret from the Feds. They know." Silence ensued, then Centurion spoke again. "What are you going to do now?"

"Whatever I have to."

"Do you want me to—"

"I want you to sit tight," Pennington ordered. "I'll get back to you." He slammed the phone down and stared at it for several seconds, letting the rage he'd suppressed earlier wash through him while he struggled for control.

"It's Callahan," he said unnecessarily, once he'd mastered himself enough to speak calmly. "He's alive."

"I know." Walsh pulled up a chair across from him and sat down. "Are you going to let him take care of it?" he asked, nodding toward the phone.

Pennington's eyes glittered. "If you'll recall, the only reason Callahan's still alive is because Centurion *didn't* take care of it a year ago. Why should I entrust this job to him again?"

There was a pause, then Walsh said, "You don't have much choice, do you? That town's too small. If you send anybody else now, they're sure to be spotted. I'd wait a couple of days, let things die down, wait for the FBI to leave." He made a placating gesture. "Let Centurion handle it, David. He screwed up the first time, and he'll make doubly sure he doesn't do it again." Walsh took a deep breath and let it out slowly. "No explosives, though. No fire. Let it look like an accident. Safer all around that way, and a damn sight easier."

"No!" Pennington pounded the heavy table so hard with his fist that the phone jumped and jangled. "No, damn it!" He thrust himself away from the table and stood, quivering with rage. "Callahan betrayed us, betrayed *me*. I won't let him get away with it." Pennington looked down at his clenched fists, forcing them to relax as his mind worked feverishly on a plan. Then he smiled.

"I swore I'd see Callahan burn in hell," he said softly. "And this time, *I'll* be the one who sends him there."

By the time night fell, Mandy's brain was teeming with the details of the sting Reilly was setting up. It would have been fascinating, in a macabre sort of way, discussing things she'd only read about in books, if not for the fact that both their lives depended on the plan's success.

"It's dangerous, Mandy," he stated somberly as she handed him the last of the dinner dishes to dry. "I wish..."

He didn't say it, but she knew he wished there was some way of keeping her from being involved. "You can't *un*-involve me," she said matter-of-factly. "So it's useless to waste any time thinking about it."

One corner of his mouth twitched into a wry smile. "My practical, down-to-earth Mandy," he said.

Not always, she thought wistfully, remembering when she'd believed that impossible dreams could come true. And they had, for an all-too-brief span of time. She'd learned her lesson, though. She no longer believed in dreams.

She shivered, from the chill creeping through the cabin or from the memory of lost dreams, she wasn't sure which.

She took the dish towel from Reilly's hands, folded it lengthwise, and draped it over the dish rack. "It's getting a little cold in here. I'll get a fire started, but we'll need more wood. Could you bring some in from out back?"

"Sure. I'll need to make a perimeter check, too. I'll do that while I'm at it." He unholstered the .45, checked the clip and the action, then reholstered the gun all in one smooth move. It reminded Mandy, as if she needed reminding, of the violent world Reilly took for granted.

He grabbed his jacket and was gone without another word. She stood there for a moment, thinking about his world, so far removed from hers, and the things he'd let slip this morning. Then she sighed, and moved to the fireplace.

When Reilly finally returned, carrying an armful of wood, the fire was going strong. She helped him stack the rough-hewn split logs beside the fireplace, then said, "I think I'll turn in early tonight. Do you mind if I have first crack at the bathroom again?"

Reilly, who had taken off his jacket and hung it up, was in the process of dusting his hands off on the sides of his jeans. "Go ahead," he said. "I don't mind."

As she gathered her things from the bureau drawer, something occurred to her, and she stopped abruptly, the bar of soap in her hand.

"What's wrong?" he asked.

"Nothing," she answered quickly. Too quickly.

"What is it?"

Her cheeks red, she mumbled, "I forgot I don't have any nightclothes." She hurried on. "But that's okay, I'll make do like I did before."

"Sorry. I didn't think of it." Their eyes met, and both knew the other was remembering long, lazy nights when neither of them wore anything at all to bed. His voice deepened as he added, "It never even occurred to me."

Mandy's breath caught in her throat as a rush of desire flooded her body. How many times had she dreamed of being with Reilly again, of feeling the helpless surge of excitement that only he created in her? How many times had she replayed their lovemaking in her mind, keeping his memory alive long after his death?

She tore her gaze away from his, grabbed her new toothbrush and added it to the little pile of things she carried, then scuttled into the bathroom. When she'd shut the door behind her, she sagged against it for a moment, weak with longing. Her chest rose and fell as her breath came quickly, and once again she had to struggle for control.

A quick bath did nothing to calm her down. Her heightened senses responded to the warm, lilac-scented water and the roughness of the washcloth as she ran it over her skin. The sensation reminded her that she was still very much a woman. Reilly's woman.

She washed her hair, remembering a time when Reilly had done that for her, his strong fingers sliding through the slick, soapy strands, lingering, teasing, tormenting....

When she realized where her thoughts were heading, she dunked her head under the tap and rinsed off quickly. Later, her newly trimmed hair wrapped in a towel, she brushed her teeth, concentrating on each brisk stroke as if she could brush her thoughts away in the process. It didn't work.

You want him, an insidious voice inside her said. *And he wants you. Would it be so wrong? This isn't a game the two of you are playing. There are people out there trying to kill you, and it could happen at any time. You might not ever have this chance again.*

How many times had she cried herself to sleep, her arms empty and aching for him? Lonely. God, she'd been so lonely for so long. No one else had ever touched her the way Reilly had. *Would* it be wrong to sleep with him once more?

"Maybe I'll finally get him out of my system," she whispered. "Maybe I've built things up in my mind because I thought I'd lost him. Maybe we weren't really that good together."

She was lying to herself, and in her heart she knew it. Sleeping with Reilly wasn't going to do anything but draw her deeper under his spell, but she wasn't going to let this chance pass her by. She wanted him, and just like before, nothing else mattered. But she wasn't going to lie to herself anymore. This time she was going into the relationship with her eyes wide open.

Reilly was going to break her heart again, and she was going to let him.

Chapter 9

The lights were off when Reilly emerged from the bathroom wearing nothing but a clean pair of jeans, and he stopped short, his heart suddenly slamming inside his chest. The only illumination in the main room came from the fireplace, and Mandy was sitting in front of the crackling flames combing her nearly dry hair. The fire's glow danced over her vulnerable profile, gilding her hair, her skin. And Reilly's mouth went dry with wanting.

Wanting. What a pitiful word for the emotions that tore at him as he watched her, mesmerized by the slow movement of the comb through the golden halo of her hair. Desire, wild and sweet, spilled into his bloodstream and surged through his veins. Love, tender and aching, washed over him in waves, leaving him shaking in its wake.

Love. Such a small word for such a devastating force but how could he not love her? From the first she'd been everything he'd never even known he was looking for: gentle, but not weak; sweet, but with enough tart edges to delight his taste; beautiful, but seemingly unaware of it. And her eyes—her eyes had looked into his soul and had seen not the man he was, but the man he'd wanted to be, for her. She had been clean and good and untouched by the horrors of his world, and she had healed him when he hadn't even known he needed healing. He'd loved her long before he'd admitted it to himself, hadn't recognized it for what it was until that night at her house when she'd looked at him with love shining from her eyes and asked him to stay.

He soundlessly mouthed her name and took an unknowing step toward her, then realized what he was doing and stopped himself with a physical effort. *Just because you want her,* he told himself sternly, *doesn't mean she wants you.*

He dropped his dirty clothes in a pile in the corner, and hung his shoulder holster over the back of a chair. Then, because he couldn't resist, he stole another glance at Mandy.

She turned at that moment. She didn't speak, but words weren't necessary. Her expression spoke of a longing that matched his, of a love that echoed what was in his heart. Without looking away, she placed the comb on the floor, then mutely held out her hand.

"Mandy?" He didn't dare trust himself to move closer, not until he was sure he wasn't just projecting what he wanted to see in her eyes.

Her tongue touched her lips, and she swallowed. "Don't make me ask," she said in a soft voice that swept through him like the wind. "Not this time."

He didn't know how he reached her, only that he was there, kneeling beside her, his arms pulling her up into his embrace. The first kiss went astray as they whispered each other's name, but then Mandy raised her face to his and their lips met.

The world exploded once more, only this time the explosion was sparked by desire. The flames in the fireplace were nothing compared to the internal conflagration that quickly escalated out of control. Heat scorched his skin as his hands roamed her body, greedy for everything he'd been denied so long. He murmured her name repeatedly, pressing frantic kisses wherever he could reach.

"Touch me," he whispered, but he couldn't wait. He grasped her hands and slid them down his bare chest, and it was like throwing gasoline on a raging fire. His manhood throbbed, swelled, threatened to burst his zipper. When her hands settled at his waist, then hesitated, he begged hoarsely. "Oh God, Mandy. Please."

His breath caught as her fingers slowly measured him inside his jeans, then fumbled with the zipper. It seemed to take forever before she released him from that strangling confinement, but once she did he had no control, no finesse left. He had one goal in mind—to be inside her—and there was no room for anything else.

His hands trembled as he slipped them inside the robe she wore, seeking the warm skin he ached to caress. He groaned when he discovered she was naked beneath the robe, and he pulled it open, tugging impatiently at the belt until it gave way. He slipped the robe from her shoulders, letting it fall behind her. Then he was pressing her down beside the hearth, settling his body on hers, kneeing her thighs apart and rolling his hips until she raised her knees and opened her legs to him.

A tiny voice in the back of his mind cautioned him to slow down, but he couldn't. He *couldn't.* He'd been without her for too long, had been tempted too often by her tantalizing nearness the last two days, and now that she'd given him the green light there was no stopping him. Air gusted out of his lungs when he sank his body into hers and came to rest in the cradle of her hips.

Reilly held himself still by sheer will, wanting, *needing* to savor the sensation of being sheathed in Mandy's warm moist depths. He'd dreamt of this moment, secretly praying to the God he wasn't even sure he believed in that someday he'd return to the woman who symbolized the home he'd never known. All his life he'd been on the outside looking in, but when he was in her arms, his body buried deep within hers, he wasn't alone anymore.

Home. He'd come home.

He couldn't hold back any longer. He withdrew slowly, his body shaking with the effort, then pressed inward, even deeper than before, desperately needing to find his place within her. He moaned a wordless apology into her mouth, then threw back his head and arched into her again.

His lips sought hers once more. Wild, rough, urgent, his kiss told her all the things he had no words for, as his hips rose and fell with increasing rapidity.

Mandy couldn't think anymore. Didn't want to. Feeling took over and she abandoned herself to it, letting it build to shattering proportions. This mad rush to completion was something new between them, she thought distantly, as Reilly's unchecked desire fueled her own. He'd never before made love to her as if he were dying and she was his salvation. Maybe he never would again, but it didn't matter. This once would live forever in her memory, and she surrendered to it, and him, willingly.

She rubbed her calves against his denim-clad thighs, urging him on, then hooked her ankles around the backs of his knees and opened herself fully to him. She was helpless then, and he immediately took advantage of it, driving into her deeper and harder than before. But she wasn't afraid. She trusted him implicitly, in this at least. Even though she was physically at his mercy, she knew he'd never hurt her.

He didn't. He made love to her, fighting his own release with each pounding stroke, panting her name as sweat beaded on his brow and rolled down his face. "Now, Mandy. Now!" he rasped. He surged into her—once, twice, thrice—and the intense, throbbing pressure finally broke.

She closed her eyes and sobbed his name, her body arching toward his as wave upon wave of pleasure swept over her. She reveled in it, tremors of completion stealing her breath and her strength. Then she opened dazed eyes. As if he was waiting just for that, he groaned her name again, and with one last, fierce thrust he finally let himself go. The naked emotion on his face ripped through her heart, and she locked around him—arms, thighs, inner depths—holding him safe as he collapsed against her.

The floorboards were rough and hard beneath her, the thin robe she lay on the only thing between her and the wooden planks. One side of her unclothed body was overly warm from proximity to the fire, the other side was shockingly cold. Her thigh muscles ached from unaccustomed exertion. And the heavy weight of the only man she'd ever loved threatened to crush her.

Mandy didn't care. Reilly lay sleeping in her arms, with an expression of such utter peace on his face that intense love for him overwhelmed her. He'd worn that same expression once before, the night they'd first made love, and her throat ached with the memory.

Remembering, she caressed him absently for long moments—light, gentle strokes over the sleek muscles of his back and hips that were meant to soothe, not awaken. Then a tiny chuckle escaped her when her roving hands touched denim. He hadn't even gotten his pants off.

"What's so funny?" The sleepy rumble of sound reverberated through her body, and her breasts responded as if Reilly had caressed them.

She shivered, from the erotic combination of the cold air and his warm body, then shifted a little, trying to let her lungs drag in enough air to answer him. He raised up abruptly, and she made a sound of protest. "Don't go," she whispered in vain, her clutching hands no match for his strength as he pulled away.

Cursing under his breath, a ferocious frown marring his features, he separated himself from her. Mandy couldn't hide the slight wince as his body withdrew from hers, and he cursed again, his expression darkening.

Before she could ask him what was wrong, he'd tugged his jeans up, scooped her off the floor and carried her to the double bed in the corner. He set her gently down on the edge of the bed, jerking the covers free almost before he'd let her go.

"Get under the blankets," he said with rough-edged concern.

Mandy hesitated, suddenly unsure of herself and of him. Then she shivered and hurried beneath the covers, pulling them up to her chin. She watched as Reilly quickly stripped off his jeans and joined her.

He plumped up a pillow beneath his head, then drew her against his body, reassuring her that whatever the problem was, it had nothing to do with what they'd just shared.

He briskly rubbed his strong hands over her chilled skin until she protested, but he kept on, insisting, "I've got to get you warm."

"I'm warm enough," she said, catching his hands and holding them in her own to make him stop. She really was warm enough by now. His big body generated a lot of heat, and the layers of sheet and blankets insulated them. Smiling, she snuggled against him, loving the feel of his naked skin next to hers. When his arms closed around her, she sighed and let herself go boneless.

"Are you okay?" he asked.

"I'm fine," she purred, rubbing her cheek against his warm, furry chest. She sighed again, little *mmms* of contentment. After a moment she asked, "Why were you so upset before?"

At first she thought he wasn't going to answer, then he said reluctantly, almost as if ashamed, "I was too rough with you."

"Oh, no," she said quickly, then sensing his need for additional assurance, she continued, "It was…special." He gave her a skeptical look, and she explained, "To be wanted like that, to know how much you needed me…it *was* special."

"I didn't hurt you?" His usual male arrogance had deserted him, and the almost humble way he asked the question gave her pause.

She shook her head. "No, you didn't hurt me." The protectiveness that came over her right then surprised her. Where had the notion come from that he needed protecting?

She didn't know, but somehow she knew it was true. He was vulnerable where she was concerned. All along she'd been afraid that he was going to break her heart again, but now she realized she wasn't the only one with something at risk here. She could hurt him, maybe even more than she knew.

"I shouldn't have made love to you on the floor like that. You deserve better."

She curled her hand around the tense muscles in his shoulder and gently massaged them. "It's not as if we've never done that before," she reminded him, a teasing note in her voice. When his muscles tightened beneath her fingers she realized he was serious, and her voice softened as she reassured him. "Honestly, I'm fine. I'd tell you if I wasn't." When she finally felt him relax, she slid her hand down across his chest slowly, eventually coming to rest at his waist.

He didn't say anything for a while, and Mandy was content to lie in his arms, feeling his chest rise and fall beneath her cheek. Her eyes drifted shut as her breathing matched the rhythm of his, but she wasn't quite asleep when he suddenly spoke.

"Damn! I didn't use anything."

Her eyes snapped open when his meaning sank in, and her heart began to pound. *Oh, my God!* she thought wildly. *I didn't even think of it. How could I forget....*

He interrupted her thoughts, his tone regretful. "I have protection for you, Mandy. I wasn't planning this, but I would never put you at risk. I bought protection when I was out yesterday. I just..."

Reilly ran his hand over his face and considered what next to say. How could he explain that all rational thought had vanished when he'd seen her sitting in front of the fire tonight, and she'd held out her hand to him? How could he make her understand that the primitive part of him had taken over, that the need to possess her had driven him to the brink where nothing else mattered?

Then something occurred to him, stunning in intensity,

and his body went hard in a rush of primeval possessiveness. He envisioned Mandy carrying his child, her body soft and rounded, vibrant with new life. What wouldn't he give for it to be true? Every male fiber of his being pulsed as he thought of fathering her children, and he pictured her with his baby in her arms, nursing at her breast. A child created from their love.

Shocked by his thoughts, he shook himself mentally. Had his subconscious desire for a child with Mandy made him deliberately forget to use a condom? How could he have done that to her?

She was shivering again, shaking with it, as if she could read his thoughts, and Reilly forced his mind back to reality. When she made little movements to free herself from his embrace, his arms tightened around her. "No, don't," he begged. "Don't pull away."

"I can't...I need to...please let me go." There were tears in her voice, and somehow he knew he'd caused them.

"I *did* hurt you," he said hoarsely. "Why didn't you tell me?"

Even in her distressed state she seemed more concerned for him than for herself, and she shook her head vehemently. "You didn't hurt me," she insisted.

He wanted to believe her, but if he hadn't hurt her with his fierce lovemaking, then why was she weeping inside?

He tried to remember what else could have triggered her emotional response. Had he done something? Said something? Then he realized she'd stiffened in his arms when he'd brought up the subject of birth control. Maybe she thought he didn't want children. Some men didn't, he knew, and since they'd never discussed it before, maybe she was afraid. Maybe if he told her how he felt...

He gathered her closer, brushing his lips against her temple, then took a deep breath and let it out again. "Mandy, if we made a baby tonight, I—"

"No!" She put her hand over his mouth as if she could stop the possibility if she stopped him from voicing it.

He removed her hand and kissed it, then gently but implacably continued. "I love you, Mandy. I know you don't really believe it, but it's true. If you're worried about how I'd react if you were pregnant, I just want you to know that I want children. Your children. I would love our child, with all my heart."

Pain welled up inside Mandy, and a shuddering sob shook her, but she fought back the tears that clogged her throat and threatened to overflow. She wouldn't cry. She *wouldn't!* If she started crying now, Reilly would demand an explanation, and how could she explain without hurting him unbearably? How could she tell him about the child he'd fathered more than a year ago, the child she'd lost the same day she'd lost him?

And how could she tell him what months of grief and despair had driven her to do?

Yesterday she could have told him. Yesterday she hadn't known he *could* be hurt by the knowledge. She could have told him this morning. She'd been angry enough to *want* to hurt him as much as she'd been hurt. But she couldn't tell him now. Not after he'd lain in her arms, his head pillowed on her breasts, his eyes closed in absolute peace. Not after his confession of a moment ago.

She wrapped her arms around him and pressed her body against his. "Make love to me, Reilly," she pleaded, her voice husky with unshed tears.

Only in his arms could she forget the remembered pain of her loss, their loss. Someday in the future she would tell him of the baby she'd carried so briefly, and mourned almost as much as she'd mourned him. Someday in the future she would confess other things, too. Someday. If they had a future.

For now, this night was all they had.

Her hands moved over him, rekindling the desire that was never far from the surface. He breathed her name and pulled her on top of him, arranging her body so that his manhood was nestled at the juncture of her thighs, but he made no attempt to enter her. His hands filled themselves with her soft curves, stroking, petting, but this time he was in no hurry.

She was. Oblivion was what she sought. Fire. Heat. Mindless, burning passion. But Reilly had other ideas.

The fire was there. Flames licked her skin wherever his hands touched, and he touched her everywhere. The passion was there, too. It sparked and sizzled with each kiss, each lingering caress. But he held back from her, as if he wanted her to know, to *know*, that he needed more from her than sex, that he craved the love they'd once shared as much as the lovemaking.

He wouldn't let her touch him. "Not this time, love," he said, fending off her seeking hands, and she whimpered in frustration.

He rolled them both over, partially pinning her beneath him, then set about driving her insane. Firelight cast dancing shadows around the room, creating an intimate setting for her seduction. And seduction it was. Reilly held both her arms above her head with one large hand on her wrists, while the other hand teased and tormented her body. Long fingers played over one pouting nipple, then the other, then his lips followed where his fingers had led.

When his mouth found her breast and began suckling, she cried out, pleasure radiating outward from the point of contact. The mustache she wasn't used to was both bristly and silky, and incredibly erotic as it brushed against her sensitized skin. He moved to her other breast, nuzzling, nibbling, until she cried out again.

While his lips played with her breasts, his hand crept downward, sliding over her damp skin like a thief in the night, stealing her breath and her sanity. His fingers tangled momentarily in the curls guarding her womanhood, then, without warning, slipped inside.

Her hips arched off the bed when his middle finger located the tiny nub he sought and flicked over it. Her thighs instinctively closed, as if she could dislodge his hand that way, but it was too late. He soothed her with cherishing murmurs, his lips finding hers for a long, drugging kiss, and his hand stayed where it was.

When he freed her arms she wrapped them around him, desperate for something solid and real to hold on to. It made no sense at all, because he was the one working his magic spell on her, but she clung to him in a world that twirled crazily around her.

Here was the mindlessness she wanted, just beyond her reach, but he wouldn't let her rush him. She was gasping for breath, her body responding to his sorcerer's touch, but his fingers kept to the same steady pace, bringing her so far, but no farther.

She moaned a wordless protest when he finally removed his hand. He kissed her once more, then his lips trailed slowly down her body. His mustache teased her breasts, the nipples already hard, tight peaks, but he didn't linger there for long. He kissed the slight curve of her belly, rubbing his unshaven cheek against it for a moment as she quivered uncontrollably. Then he continued on, parting her legs with his body.

When his warm breath touched the petals of her womanhood, she finally realized what he intended, and her whole body clenched. This was something else he'd never done with her before, and the incredible intimacy of it shocked her.

"No." She struggled to free herself, to close her legs and her body to him before he could go any further, but he held her down with ease.

"Don't fight it, darlin'," he whispered. "I've dreamed of doing this for you." And he lowered his head.

She'd read of such things in books, in the romances she loved, and each time she'd skimmed over the details, uncomfortable with the whole idea. It didn't seem right, somehow, as if the focus on purely physical sensation detracted from the emotional involvement between a man and a woman.

She'd been wrong. So wrong. This wasn't a physical act.

It was a gift of love, from him to her, and it shook her to the core.

She shuddered under his caressing tongue as he led her ever upward, taking her from peak to peak with no respite. Her hands fisted in the sheets, her body writhing and her heart pounding, as blood roared in her ears.

Then she was perched on the edge of a wave-battered emotional cliff, wanting to fly free, but terrified of falling on the jagged rocks below. The windblown waves were beating higher and higher, a siren song of desire, and she swayed toward them, then pulled back, afraid.

It was almost as if he understood, because his reassuring whisper came to her out of the storm-tossed shadows. "It's okay, Mandy. Let go. Let go, love. I'm here. I'll catch you." And he touched her again.

She closed her eyes as the tidal wave swept over her. Then she was soaring, floating, plunging in a bottomless free-fall vortex of sensuous delight, down, down toward the rocks she no longer feared. Strong arms caught and held her tight as she knew they would, and she clung to them, trusting those arms and the man to whom they belonged to keep her safe.

Somewhere beyond her consciousness someone was calling her name. She had no strength, no breath left to answer. Tiny Catherine wheels were still bursting behind her closed eyelids, and her body still trembled in the aftermath of a cataclysmic explosion that defied description.

"Don't cry, Mandy. God, baby, please don't cry."

Was she crying? Her limbs didn't seem to be attached to her body, but her brain sent the message anyway, and she raised a hand to her cheek to check for herself. Her fingers came away wet. Her eyes blinked open in astonishment, and she found herself gazing into the concerned face of the man she loved.

She couldn't hold the words back any longer. "I love you," she said on the tail end of a sigh, and it felt so right that she said it again. "I love you, Reilly."

His eyes closed, and when they opened again there was

so much longing in their shadowed depths that Mandy caught her breath. "Ryan," he said with a husky catch in his voice. "Just once, I..."

She understood, and cupped his face with her hands. She kissed the corners of his eyes, then his lips, little butterfly kisses, and said softly, "I love you, Ryan."

A great sigh shuddered out of him, then he laid his head against her breast, like a tired warrior returning home. In a raw voice, he said, "I've waited so long to hear you say those words."

"I know."

"I thought you hated me for leaving you."

Mandy's hands trembled as they caressed his hair, his back, everywhere she could reach. "I thought I hated you, too," she answered honestly.

"I didn't want to leave." His arms tightened around her, as if he could change the past by holding on to the present.

"I know."

Minutes passed in silence, and as the room turned steadily colder, she suppressed a shiver. With Reilly as her personal blanket, parts of her were warm enough, but now that passion had cooled, the chilly air pressed all around them, and the fireplace was too far away to do much good. She wasn't going to move, though, not for anything. But when she shivered again he felt it, and he rolled over, bringing her with him. Then, still holding her, he dragged the tumbled covers over both of them as best he could.

She snuggled against him, listening to the slow thud of his heart. For a while the only other sounds in the room were the crackling fire and the soft rasp of their breathing. Then he asked, "What made you change your mind?" He didn't wait for a response before clarifying, "I mean, why tonight?"

Mandy thought a long time before telling him the only truth she could. "I lost you once, and it almost killed me. If you had trusted me a year ago—"

"I couldn't." The harsh growl didn't fool her. Not anymore.

She hadn't known when they first met just what a loner he essentially was. She'd fallen for the facade at first, the reckless, flirtatious persona he presented to the world, but it had been those tantalizing glimpses of the lonely inner man that had drawn her under his spell, that had made her fall in love with him. But she hadn't really known him.

She knew more about him now, and it explained so much. Like a lot of cops, he was a throwback to the days when men sacrificed their lives to protect those weaker than themselves. His personal code of honor had strict rules—a man didn't put the woman he loved in the line of fire. Looking back, she realized their time together had been too short for her to teach him that she could be trusted, that telling her of the danger threatening him wasn't the same as putting her in jeopardy. According to his code of honor he'd done the only thing he could to keep her safe, not comprehending the devastation he'd left behind.

She sighed. "I know you believe that," she said softly, referring to his earlier statement, "but it doesn't change how I felt when I lost you, or what I thought when you turned up alive."

"Mandy—"

"No, let me finish. I realized tonight that if I let you go on believing I didn't love you anymore, I'd be doing the same thing to you that you did to me." She kissed the underside of his chin. "How will I ever teach you to trust me if I don't trust you?"

As the words left her mouth her conscience gave her a small pang. If she truly trusted him, if she were completely honest, there were things she needed to tell him, and it wasn't just about the baby. *Not tonight,* she pleaded with herself. *Not when we've just found each other again. I'll tell him,* she promised her conscience, *but not tonight.*

"It's not easy for me to trust, Mandy," Reilly said diffidently. "I wasn't raised that way." His voice was brusque as he explained, "When I first teamed up with my partner, Josh, it took me almost two years before I trusted him enough to let him guard my back."

Mandy didn't say anything, just stroked a hand over his chest, encouraging him to go on.

"Both my parents died when I was young," he said, the tight-edged words dropping into the silence, "and I grew up in foster homes."

"You never told me that before."

"I couldn't. I'd taken on a new identity, a new life. Reilly O'Neill's past wasn't Ryan Callahan's."

She rubbed her cheek against his shoulder in empathy and understanding. And after a moment, Reilly continued.

"I don't know why I wasn't adopted. They never tell you things like that. But trust wasn't a big part of my formative years."

He shifted restlessly beneath her, and Mandy knew these confidences weren't easy for him to reveal. As much as she wanted him to share the intimate details of his past, she didn't want them grudgingly given. Someday, when the danger was behind them, when they had time, she'd teach him that it was safe to confide in her. For now, she'd settle for what he could give her.

She ran her hand down his chest and lower. He was already half-aroused, and it didn't take much to bring him to full readiness. But when she would have taken him into her body he stopped her.

"Not this time," he said in a husky voice that was far from steady. He slid from the bed and padded across the room to his knapsack. When he returned, he'd protected her, just as he'd promised.

He had no way of knowing that protection was the last thing she wanted now.

Chapter 10

Mandy woke with a start, her heart pounding. She didn't know what had awakened her, but the minute she opened her eyes in the darkness she knew something wasn't right.

Where was Reilly?

She turned sharply, seeking him, and a hand covered her mouth. "Shh." The sibilance was pressed against her ear. "Don't move. There's someone out there."

Seconds later Reilly slipped from her side, and Mandy watched in terrified silence as he crept across the floor, keeping well below the line of sight of the windows. The fire had died down to glowing embers, and Reilly was little more than a shadow in the watery moonlight filtering through the kitchen window. He crouched by the chair where he'd slung his shoulder holster earlier and slid the .45 out, chambering a round with deadly ease.

The sounds outside were louder now, more distinct, and Reilly froze, his head turned to one side as if he were gauging the direction the sounds had come from. Then he backed toward the bed, gun raised, grabbing his clothes from the floor on the way.

When he reached the bed he lowered the .45 and reversed his grip, holding the gun out to Mandy, saying, "Hold this for a second." She sat up to take it, but he snagged her around the waist and lifted her to the floor, whispering a fierce "Stay down!" before turning the .45 over to her.

This gun was much heavier than the one he'd given her yesterday, and she wrapped both hands around the stock for a more secure grip, then curled a forefinger around the trigger, wondering if she'd have the strength, and the nerve, to fire it if she had to.

Reilly had already tugged his jeans on and shrugged into his shirt by the time she glanced his way again. His zipper rasped shut, the small sound magnified in the stillness of the room.

He transferred the .45 back into his possession and mouthed, "Stay here."

She blinked and he was gone, melting into the shadows and slipping out the back door with scarcely a sound.

Her heart jolted as the door closed behind him. She remembered Reilly's earlier statement that he'd kill anyone who tried to hurt her, and finally understood. Her teeth clenched as anger surged through her body, breaking terror's hold on her. *I won't let them hurt you either, Reilly.*

She scrambled around the bed to the other side and reached for the dresser drawer, pulling out the first clothes that came to hand and jerking them on. She didn't bother tucking her shirt in or looking for her shoes—she didn't have the time to waste. She needed to find Reilly's other gun.

On hands and knees she crawled across the floor toward the kitchen counter, expecting any moment to hear gunfire or the now-too-familiar whoosh of explosives, but none came. Without raising her head above the counter, she reached up and felt around until her fingers brushed against cold steel.

Shaking, she closed her hand around the semiautomatic's grip, brought it down and checked it over frantically. She couldn't see very well in the dark, and was grateful Reilly had warned her there was a round already chambered. She fingered the safety and clicked it off, then lurched toward the back door.

Reilly had closed the door behind him, making it safer for her but more dangerous for him should he suddenly need the shelter of the cabin. Mandy eased the door open a little way, peering out into the night.

Moonlight cast an eerie glow over the landscape, illuminating the empty clearing behind the cabin. No intruders. No Reilly. She ignored the small, scared voice inside her that said, *You're not cut out for this,* just as she ignored the blood pounding in her ears and her suddenly dry mouth. Maybe the voice was right, she thought, but Reilly was out there somewhere. She had to keep going.

She gripped the gun tighter and stepped outside, expecting the worst. No gunfire greeted her. Relieved, she sagged against the wall for a second, then straightened with a jerk, angry at herself for the momentary weakness.

She crept through the shadows cast by the generator shed. At the edge of the cabin wall she paused and took a deep breath. Then she darted around the corner, moving into a two-handed firing stance.

Nothing confronted her.

Relief washed through her again. Her knees quivered like gelatin and her brain registered that her already injured left foot was standing on a jagged rock. She shifted the bruised foot and gulped air, trying to control the shakes. It didn't help.

Voices broke the silence, deep male voices carrying clearly in the stillness of the night. She gasped as she recognized both—one angry, the other deadly in intent. She bolted toward them, heedless of the cold, damp ground beneath her bare feet.

"Damn you, O'Neill, I said cut me down!"

For a moment, Reilly contemplated the man in front of him. Suspended upside down from one booted foot at the end of a rope noose, the intruder swung helplessly to and fro a few feet off the ground.

Reilly lowered his gun hand to his side. "First tell me what you're doing here, Walker."

A stream of curses exploded from the trapped man, followed by a fruitless attempt to right himself and free his foot.

"Thrashing around like that only makes things worse," Reilly observed dispassionately. More invectives were hurled at him, but the struggles ceased. "That's better," he approved. "Now, what are you doing here?"

Walker visibly gritted his teeth. "You seem to forget that this is *my* land you're standing on, damn it. *Now cut me loose!*"

"Let him go, Reilly."

Reilly swung around, stifling a curse of his own. He should have known better, should have heard the approach, but **he**'d relaxed his guard when he'd found Walker in the trap. Lucky for him the gun-toting woman confronting him at the edge of the clearing was his own.

"What the hell are you doing out here?" he demanded. "I told you to stay inside."

Mandy didn't answer. "Let him go," she repeated. "Cody's a friend."

He didn't like the way she said that. All his primitive instincts went on the alert, his nostrils flaring as if he scented danger. After a tense few seconds he conceded that there wasn't a damn thing he could do about it. Not now, anyway.

He turned back to Walker and assessed the situation. The trap had worked better than he'd expected. He'd had to use more weight than usual to force the branch down in order to set the trap, and he hadn't been sure that the trip wire would release it. Also, because the surrounding vegetation was relatively sparse, he'd worried that this particular trap would be too easily spotted. But then, darkness hid a lot of faults.

It was too bad that the fastest way to free Walker was

to cut him down. A shorter rope meant changing the angle of the trap when he reset it, and it might not work as well. Reilly hated to do it, but he didn't see much of a choice.

"We'll need a knife," he told Mandy, glad of the excuse to get her out of the way for a couple of minutes. He had a few things he wanted to say to Walker he didn't want her overhearing.

"There's a hunting knife in my boot," Walker volunteered. "But I can't reach it."

Reilly cast him an acerbic look, then shoved his .45 into the waistband of his jeans and reluctantly moved toward Walker. He had no other option, not with Mandy looking on.

"I'll take this first," he said, relieving the sheriff of the revolver in his gun belt and tossing it safely to one side.

"That's two I owe you," Walker said for Reilly's ears only. The men's eyes met, both acknowledging that payback time would come for this second disarming.

Reilly located the concealed knife and drew out six inches of wicked steel. He hefted it in his hand for a moment, grudgingly approving the weight and balance of it. This was no ordinary hunting knife. This was a weapon of attack as well as defense.

Mandy laid her gun down and stepped forward to help. "Hurry up," she urged. "Can't you see Cody's in pain?"

Reilly bit back a growl, but complied. He reached up with his left arm and wrapped it around Walker's bound leg, using his weight to pull the other man down to the ground. Then he sliced through the taut rope with one swift, efficient stroke.

The free end of the rope hissed into the air, then danced and bobbed along with the swaying branch it was attached to, before eventually settling into a still, black line against the night sky.

Reilly grimaced and rubbed his face, thinking about how much work it was going to be to reset this trap. For a few seconds he considered using something else this time, then decided against it.

He turned at a sound from behind him, and forgot all about the trap. Grimly he noted that Mandy was kneeling at Walker's feet, tugging futilely at the hemp noose still bound around Walker's ankle.

"Here, I'll do it," Reilly said, kneeling beside her. He slid the knife between rope and boot, and sliced upward, then jerked the rope free and tossed it to one side.

Walker drew his knees up and hunched over them, rubbing the circulation back into his legs, and Mandy scooted closer, making soft, sympathetic sounds. Walker gingerly removed his boot, testing his ankle for injuries, and Mandy helped. But when her slender hands moved from Walker's ankle to his knee, Reilly told himself enough was enough.

He lifted her out of the way and knelt in her place. He'd had first-aid training as a cop back in New York, and after handing Walker's knife back to him, he ran his hands over the other man's knee with impersonal professionalism. "Anything broken?"

Walker flashed him a look that would have torn strips off Reilly's hide if he'd been thin-skinned, but shook his head. "No thanks to you," the sheriff snapped, tugging his boot back on and returning his knife to its sheath.

Reilly picked up Mandy's gun from where it lay, forgotten, beside Walker. He slipped the safety back on and stood, tucking the gun into the back of his jeans. He hesitated a moment, then held out a hand to the other man. Walker stared at it, obviously debating with himself, then grasped it and let Reilly pull him to his feet. The sheriff brushed himself off, then walked around a bit, scowling, favoring one knee.

When he finally halted, Reilly asked silkily, "What are you doing here?"

Walker sputtered. "Isn't that supposed to be *my* question?" He glanced at Mandy, but Reilly moved, partially blocking her from view. "I take it the two of you have been hiding out in my cabin?"

Reilly started to answer, but Mandy stepped around him and said, "I told him you wouldn't mind, Cody." Exasperation edged her voice, and Reilly knew it was aimed at him.

He couldn't help his response, though. Something was raising his hackles, and that something was Cody Walker. He shot a belligerent look at Walker that said the other man better *not* mind.

Walker's speculative gaze wandered from Reilly to Mandy, and Reilly's gaze followed, his eyes narrowing. When he'd left the cabin, Mandy had been wearing nothing but a sheet and moonlight. Now she was dressed in clothes that shouted they'd been donned in haste and in the dark. Her blouse hung loose, the front misaligned and only partly buttoned, as if she hadn't taken the time to worry about getting it right. Her nipples' reaction to the cold air made it plain she wasn't wearing anything under the blouse, either. Her hair was tousled, too, and hung in a pale gold cloud around her face, and the feet peeping out from beneath her jeans were as bare as his own. She looked exactly like a woman who'd just tumbled out of a man's bed.

Reilly's gaze snapped back to Walker, daring the other man to say a word. A *word*. The two men exchanged speaking glances, and the line was drawn between them as clearly as if they'd scratched it into the dirt.

Mandy intervened when she crossed her arms and began rubbing them against the cold. Both men turned at the movement, concern for her taking precedence over their private quarrel.

"Go back to the cabin," Reilly told her, then could have kicked himself when she just raised her stubborn chin at him in response. Mandy never had taken well to orders. He should have remembered that.

"It's damn cold out here, honey," Cody interjected. "You really shouldn't be outside dressed like that. You'll catch your death."

Reilly was pleased to see that Mandy ignored Cody's instructions, too, although he *wasn't* pleased with the endearment the other man had slipped in.

"I'm not going anywhere until the two of you cut it out," Mandy said firmly.

Reilly raised his eyebrows in an innocent "Who, me?" gesture, then glanced over at Walker and caught him doing the same. "What are you talking about?"

Mandy's eyes glinted. "You're acting like a couple of prizefighters about to go at it for a few rounds."

Although she didn't add *and I'm the prize,* Reilly heard the words inside his head. And in his heart.

"I'm cold and I'm tired," she said in a flat voice, "but I'm not leaving until you both get it through your thick skulls that we've got more important things to worry about."

She glared at them. "Now, I'm going inside. If there's any other baggage you two are carrying, I suggest you leave it at the door." She turned on her heel and started for the cabin.

Reilly watched her for a few seconds, then realized Walker was doing the same. He bristled before he was aware of it, then put a curb on his emotions. Mandy was right. It galled him to admit it, but they needed Walker's help. He had to put personal animosity aside for now.

There will be a reckoning, though, he promised himself. *When this is all over, I'll find a quiet spot and have it out with Walker. That's for damn sure.*

Walker had other plans. He waited only until Mandy was out of sight, then said bitterly, "It didn't take you long."

The muscles bunched in Reilly's arms. "Just what the hell is that supposed to mean?"

Walker threw him a burning look. "I'm not blind, O'Neill."

"What's between Mandy and me is none of your business," Reilly warned. "You'd better remember that."

"And if I make it my business?"

Reilly's adrenaline level shot up at the challenge, and he edged his weight onto the balls of his feet, alert to the changes in Walker's stance, too, watching for any sudden movement. "Don't try it," he advised.

A twig snapped about thirty feet away, and both men whirled toward the sound. Walker hit the ground in a controlled roll, and bounced up, armed with his knife. Gun already drawn, Reilly dropped to one knee and took aim, balancing his shooting hand on his other forearm for greater accuracy.

A scurrying sound was followed by a disappointed yelp as some small creature evaded a night predator, and the two men heaved sighs of relief. They looked at each other. Words weren't necessary as they acknowledged how careless they'd been. If the sound that interrupted their confrontation had been caused by a *human* predator, they might both be dead by now.

Reilly tucked the .45 back into his waistband, then searched the clearing until he found Walker's revolver. "Here," he said, handing it to him. "You're pretty fast with that knife, but if something really goes down you'll need this, too."

"Yeah." Walker holstered the gun, then caught Reilly's arm when he turned away. "This doesn't change anything, you know."

Reilly's glance at the hand on his arm was an implacable demand, and Walker released him, but didn't back away. Their eyes met, steel clashing against steel, then Reilly nodded. "I know."

"If you break her heart again, you won't get another chance. I'll make sure of it. The next time you leave her will be the last."

"There won't be a next time, Walker. When I leave, I'm taking her with me." Reilly shouldered past the other man and headed for the cabin.

He'd taken only a few steps before Walker called after him. "Are you so sure she'll go with you?"

Reilly stopped short. No, he realized, with something akin to shock, he *wasn't* sure. Not completely.

But he'd be damned before he let Walker know it.

Mandy put a pot of coffee on the stove while she waited for the men to come to their senses and join her. She didn't know which man she was more upset with. Reilly, she decided after a moment, as she rebuttoned her blouse and tucked it snugly in her jeans. He should have known better, should have realized Cody was no competition. Not after what they'd shared tonight.

She turned around and her eyes were drawn to the spot in front of the fireplace where she and Reilly had made love earlier. Her pulse quickened. No, Reilly had nothing to worry about where she was concerned. She'd given him ample proof.

Her gaze slid away, and she surveyed the bed in the corner, its rumpled condition mute testimony to the fact that two people had shared it recently. She made an indecisive face, then straightened the bedding with brisk motions, all the while telling herself it was a waste of time. Cody wouldn't be fooled. He knew her too well, and he'd probably already guessed that she and Reilly were lovers again. Still, she'd been raised in Black Rock, with its small-town values and standards. She'd never flaunted her physical relationship with Reilly before, and she wasn't about to start now.

Her hands trembled as she smoothed out the indentations on the pillows, then tugged the blanket over them. *It's just delayed reaction,* she reassured herself. All that adrenaline her body had pumped out earlier had sapped her strength, leaving her weak as a baby. Lack of sleep over the past two nights didn't help either, and her body ached in places she didn't care to think about right now. She didn't know what time it was, but judging by the position of the moon, she and Reilly couldn't have been sleeping for very long before Cody's arrival.

What if Cody hadn't been caught in that snare? she thought. *What if he'd arrived while Reilly and I were making love?* Her cheeks grew warm just thinking about it.

The front door opened suddenly. Startled out of her thoughts, Mandy swung around and bolted away from the bed as a cold gust of air ushered Reilly in, followed closely

by Cody. She studied both men and saw little of their earlier hostility towards each other reflected in their faces, but
she was still wary. She wasn't going to let them make her
the cause of trouble between them, not if she could help it.
If they started up again, she'd set them straight pretty darn
quick.

Reilly encompassed the whole room in a glance, his eyes
narrowing as they took in the neat state of the bed. Mandy
knew by his expression that he realized what she'd done,
and why. He'd also noticed that she'd straightened her
clothing, because his gaze travelled over her, lingering on
her blouse before moving up to meet her eyes. He didn't
say anything, though. Probably because he didn't want to
draw Cody's attention to it.

She shivered. Was it was from the cold? she asked herself, or from the blatantly sexual look in Reilly's eyes?
"It's chilly in here," she muttered, and started for the fireplace. Cody beat her to it.

"I'll take care of that," he told her as he knelt and stirred
up the coals before adding a couple of logs.

Not to be outdone, Reilly strode across the room and
switched on the space heater, to add its meager heat to the
task of warming up the room. He would have slid a possessive arm around her then, but the coffeepot boiled over
at that moment, and glad of the excuse, Mandy hurried to
turn off the flame.

She took three mugs down from the cabinet and set them
on the counter in readiness. As she poured coffee into them,
she asked, "Cody, what are you doing here in the middle
of the week? Aren't you on duty tomorrow?"

He accepted the mug she held out to him and shook his
head. "I switched with one of my deputies. There was talk
of a memorial service for you tonight, even though nothing's been confirmed yet, so I hightailed it out of there. It's
hard to fake grief when I know you're not dead. I played
the stoic mourner, and told people I was going to the cabin
for a couple of days to…you know…" The corner of his

mouth twitched ruefully. "Everyone was duly sympathetic."

She shot a warning look at him, and with a sideways glance at Reilly he added, "You being my oldest friend, and all."

Mandy handed Reilly his cup of coffee, avoiding his sharp-eyed gaze. "I wish..." she started, then fell silent. What was there to say? She hated the thought of her friends grieving for her, knowing how she would feel if it had been Alice or Judy or any of the other friends she'd grown up with who was presumed dead. She wished there was some way she could let them know she was still alive, without endangering Reilly or herself. There wasn't, though, and she knew it. What good would voicing the wish do, except make Reilly feel worse than he already did for having brought all this down on her?

She also wished there was some way to escape the questions she sensed Reilly was just itching to ask. She had the sick, bottom-dropping-out-of-her-stomach feeling that her answers were going to hurt him far more than she'd ever believed possible. She wouldn't lie to him, though. There'd been too much secrecy and deception in their relationship already. How could she ever make Reilly understand how wrong he'd been before, if she did the same thing now?

There would be a time and place for the explanations she needed to make, but this wasn't it. Not with the latent hostility between the two men just waiting for an excuse to flare up again.

She picked up her own cup of coffee and took a long swallow, letting the warm brew chase the cold away. The tension in the room was so thick it was a tangible thing, and she prayed that neither man would do anything to set the other one off.

Cody chose that moment to speak up. "So O'Neill, have you changed your plans since you heard the news?"

Reilly tossed him a questioning glance, and Mandy said, "What news?"

"You mean you haven't heard?" Cody straightened,

then grimaced and eased the weight off his bad knee again. "Pennington's out of jail."

"What?" Reilly's eyes narrowed dangerously. "That's not possible."

"The appellate court overturned his conviction, and he's out on bail. It was all over the news this morning."

Shocked, Mandy asked, "How could they do that? He tried to kill Reilly a year ago!"

"None of that has been proven, honey," Cody said, with a guarded look at Reilly that Mandy saw but didn't understand. A silent message seemed to pass between the two men, and she opened her mouth to ask about it, but Cody explained, "It's a catch-22 situation. O'Neill was supposed to be dead, but really wasn't. Pennington couldn't be prosecuted for ordering a murder that never occurred, and if the charge had been *attempted* murder, Pennington would have known O'Neill was still alive. That would have defeated the whole purpose of faking O'Neill's death."

"But..." Mandy set her coffee cup down and fumbled to put her thoughts into some kind of order. "He must have known Reilly wasn't dead. I mean, Pennington wouldn't have tried again now if he didn't."

Reilly's voice sent icy shivers down her spine. "Yeah. You're right. But whoever sold me out did it recently. Now that I know Pennington's original conviction was overturned, the list of possible suspects just expanded."

Mandy's forehead wrinkled. "What do you mean?"

Cody answered. "A new trial, honey, means the prosecution has to reassemble its case. Witnesses have to be lined up. Without O'Neill's testimony, the original case against Pennington falls apart."

Reilly added, "Only two men in the witness protection program had the knowledge to betray me this time. They both knew about you and they both knew I was headed this way when I left California three weeks ago. Up 'til now I thought one or the other, or both, had to be guilty.

"Under the circumstances, though, they probably had no choice but to reveal to the prosecutors that I'm still alive, still able to testify." He stared at the contents of his coffee mug as if he didn't like what he saw, then dumped the remains in the sink and left the cup there. "That means anyone on the prosecution team could have done it. And if they sent federal marshals after me to bring me in, any one of them could have sold me out, too."

"Federal marshals?" Mandy was appalled.

"I told you Pennington has men everywhere," Reilly gently reminded her, "at all levels of our government. We'll never discover them all. It doesn't really matter, though, because they're relatively harmless without the organization. Pennington's the key. Without him, without his money and his contacts with the underworld, the New World Militia can't survive."

"That's the one good thing about Pennington," Cody threw in. "If you can call it that. He's a megalomaniac. Always kept the real power in his own hands. Any good military organization has a chain of command, men trained to take over even if the top man goes down, but Pennington didn't set up the militia that way." He tossed off the last of his coffee and set his cup beside Reilly's, then leaned against the counter and crossed his arms. "There's no one trained to take Pennington's place. He's indispensable to them, and that's exactly how he wants it."

For just a moment Mandy wondered how Cody knew so much about the New World Militia, then shrugged it off as unimportant right now. She sipped at her coffee, her eyes seeking Reilly's over the rim of the cup. "So what are you going to do?"

"Whatever I have to." His expression was grim, forbidding, his lips set in uncompromising lines. "He won't get another chance to hurt you."

Mandy shivered again, despite the hot coffee she'd just swallowed and the growing warmth of the room. She was afraid when Reilly looked like that. Not for herself, but for him. She still balked at the knowledge that the man she loved was capable of premeditated murder, even if it was to protect her.

What about you? her conscience demanded. *When you went after Reilly tonight, gun in hand, you were just as willing to kill for his sake. What's the difference?*

Was it the same thing? She wasn't sure. Her world had been turned upside down in the forty-eight hours since Reilly's return, and she hardly recognized herself. The woman who would have fired that gun without hesitation tonight wasn't the same woman who'd walked into her bedroom two nights ago. Or was she?

She didn't know anymore. All she really knew was that she still loved Reilly. It hadn't been easy admitting it to herself, or to him, but now that she had, did she have any other choice but to accept him as he was?

"There are other ways of taking Pennington down without killing him," Cody said bluntly, stating what was in all their minds. "But we aren't going to solve anything tonight." He rubbed a hand over his face, stifling a yawn. "I don't know about you two, but I'm dead tired. I've got to get some shut-eye." He cast a not-so-casual glance at the bed in the corner, then caught Reilly's eye and coughed.

Warmth crept up Mandy's cheeks at the possessive expression on Reilly's face. If he hadn't already made it plain by his earlier behavior, he wasn't leaving any room for doubt in Cody's mind that they were lovers again. Embarrassed, and trying not to show it, she busied herself with rinsing out all three coffee cups and avoided looking at either man.

What was she going to do about the sleeping arrangements? She only had a few seconds to decide. She didn't think Reilly would understand if she refused to share his bed, but she didn't know if she could sleep with him while Cody was in the same room. It would be awkward, to say the least. And she had no idea what Cody's reaction would be if Reilly pushed the issue.

Reilly's voice, deep and compelling, spoke her name. It wasn't a question but a demand, and it forced her to turn around and look at him. He hadn't moved, but he seemed to loom over her, and his aggressive stance told her he wasn't going to be understanding about this. Her eyes pleaded with him, but the message didn't get through.

She wanted to explain, *needed* to explain, but it was impossible with Cody right there listening to everything they said. Besides, what would she say? Reilly had no way of knowing how things stood between Cody and her, and she really didn't think now was the time to tell him.

She shot an imploring look at Cody, but he just folded his arms, tightened his lips, and gave her a tiny shake of his head, as if to say he wasn't about to make it any easier for her by leaving the room.

Her gaze flashed back to Reilly, standing so still and unyielding. He'd caught her momentary exchange of glances with Cody, and she saw the dawning comprehension in his eyes. Her hand moved toward him in a futile gesture. "Reilly, I..."

He swung around, not waiting for the rest. "I'm going to check the other traps," he tossed over his shoulder as he headed for the front door. "I'll be back shortly." He paused on the threshold, one hand on the doorknob, and threw her one last burning look. "Whatever you decide, decide by then."

Mandy covered her face with both hands, wishing she could blot out the sight of Reilly's face as he left, but knowing it would stay with her forever.

He knew. Somehow he knew about Cody and her.

I should have told him. I shouldn't have let him find out like this! She rubbed her hands over her face and pressed her fingertips in the corners of her eyes to hold back the threatening tears.

But what could I have said? When could I have explained? There hasn't been a chance, really. If only Cody hadn't shown up! I could have explained everything in the morning. Oh God! Before, I wanted to hurt Reilly because he'd hurt me. But not like this. What am I going to do?

"Mandy?" Cody's voice intruded on her pain, and she dropped her hands to look up at him.

"I never stood a chance with you, did I?" A trace of

bitterness sharpened his tone. "It was always O'Neill. Even when you thought he was dead, you still loved him."

She nodded, her throat too tight to speak.

Emotion flickered over his irregular features. "You haven't told him about us, though, have you?" When she turned away without answering, he grabbed her arm and swung her around. "Or about anything else?"

"I *couldn't*."

"Damn it, Mandy. I'm the last one to plead his case, but you owe him the truth at least."

Reilly's voice, cold and hard, came from the doorway. "And what truth would that be?"

Chapter Eleven

Mandy and Walker whirled around, guilt written on both their faces. Reilly waited a moment, and the thought ran through his mind that maybe he didn't want to hear the answer, but he pressed on doggedly. "The truth that the two of you are lovers?"

Mandy caught her breath. "No!"

Walker's eyes steadfastly met Reilly's. "Yes."

"Cody, no!" Mandy's gaze darted to the man at her side and then back to Reilly, her eyes huge in her pale face. "It wasn't like that, Reilly. I swear."

The blow rocked him with unexpected power. One hand grasped the door frame for support, until the knuckles turned white. Emotions roiled within him, anger battling revulsion and betrayal for dominance. Hot words pressed against his lips, and his jaw ached as his tightly clenched teeth fought to keep them back. *How could you, Mandy?* he raged silently. *Is that all I meant to you? You didn't even have the decency to wait a year before—*

His hands curled into fists and his muscles tensed as he curbed the urge to strike out.

He'd refused to believe it earlier. When he'd walked out, his initial certainty had quickly turned to doubt, and he'd taken himself to task for not trusting Mandy. He'd all but convinced himself that his suspicions were unfounded, that the meaningful glances between Mandy and Walker and the significant pauses in their conversation didn't mean what they seemed to mean. He'd made short work of checking the perimeter, eager to return to the cabin.

Eager. He mocked himself with the word. He'd always been eager where she was concerned. Eager for her companionship as well as her bed. Eager to share the wonder, the joy of a love that had come to him after so many years of waiting for the one woman who would be to him what his mother had been to his father. Eager to protect her when danger threatened, even though it meant sacrificing his dreams. Eager, so *damned* eager to return to her when it finally seemed safe.

And all this time, while he suffered—submitting the face God gave him to a surgeon's altering scalpel, counting the days, weeks, *months* that passed, hoping against hope—all this time she'd been sleeping with Cody Walker.

After a moment fraught with tension, he concealed the mortal wounds he'd received behind a mask of contempt and said, "I guess that settles the question of who's sleeping where."

He knew the barb had hit home when Mandy flinched as if he'd struck her across the face. She closed her eyes for a moment, and when she opened them again, they glistened with pain, anger and unshed tears.

"Damn you," she said. "You have no right to judge me! No right, do you hear?" She looked at Walker. "And damn you, too. Damn both of you!" She was shaking, but her head swiveled toward Reilly again and she took two steps toward him. "You don't know what I went through. You stand there in judgment, like God Almighty, but you don't know anything about it." Tears trickled down her cheeks and she angrily dashed them away. "I almost died when you did. Does that make it easier for you? Does that make you happy?"

Deep inside, far beneath the smothering ashes of his own pain and the shield of wounded pride, another emotion breathed into life once more. "No," he managed to say, shaking his head, his throat aching.

More tears trembled on her lashes, spilling over as he watched. "Yes, I slept with Cody. Once. I'm not proud of it, but I'm not ashamed, either. I won't *let* you make me feel ashamed." She drew a ragged breath and expelled it in a rush. "He was there when I needed someone," she said in a desolate, heartbreaking voice. "Do you want to know why? Do you?"

Walker reached out and snagged her arm. "No, Mandy. Not like this."

She shook off his hand. "What do you know about it, Cody?" she asked bitterly. "You don't understand. Neither of you understands anything."

"I understand enough to know you'll regret it later," Walker said.

As little as Reilly was enjoying this scene, he hated being kept in the dark even more. "Leave her alone, Walker," he threatened. "Whatever her excuse is, let her tell me."

Mandy tossed back her head, her blue eyes blazing at him. "Excuse? I don't need excuses. You let me think you were dead. Any claim you had on me died with you!"

Reilly's anger flared, rising to match hers. The desire to wound as he had been wounded made him say softly, "So much for your deathless love, Mandy."

She slapped him. She put her whole arm into it, but the shock that he'd baited her into striking him was worse than the sting. Shame scorched him as he touched the red imprint of her fingers on his cheek, and he acknowledged that he deserved it, and more.

"Believe what you want," Mandy said, throwing the words at him like tiny poison-filled darts. "I don't have to justify myself to you. No, don't touch me," she told Walker as the other man reached to restrain her. "I'm sick to death of men right now."

She squared her shoulders and said defiantly, "I'm going to bed. Alone." She glanced at the bed in the corner, and Reilly thought he detected an instant's yearning regret in her expression before she looked away, but it could have been just a trick of the light. "I'll take the cot," she said. "The two of you can fight over the bed."

There wasn't a chance in hell he would get any sleep in that bed tonight, Reilly thought. Mandy's sweet fragrance, combined with the more earthy scents of their recent love-making would be lingering reminders of the passionate heights they'd reached earlier, underscoring the despairing depths to which he'd now sunk. But there was no way he was going to let Walker sleep there, either. "You take the bed, Mandy," he said in a voice that brooked no argument, casting a forbidding look at Walker to ensure his assent. "Walker can have the cot, since it's his cabin. I'll doss down on the floor."

Mandy shivered in the darkness. The fire Cody had built up earlier had died down, leaving a definite chill in the air, but it wasn't the cold that bothered her. Even though they'd had to share the available blankets between the three of them, she'd managed to make a cozy little nest of warmth for herself under the remaining covers.

No, she wasn't shivering from the cold, but from the delayed reaction to her earlier confrontation with Reilly.

I almost told him, she thought, horrified that she could even contemplate using the baby she'd lost as a weapon against him. *That's beneath contempt.* She closed her eyes and her lips moved silently as she sent up a prayer for forgiveness from heaven and her baby.

When she was done she sighed and turned over, hoping for sleep, but every time she breathed she smelled Reilly's dark, masculine scent on her pillow, and her heart ached.

She searched her soul for answers and found none that satisfied her. She'd thought she had already dredged out the

well of anger and resentment she'd discovered in herself
earlier, but it must have gone deeper than she'd known. It
had only taken a few condemning words from Reilly to
bring it welling up again.

*It's all gone so horribly wrong. I should have told Reilly
about Cody before we made love. It wasn't fair to let him
find out afterwards, when he was most vulnerable. Even
then, I should have explained calmly, rationally. Instead, I
hurt him and kept on hurting him. I wanted to see him bleed
as I was bleeding inside when he looked at me that way.*

She shifted her head on the pillow, Reilly's earlier words
taunting her. *So much for your deathless love, Mandy.* She
flexed her hand, imagining she could still feel the sting
from when she'd struck him.

*He was right to say that. At least that's how it looked to
him. I did sleep with Cody when Reilly had been dead only
a few months. It's not much of an excuse to say I was
grieving for him and for—*

"No," she whispered to herself, fighting tears and memories both. She wouldn't think about the baby now. She
couldn't bear it. Losing Reilly had torn out her heart. Losing his baby, losing that last precious link with the man she
loved, had ripped out her soul, leaving her bereft of hope.

Even now she wouldn't let herself think of that time. She
wouldn't, *couldn't* go down that road again, not when her
emotions were already raw.

She turned over restlessly, punching her pillow, and telling herself that if she didn't get some sleep she was going
to be useless in the morning. Both men had long since
fallen asleep; Reilly's steady breathing in the still room was
punctuated by Cody's gentle snores, both sounds coming
and going with regularity through the darkness.

Her thoughts gave her no respite. *I said I wasn't ashamed
of sleeping with Cody, but I am. Not just because of Reilly,
but because I used Cody. I used his love for me to try to
block out my pain. It didn't work, of course, but I didn't
deserve to have it work. And because I was a coward, I
didn't have the heart to tell either man the truth. I didn't*

*tell Cody he could never take Reilly's place. And I didn't
tell Reilly about Cody, or about the baby.*

The baby. Conceived the first time she and Reilly had
made love, when they'd been so wrapped up in each other
that neither had spared a thought for protection. They'd
always been careful after that, but neither had known it was
already too late.

Despite her determination not to think about that time,
she'd never been able to control her dreams. As sleep stole
over her, her mind skittered willy-nilly back to memories
of the baby. Her precious baby that never was.

She hadn't suspected anything when she skipped her first
period. She'd never been all that regular to begin with, so
she never marked her calendar as other women did, and the
weeks slid by without her noticing. Around the time her
next period was due she had an extremely light flow for a
couple of days, little more than spotting really, and thought
nothing of it. By the time she missed her third period, however, she'd already noticed other symptoms—extreme tiredness for no reason, heightened sensitivity in her breasts, a
slight thickening of her waistline—and she grew concerned.
When she started counting back, she knew.

She'd been unsure of Reilly's reaction to the news. As
often as he told her he loved her, he never mentioned marriage or children, and she didn't want him to think she was
trying to trap him this way. She also wanted medical confirmation before she said anything, but she could hardly
walk into Black Rock's only drugstore and buy a home
pregnancy test. The gossip would have blazed through town
like wildfire before she returned home. And since Black
Rock had no doctor of its own, she had to make an ap-
pointment with her doctor at the clinic in Sheridan without
letting Reilly know.

Four months. Her baby had been almost four months
along when the doctor confirmed her pregnancy, although
in her heart Mandy had already been sure.

She drove home from Sheridan in a state of nervous ex-

citement: excited about the baby, nervous about telling
Reilly. She couldn't put it off any longer now. In truth, she
yearned to share this precious secret with him. Lately his
beloved face had worn a distant, almost sad, expression at
times, when he thought she wasn't looking. When she
asked him if anything was wrong, he denied it, but she
wondered if he suspected she was keeping something from
him and was hurt by her silence.

She turned off the highway before reaching the road to
Black Rock, deciding not to wait until this evening to tell
Reilly about the baby. Saturday was her busiest day at the
bookstore and she rarely took it off, so he'd be surprised
to see her. Surprised and, she hoped, pleased.

When he'd kissed her goodbye that morning, he'd told
her he would be working at the reservoir, repairing the
pump station's frame housing. She took the steep road that
wound up the north side of the mountain and led to a short-
cut, rehearsing exactly what she would say to him.

She never got the chance to say anything. A little way
above the reservoir she caught sight of him, saw him put
his tools in the back of his Blazer, and she sped up to catch
him before he left by the main road. She didn't want to
miss him now that she'd come all this way.

A bend in the road blocked her view for a minute, then
she rounded another turn and spotted the Blazer again, seconds before it exploded into a ball of smoke and flames,
sending shards of twisted metal flying. She screamed his
name, knowing he was inside, knowing she was too far
away to save him from a horrible death. That didn't stop
her from trying. Praying as she'd never prayed before, she
jammed her foot on the accelerator, and her car shot forward, rocketing dangerously around the downward turns.

That was the last thing she remembered before waking
up in the little hospital in Sheridan. Cody sat in a chair
beside her bed, holding her hand. He never said a word,
but she didn't need him to tell her that Reilly was dead.
She knew. And by the hollow, empty feeling inside she
knew the baby was gone, too....

* * *

Mandy moaned in her sleep and thrashed, then jerked awake. She lay there for a few seconds, disoriented by the familiar nightmare and the strange bed. Then she heard the rhythmic breathing of the two men in the room, and one nightmare replaced the other as she realized where she was.

Grief rolled through her in waves, accompanying the memories evoked by her dreams. She squeezed her eyes shut and fought the memories off before they went any further. It was a trick she'd learned in the past few months, a way of accepting only as much as she could deal with at one time. It didn't always work, but it worked better for her than the more traditional grief therapy, although she'd gone through that, too.

She wondered if she'd ever reach the point where her memories no longer had the power to invade her dreams. Maybe, she thought. Now that she knew Reilly wasn't dead, maybe those memories would fade away eventually.

She didn't think she'd be so lucky with the rest of them.

She sighed, a broken sound that trembled on the brink of tears. The saddest thing of all, she thought, was that her baby hadn't had to die. If she'd known the truth, if Reilly had trusted her, she would never have crashed. But there was no turning back the clock, no way to change what had happened when she'd seen his Blazer burst into flames.

There were no second chances for her baby.

She couldn't hold the grief at bay any longer. A sorrowful sound welled up in her throat, and she muffled it against her pillow as sobs shook her body.

It was a long time before she slept again.

Reilly woke before anyone else, the quiet of the early morning out here in the middle of nowhere intruding on his sleep in a way that the hustle and bustle of a big city would never do.

He lay there for a few minutes, getting his bearings, his big body aching all over. *I'm getting too old to sleep on floors,* he thought, focusing on the physical, putting off the moment when he would have to face the emotional ache deep inside.

God, he'd wanted to kill Walker last night when the man had looked him straight in the eye and admitted to being Mandy's lover. *Lover.* Maybe he should have killed him. Maybe then he wouldn't have lain awake for most of the night, tormenting himself with pictures of Walker holding Mandy, Walker touching her lips, her breasts, the softer-than-soft place between her thighs. *Mine,* he told himself, gritting his teeth. *My* woman.

He drew a sharp breath as pain stabbed through him. It was a physical thing, this pain, as if Mandy had reached into his chest and squeezed his heart with callous hands before tearing it out altogether.

Was it all lies, Mandy? he'd asked her in his mind last night. *Did you ever love me?*

He'd known the answer, though, even without hearing her say it. She couldn't have loved him, at least not the way he loved her. If she had been the one who died, he'd told himself last night, he would have died, too. Oh, his heart would have kept on pumping blood to his vital organs, but he would have been dead inside. He could never have assuaged his grief over losing her with another woman. There was no other woman for him. It was Mandy, or no one.

A scornful sound issued from his lips. *I guess it's no one, then,* he mocked himself. *Do you really want her after she's been with Walker?*

He rolled over onto his side, unwilling to answer that question just yet.

He'd heard her muffled weeping during the night, when she thought everyone else was asleep. Despite everything, he'd been hard-pressed not to go to her, not to hold her, comfort her, and discover the cause of her tears. He'd managed it only by reminding himself that she was probably just feeling sorry for herself now that her guilty secret had come out.

But when he'd finally fallen asleep in the wee hours, he'd

dreamed of her. Not as she'd looked when he'd returned to the cabin and found her with Walker, but as she'd been earlier, lying in his arms, fighting back tears as he spoke of having children with her.

He couldn't erase that picture from his mind, or her expression earlier as she'd sat by the fire and held out her hand to him, love and longing chasing the shadows from her eyes.

Nor could he forget her soft voice saying, "I love you, Ryan." She hadn't been faking then. He was damned if he could make himself believe it.

I should have let her explain last night. But I was too proud, too hurt, and I struck back without thinking, condemning her without giving her a chance.

Well, that wouldn't happen again. Maybe she didn't love him as he wanted her to, but she *did* love him, and a part of Mandy's heart was better than nothing.

He had his answer to his earlier question, too. Walker or no Walker, he wasn't giving her up without a fight. He'd never be able to forget; no, that was asking the impossible. But he might be able to forgive. Someday.

At least he'd have Mandy, and he'd know she was safe. The last thought made him throw off his blanket and stand up, his muscles protesting. He yawned and stretched wearily, then picked up his shoulder holster and made his way to the bathroom as quietly as he could, so as not to wake Mandy.

When he came out, Walker was up and moving around as stealthily as he himself had done. Reilly ignored him and strapped on his gun. He'd slept in his clothes last night, as had Walker and Mandy. He could have used a shower, but it was more important to check the perimeter right now. Especially since Walker was awake. He didn't trust himself not to take the other man apart, piece by piece.

Reilly stepped into his shoes without bothering to unlace them, then headed for the door. Walker stopped him.

"Hold on a minute," the man said in a deep undertone. "I'm coming with you."

Walker didn't wait for Reilly's answer, just disappeared into the bathroom, emerging a moment later. At a soft sound from the bed, both men froze, then turned toward it. They watched as Mandy's head tossed restlessly on the pillow, then subside, the tousled golden strands of her hair glinting in the early-morning sunlight that crept through the window.

Reilly's hands clenched at the brief flash of naked emotion that crossed Walker's face, emotions that mirrored his own. *You have no right to look at her like that,* he wanted to say, but he didn't know if it was true. Maybe Mandy had given Walker that right. He wouldn't know for sure until he talked with her.

They waited for several heartbeats, but Mandy didn't stir again. Finally Walker tore his gaze away. "Let's go," he said tightly.

Outside, Reilly set the pace, with Walker only a half step behind him. Neither man said anything as they walked the line, the crisp mountain air bringing them both wide awake. Walker watched as Reilly checked each trap, and Reilly knew he was noting their location against future need.

It wasn't until they were heading back toward the cabin that Walker spoke. "You know your stuff, O'Neill. I have to give you that."

Reilly grunted, a noncommittal response. He didn't need the other man's approval. And all things considered, he didn't want it, either.

"Yeah," Walker continued, "You know this stuff like the back of your hand, all right. But you don't know squat when it comes to Mandy."

Reilly swore and swung around, his right fist making contact with Walker's mouth before he knew it, sending the other man sprawling in the dirt. His knuckles ached, but Reilly didn't care. It gave him great satisfaction to see Walker wiping blood away with the back of his hand; he'd been wanting to mess up Walker's face for him, among other things.

When Walker jumped to his feet, Reilly expected him to

try to return the favor, and he held himself at the ready—body crouched in a defensive stance, weight balanced on the balls of his feet, hands up to ward off one blow or a dozen.

The two men were well matched, and Reilly welcomed the chance to relieve some of his anger and frustration in a set-to with Walker. The sheriff was perhaps a shade taller and a couple of pounds heavier, but Reilly knew he could take him. This wouldn't be a finesse fight with rules and time limits, and Reilly hadn't grown up a street brawler for nothing. He had no hesitation about fighting dirty, especially given provocation.

Instead of rushing Reilly, however, Walker stood with his hands balled into fists for a tense moment, his alert eyes narrowed to slits as if gauging the weaknesses in Reilly's defenses. Then, with a visible effort he relaxed, muscle by muscle, and straightened up. He looked at his fists as if he didn't recognize them, then uncurled them and dropped his hands to his side. He raised his face, and there was a grim set to his mouth as he said, "That's your free one, O'Neill." There was a watchfulness about him still, as if he didn't trust Reilly to accept the offered truce, then he added, "But don't even think about doing it again, because I won't hold back next time."

"What's holding you back now?" Reilly taunted.

"The same thing that held us both back last night."

The blood lust faded. Frustration mounted at being deprived of the fight he craved, but he could hardly hit Walker again when the man had dropped his guard. The first blow, yes. Walker had deliberately provoked him into it; he deserved what he'd gotten. But even though Reilly had been a street fighter, he'd never been a bully. The fight was over. For now.

Reilly dropped his fists, but remained on the defensive. If Walker thought to catch him off guard with his not-so-subtle reminder, Reilly would be ready for him.

Neither man spoke for a moment or two, each taking the measure of the other, then Walker's gaze slid away from

Reilly's, and his eyes clouded as though he were seeing something only he could see.

When their eyes finally met again, Walker said, "You think you're the only one to suffer in all of this?" Self-mockery twisted his lips. "It's no secret that I love Mandy. I've loved her for years, ever since we were kids. Long before you showed up. She never 'saw' me, though. I was her *friend*." A bitter smile replaced the mockery. "But I was willing to wait. Time was on my side, I thought, and it could still happen. Maybe one day she'd turn around and really see me."

His nostrils flared. "Then you came to town. I had to watch her fall in love with you, and there wasn't a damn thing I could do about it."

"Except sleep with her when my back was turned," Reilly answered in a soft, deadly voice.

"Is that what you think?" Walker's bark of laughter grated on Reilly's ears.

"What else am I supposed to think? You knew I was alive. I trusted you to watch over her, to keep her safe while I led the wolves off the scent." He was breathing hard as his anger built again. "That didn't mean she was yours for the taking!"

"That wasn't how it was, damn it!"

"Yeah, right." Reilly expression was as derisive as his tone.

Walker shot back, "She saw the explosion." He held up his hand as Reilly started to interrupt. "I know, I know," he insisted, "she wasn't supposed to be anywhere around, but she was. She was coming down the back road toward the reservoir when your 4x4 burst into flames."

Reilly remembered Mandy saying something of the kind, remembered her statement that she'd seen him die. It cost him something, but he put his pride in his pocket, and asked, "Why? What was she doing there?"

"It would be better if she told you herself."

"Damn it, Walker! Spit it out!"

Walker glared at Reilly. "She was pregnant, you son of a bitch! Pregnant with your child!"

As the meaning of the words sank in, Reilly had the same sensation as the time he'd been shot in the line of duty, the same disbelief that this was actually happening to him, before he turned numb and cold. "A baby?" He managed to get the question out. "She had my baby?"

Pity replaced Walker's belligerent expression, and he shook his head. "No," he said with real regret. "I wasn't going to tell you like this, but she lost the baby the same day. She crashed trying to reach you after the explosion."

The numbness that had started to wear off returned in full force, cushioning the blows to his heart, but Reilly fought against it. Underneath the shocked numbness was pain that rocked him to the core, but at least that was *real*. His lips moved, forming one word. "How?"

"No one travels that old back road much," Walker answered, "because the new one is safer, even if it is longer. But I guess she was in a hurry to reach you. I don't know all the details—Mandy doesn't remember the accident, of course—but the skid marks told their own story. She lost control on a sharp turn and went off the road. Her car broke through a guardrail, rolled halfway down a ravine, then ended up wedged sideways against a stand of aspens. It was a miracle that the gas tank didn't explode." Walker's voice wasn't quite steady now. "She wasn't found for hours, and by the time she was, it was too late to save the baby." His eyes darkened as he remembered. "It was touch and go with Mandy herself for a while there."

It was too much to take in at once. Reilly struggled to put the pieces together in a way that made sense, but all the while the thought kept running through his mind that she had almost died. She had said as much to him last night. *I almost died when you did,* she'd thrown at him, but he'd thought she was talking figuratively.

He shook his head to clear it of the memory. "Why didn't you contact me?"

"How was I supposed to do that? You were in the program, remember? They whisked you away and told me nothing.''

Reilly wasn't ready to accept that explanation. "There were ways. If I'd known…''

"What could you have done? Come back? Put Mandy in danger again so you could tell her the explosion was a setup, and that she didn't have to risk her life and her baby's to save you?''

The blow landed, and Reilly struck back. "You could at least have told her I was still alive. But that didn't fit in with your plans, did it?''

Walker flinched, and Reilly closed in for the kill. "You saw your chance to move in on her, and you took it. Never mind that I trusted you to watch out for her. Never mind that she was grieving for *me*, that she was mourning the loss of *my* baby. No, those things weren't important. You wanted her….'' Bile rose in his throat as the image of Mandy in Walker's arms floated before his eyes, and he couldn't finish.

"I *couldn't* tell her, damn you!'' Walker was furious. "By the time she was strong enough to be told, I didn't know if you *were* alive. And even if you were, there was no guarantee that you were ever coming back. She had already suffered enough. There was no way I could tell her the truth!''

A harsh voice intruded from the other side of the clearing. "You should have found a way, Cody.'' Both men swung around to face the direction the words had come from. Mandy was standing about ten yards away from them, and they'd never heard her approach. They'd been so caught up in their argument, they'd blocked out everything else.

"All this time, you let me think Reilly was dead. You *knew*, Cody, and yet you said nothing.'' Bewilderment replaced the shocked comprehension of a moment ago, and she stared at him as if he were a stranger. "You were my friend. I trusted you. How could you do that to me?''

"Mandy, I—''

She cut him off. "And you," she said, turning that bewildered gaze on Reilly. "You said you loved me, then you went away and let me think you were dead, but you trusted *him* with the truth?" She shook her head, as if she could somehow make sense of it that way. "I was right the first time." She took a step forward, her hands tightly clenched. "Who gave you the right to play with my life that way? My life, and my—" Her voice wavered, then quit before she could get the word out.

She swallowed, the movement visible to Reilly even from a distance, and her name was torn from his throat. "Mandy, don't."

She found her voice again and continued, her bitter words flaying him. "You don't deserve an explanation, but I'll give you one anyway. When you died, and I lost the...baby..." She quivered and wrapped her arms around herself as if for moral support. "I wanted to die, too. I had nothing to live for. Can you understand that? Nothing. You talk about deathless love as if you understand it, but you don't have a clue." She laughed a little, the forlorn sound slashing at Reilly's heart. "I don't know what all Cody told you, but I'm sure he didn't tell you this." Her voice lowered, but her next words came to him clearly. "When you died I tried to kill myself."

Chapter 12

Reilly's throat worked, but no sound came out. "No," he mouthed, taking a step backward, as if he refused to believe the unforeseen results of his actions a year ago. "I was only trying to protect you."

Mandy didn't hear him. For a moment she was back in the hospital, waking up to a world devoid of hope. Reilly and her baby were dead. She might as well be dead, too. Surrounded by equipment meant to save her life, one thought had run through her head like a sad refrain: *Nothing to live for. Nothing to live for.*

Dry-eyed, she'd deliberately ripped the IV needle out of her arm and turned off whatever equipment she could reach. And waited to die.

The flashback receded, and Mandy repeated, "I tried to kill myself. When I finally came to my senses I realized that I *couldn't* die. It's funny," she said, her gaze turned inward as she contemplated the past, "but even though I knew I would never love again, never carry a child again, I still found a reason to live."

"What—" There was a catch in Reilly's husky voice, then he managed to ask, "What was it?"

"To keep you alive." She smiled sadly. "I thought, as long as *I'm* alive, Reilly can't ever really be gone. My memories of you, of us, were too vivid, too vital to let you fade into oblivion. I'd lost your baby, your chance for immortality. *My* chance to see you live on in your child. I knew the only other way to keep you alive was in my heart. And for that I had to live."

"I can't listen to this." The clipped words were Cody's. He turned on his heel and strode toward the cabin.

As she watched him go, Mandy couldn't help but feel a quick pang of empathy for him, despite his betrayal of their friendship. She had her own wounds to deal with, though, and Reilly's. Cody's came a distant third.

Her gaze swung back to Reilly. After the less than stoic response he'd been shocked into revealing, he'd retreated behind an emotional stone wall again. A spasm of anger shook her. She wasn't his enemy. All she wanted was to make him *see* how it had been.

"How about you?" she challenged. "Or can't you deal with the truth either?"

If he was surprised by her question he didn't show it. "I want to know," he said. "Everything." And for an instant she saw the rare vulnerability in his eyes, the vulnerability he only showed to her.

Mandy let out the breath she'd been holding. "I lived. It wasn't easy," she said slowly, searching for the right words now. "Even though I'd found a reason to go on living, don't think it was easy." She glanced away, seeing not the sun peeking warmly over the horizon, nor the faint green traces of spring in the foliage around the clearing, but rather the endless winter of loneliness she'd endured.

"The nights were the worst," she said softly. "I'd lie awake for hours, remembering, pretending you were in bed next to me, then finally fall asleep and dream. The dreams started out fine, but they all ended the same way, watching you burn to death. I'd wake up, and for a second or two

I'd think, *Thank God it was only a dream.*'' She breathed sharply, then met his eyes again. "I'd reach for you, to reassure myself, but you were never there. And I'd grieve all over again.''

Reilly made a restless movement with his hand, as if to deny the past, but Mandy pressed on relentlessly. "Then there came the night when I didn't dream your death, and I woke up crying. I knew you were truly dead then, and nothing—not my love, not my memories, nothing!—could keep you alive.'' Her breathing was ragged now, but she knew if she stopped she'd never be able to bring herself to this point again.

"That was the worst day since I'd woken up in the hospital. It was New Year's Eve. Symbolic, in a way, saying goodbye to the best and worst year of my life.

"We were in the midst of a three-day blizzard, but even if we hadn't been, I couldn't have gone in to open the store. I cried off and on that whole day and far into the night, knowing I had to let you and our baby go.'' As she was talking, a small part of Mandy wondered why, when the memory still had the power to rend her heart, her tears were absent.

She licked her dry lips. "I even tried to drink myself into a stupor that night with the bottle of Irish whiskey I'd bought for you months before. I just wanted to forget, even for a little while. I thought if I could just blot everything out for one night...'' She paused, reliving the memory as if it were just happening, and her voice dropped to a whisper. "I was so cold that night. So cold, from the inside out. I built a roaring fire in the fireplace and brought blankets and pillows to lie down in front of it, but I couldn't get warm.'' She shivered with the memory. "Cody came to check on me the next day.''

"That's enough.'' The harsh voice startled Mandy out of her trancelike state, and her eyes focused on Reilly's face. "I don't think I want to hear the rest, after all,'' he said, an expression of what she thought was revulsion casting a grim shadow over his features.

She dropped the arms she'd wrapped around herself earlier and lifted her chin. "I wasn't going to tell you any more than that," she said, gathering her dignity around her like a cloak. "What passed between Cody and me is private, and no one's business but ours. I would no more tell you about him than I would tell him about you. Even if you and I were—" She broke off, paused for a second, and tried again. "Even if we...I know it's not very likely now, but if...somehow...we were together again, I couldn't tell you."

"You don't have to go on," Reilly said brusquely. "You've made your point."

She studied him for a moment, but found no hint of softening, no sign that he had even tried to understand. *It was all for nothing,* she told herself bleakly. *I could have saved myself the trouble, spared Cody the humiliation.*

Her shoulders sagged and she turned to go, then changed her mind and faced him again. "I have to ask you something. You don't have to answer, but I hope you will."

"What is it?"

"Would it have made a difference if...if I'd told you about the baby and...Cody before we...you know. Would you feel differently now if I had?"

He considered the question for a few seconds, then slowly shook his head. "No. It wouldn't have made a difference. None at all."

She nodded. *I was wrong about that, too,* she thought. *Wrong all across the board.* "Thanks for being honest, at least," she said out loud, forcing a tiny smile. It probably looked as phony as it felt, but she couldn't do any better. Not right now. Maybe later, when she'd had a chance to pull herself together, maybe then she'd be able to put up a brave front. For now, she'd be satisfied if her legs held out until she could put some distance between herself and Reilly.

Reilly watched Mandy walk away from him—shoulders squared, head held high—and fought the urge to call her

back. She hadn't understood what he'd meant when he answered her question, and his first impulse had been to set
her straight. He'd curbed that impulse, realizing that maybe
it was better this way. He'd been blown away by the discovery of the baby she'd lost because of him, and her subsequent revelations had shattered his conviction that he'd
only done what was best for her.

He needed time to sort things out in his mind, time to
come to terms with Mandy's home truths, but time was
something he had precious little of right now.

Assuming Walker was still willing to help him take Pennington down—and that was a big assumption—things
were going to heat up pretty damn quick. It would be better
all around if he kept emotions out of it until everything was
settled.

Before he'd met Mandy, he'd had a lot of experience
doing just that: compartmentalizing his life, locking his
emotions away. It shouldn't be too hard this time. All he
had to do was focus on his target—Pennington—and the
rest would follow as it always did.

He hoped.

In the cabin, Mandy found Cody standing over the sink,
wolfing down a bread-and-butter sandwich. Normally she
would have made a teasing comment about his unbalanced
diet, but not this time. She had a few things to say to him,
and none of them concerned food.

She didn't even wait for him to finish. "You had no right
to tell Reilly anything," she said, watching him swallow
the last bite and brush the crumbs from his hands before
he turned to face her. "Not last night, and not this morning."

"He asked."

"That's no excuse, and you know it. I was going to tell
him myself when the time was right."

"There's never a right time for that kind of thing. If there
was, you'd have found it before now." Cody's voice had
an edge to it.

"It was still my choice. *Mine.*"

"He'd already figured it out last night, and he wouldn't have believed me if I'd lied. And this morning he was a walking time bomb. I didn't want *you* to get hurt."

"Shielding me again," she said, her anger flaring. "You and Reilly, you're both the same. Both of you lying to me, both of you trying to *protect* me, as if I'm some halfwit who can't protect herself. Well, I have a news flash for both of you—I can. I'm stronger, *tougher* than either of you will ever be."

Reilly strode into the cabin as the last sentence left her mouth, and he answered her before Cody could. "Maybe you are," he said abruptly, and though he faced her, he avoided meeting her eyes. "Maybe we were wrong not to tell you what was going on a year ago, but what's done is done. We don't have time for recriminations. Pennington is out there, still gunning for me, and you already know he doesn't give a damn about who else gets killed in the process. He won't stop unless we stop him first." Reilly's gaze moved beyond Mandy to Cody. "Are you still in?"

Cody's brows drew together in a frown, but he said, "That hasn't changed."

"Good," Reilly said. "The sooner we start, the sooner it'll be over. And now that I know Pennington's out of jail, we need to revise our plans."

"Are you thinking what I'm thinking?"

"Probably. The timing will be tricky, but I'm betting we can pull it off."

Mandy looked at Reilly's face first, then Cody's. There seemed to be an understanding between the two of them that transcended their earlier hostility toward each other.

"You'll be taking a big risk," Reilly warned.

Cody shrugged. "So will you."

"Yeah, but I don't have a choice. You do."

Cody glanced at Mandy, then back at Reilly. "No," he said softly, with a crooked smile. "I don't have a choice either."

Reilly stiffened for a second, then acknowledged, "I don't guess you do, at that."

Mandy had had it with being left out of the discussion. "If you think either of you is leaving here without telling me what you're talking about, think again."

The men's eyes met over her head, then Reilly nodded toward the kitchen table. "Have a seat," he said. "This'll take some time."

Night had fallen. Reilly sat at the table, a soft rag in one hand, the pieces of his gun spread out in front of him for cleaning and oiling. His second gun, the one he'd given Mandy to use, was already finished and laid to one side.

Mandy sat in front of the fireplace, her arms wrapped around her knees. She glanced over at Reilly, but something in his intense concentration prevented her from interrupting him. He'd been like this all day, shutting her out, his closed expression forbidding her to approach him in any way.

She sighed soundlessly, then turned back and again stared into the dancing flames, wondering what it would take to break through that shell of his, and wondering even more if she had the courage left to try. He'd as good as told her this morning that he didn't love her anymore, and she wasn't a masochist. Why give him the chance to tell her again?

Her thoughts shifted to Cody, who'd long since left. Before he'd gone, however, he'd managed a private moment with her while Reilly was outside. Now she blocked out the crackling fire and the methodical sounds from the table behind her and replayed that scene in her mind.

"I'm sorry," Cody said, his blue eyes contrite, reminding her poignantly of apologies they'd exchanged over the many years of their friendship, and her heart softened toward him despite herself. "I know it doesn't change things, but I am sorry."

"I know," she said.

"I wanted you to know—not that it changes things either—but O'Neill was wrong. I didn't plan what happened on New Year's Day. You were vulnerable, but I didn't set out to take advantage of you. It just…happened."

"I know that, too." She paused, then added, "I always meant to apologize for using you that way. For using you to try to forget Reilly." Her gaze wavered, but she hung in there and continued looking up at him. "By then I knew how you felt about me, and I knew it wasn't fair to you. But I did it anyway. I'm not proud of myself, but like you said, it doesn't change things. It happened. I never for a moment blamed you."

Cody swallowed, then touched her cheek briefly. "Thanks."

"Be careful out there, okay?"

"Okay." He hesitated a moment, as if making a decision, then asked lightly, "There's no chance for me, is there?"

"Oh, Cody." Her soft heart ached for him, but there was no point in giving him false hope. Even if she and Reilly never patched things up, she would never love Cody the way he deserved to be loved. She shook her head.

"That's okay, honey." He gave her a lopsided smile. "I didn't really think so."

He'd gone before Reilly returned, and Mandy had watched him until he was out of sight. Cody had hidden it well, but she knew she'd hurt him anew, and she mourned the loss of a friendship that would never, *could* never, be the same.

She sighed again, out loud this time, and stole another glance at Reilly. Without raising his head from the job in front of him, he suggested, "Why don't you go on to bed? I know it's early, but you didn't get much sleep last night."

"No less than you."

"I'm used to it. You're not."

Something snapped inside Mandy. "You don't know what I'm used to. Not anymore. You haven't exactly been around to see." The hands carefully reassembling the gun froze for a second, then continued their task. For some reason his control made her lash out at him. "For that matter, you don't have to pretend you're concerned about whether I get enough sleep or not.''

The gun thudded to the table, and the eyes that met hers were dark and dangerous. "What the hell is that supposed to mean?"

"Just what I said. I know you're stuck with me for now, until you catch David Pennington, but you don't have to pretend you care. It's not necessary, and frankly, I'd just as soon you didn't.''

He was out of his chair and grasping her shoulders before she knew it, pulling her to her feet. Warmth pulsed off him in angry waves, and Mandy's head swam dizzily for a moment.

"Don't push me," he warned, and a frisson of fearful excitement ran down her spine. His grip tightened, and she knew there would be faint, smudgelike bruises on her arms come morning, but she didn't mind. At least Reilly was showing her some honest-to-God emotion, rather than that wooden detachment he'd displayed earlier.

"Let me go," she demanded, struggling just enough to show she meant business, but not enough to actually break free. "You've made it very clear what you think of me and I don't want you touching me anymore.''

He ignored her struggles and pulled her closer. A fine tremor ran through him and transferred itself to her. "Is that what you really think? That I don't care?" When she didn't answer he shook her and said in a tortured voice, "I wish to God I *didn't* care. Then maybe I could forget." He paused for a harshly drawn breath, then whispered, "Maybe I could forgive."

That stung Mandy on the raw. She fought Reilly for real this time, with all her strength, and finally wrenched free. She backed away, panting a little, the pain in her arms nothing to the pain in her heart. "I can't make it go away." Her breath caught, but the words kept coming. "I can't go back in time and make it never happen, just as I couldn't change what supposedly happened to you.''

He flinched, but she was past caring. "You're not the

only one who can't forget, you know," she flung at him. "I tried. I thought Cody could make me forget what it was like to make love with you, what it felt like to sleep in your arms, but—"

"Is that what you thought I meant? That I couldn't forget about you and Walker?" Reilly shook his head and laughed without humor. He passed a hand over his face, and when he looked at her again she was shocked by the bleakness in his eyes. "No, Mandy," he said, shaking his head again. "It's not what *you* did I can't forget. It's what *I* did."

"What do you mean?"

His face twisted, but he didn't spare himself. "I killed our baby."

A denial sprang to her lips, but before she could speak he said, "Don't bother denying it. You almost came right out and accused me of it this morning."

"I was upset, but—"

"No. You were honest. Brutally honest, but..." He shrugged his shoulders. "You blame me for losing the baby, and I understand that." His voice shook with repressed emotion. "I blame myself, too."

She didn't know what to say. He was right in a way, and she'd be lying if she said otherwise. A part of her *did* hold him responsible, but in her heart of hearts she knew the fault wasn't entirely his. If she'd told him about the baby sooner, when she'd first suspected she was pregnant, maybe things would have been different. If she hadn't been such a coward...

She had to know the answer. "If I had told you about the baby before you left, would you have taken me with you?"

Because she was half expecting an emphatic confirmation, she was surprised when none was forthcoming. "Reilly?" she asked, hesitant now. "What would you have done?"

His lips thinned beneath his mustache. "I know what you want me to say," he said curtly. "I wish I could say it. The truth is, I don't know. A baby would have made you even more vulnerable, and I was a hunted man. Given the situation with Pennington…'' He met her eyes squarely. "I just don't know if I would have done anything differently.''

It made absolutely no sense, Mandy thought. She should be angry with him. Or hurt. Or any of a dozen emotions other than what she was feeling.

Loved. Cherished.

The memory of the night he returned flashed through her mind. Reilly covering her body with his own when the first firebomb crashed through the window. Dragging her after him with a death grip as he crawled toward safety. Braving the wall of flames in the kitchen to rescue her when the second firebomb trapped her without an escape route. Shielding her in the tunnel when the propane tank blew.

Reilly was a born protector. She'd had some inkling of it after they'd made love last night, but she saw now that it went far beyond just being a cop.

There were other signs, too, obvious now that she thought of it. Reilly jury-rigging a security system for her out of little more than rope and wire. Leaving her his spare gun and making sure she knew how to use it. Going after last night's intruder alone, leaving her behind in the relative safety of the cabin.

Protector. That one word defined him in ways she was only beginning to understand and accept. It was what made him go after Pennington in the first place, what made him willingly take risks other men balked at.

It even explained why he'd resisted taking what she'd shyly offered him only a couple of weeks after they'd first met. Most men would have jumped at the chance, but not Reilly. He'd turned her down so gently that it hadn't seemed like a rejection, but a compliment, and had only made her love him more. He'd held off for almost two months—even though she'd made it perfectly plain how much she wanted him—protecting her from him and his secret past.

And because he *was* a protector, he couldn't forgive himself for the loss of their baby.

He wouldn't take the easy way out, either. She'd given him the perfect opportunity to sidestep responsibility, but he hadn't taken it, preferring the honesty between them that she'd demanded. Could she be any less honest with him?

"It wasn't all your fault," she whispered.

"Yes, it was. I should never have involved you, back then or now. If I'd never touched you, none of this would have happened."

Mandy shook her head. "You talk as if I had no say in the matter. Let me remind you that *I* seduced *you* the first time." She blushed a little, but went on. "I was the one who wouldn't let you leave."

A tender smile softened his face momentarily, tilting up the corners of his mouth in the way she'd always loved, and she sensed that if things had been different between them he would have reached out and caressed her cheek. "I remember," he said. The smile faded and he just stood there watching her. He didn't say or do anything else, but his vivid tawny eyes betrayed him.

"Reilly?" She took a step toward him and spoke his name before she was aware.

"What?"

Suddenly flustered and unsure, she shook her head and said, "Nothing."

An age-old weariness seemed to settle on his shoulders. "Can't you tell me?" he asked gently. "Have I killed your trust along with everything else?"

The vulnerable expression in his eyes freed her tongue, and she blurted out the question she'd longed to ask. "You don't really hate me, do you?"

Pain flickered across his features, a response he didn't even try to hide. Then he shook his head.

"Then why did you say what you said this morning?"

"I said a hell of lot of things this morning. Which one in particular?"

"That it wouldn't have mattered if I'd explained about the baby and Cody before we made love last night."

His harsh laugh startled her. "That wasn't what you

asked," he said. "You asked if it would have made a difference in how I felt."

"It's the same thing."

This time he did reach out and touch her, brushing a tangled curl away from her face and tucking it behind her ear. "No. It's not."

"I don't understand."

He hesitated. "I don't know if I can explain. I told you before, I don't have a lot of experience in talking about my emotions."

Mandy remembered Reilly's confession last night that he'd grown up in orphanages and foster homes, and understood. It was hard to break the habits of a lifetime. She needed an answer, though, so she pleaded, "Please try. I have to know."

"I went over and over it in my mind last night," he said after a moment. "I was angry, angrier than I'd ever been in my life. I couldn't believe you'd betrayed me like that, not after..." He ran his fingers over his face, feeling the changes plastic surgery had wrought. "This was for you, so I could come back for you someday. I wouldn't have done it otherwise."

"I...I think I knew that."

He didn't acknowledge her interruption. "I thought you'd been lying to me all along. That you never loved me."

"Oh, no!"

"Yeah." His eyes darkened. "I wanted to kill Walker for touching you, as if wiping him out could wipe away the images of you in his arms."

She'd asked for the truth, Mandy thought, but she didn't know if she could bear seeing Reilly lay his heart open like this.

"When Walker told me about the baby this morning," he continued, "and that you'd almost died, I knew deep down that I had no one but myself to blame for all of it."

She couldn't let him suffer like this. She threw herself

at him, wrapping her arms around his waist and pressing her face against his shoulder. "It was my fault, too."

She felt the struggle within him before his arms reluctantly closed around her, almost as if he thought he didn't have the right to hold her anymore. "I thought nothing could hurt worse than hearing about the baby," he said in husky tones that reverberated through her body. "Then you told me you tried to kill yourself."

It was past midnight on the East Coast, but David Pennington wasn't asleep. When the phone rang he picked it up and waited impatiently while the man known as Centurion identified himself with the proper code sequences. Then he listened intently to the information the man imparted, nodding his head in silent agreement with the plan sketched out for him.

After a couple of minutes he frowned and said, "No, that's not necessary. I'll find my own way there. You just make sure Callahan shows up on time and not before."

"Yes, sir."

"Don't screw it up this time. If the operation goes smoothly, I'll consider removing the black mark from your record." He didn't have to add the unspoken threat that accompanied his statement. He seldom had to. Few men received second chances from him.

"Thank you, sir. You don't have to worry. Everything will go like clockwork tomorrow night."

"Make sure of it," Pennington said, then hung up abruptly and dialed another number. Minutes later, his flight to Wyoming was arranged.

He sat back in his chair, sipping his brandy, mulling the plan over in his mind and finding no flaws. Then he considered his adversary.

Callahan was a fool for going back to Black Rock, he decided. With his new face, Callahan could have escaped detection if he hadn't returned for the woman. But every man had at least one weakness. It hadn't been too difficult to spot Callahan's.

Pennington chuckled to himself, a sinister sound made all the more so because he was alone in the room. *I can't wait to see Callahan's expression,* he thought, *when I tell him who betrayed him. When I tell him that he and Centurion share the same weakness.*

Chapter 13

Mandy rubbed her cheek against Reilly's chest as if she could erase her confession of attempted suicide that way. "I shouldn't have told you."

"It was true, wasn't it?"

"Yes, but—"

"Then you should have told me."

"Not like that. Not as a way to hurt you."

"Oh, Mandy." The sadness in his voice made her lift her head to gaze up at him. "I would have been hurt no matter how I learned about it."

She closed her eyes to shut out the naked emotion reflected in his face, then rested her head against him once more. They stood like that for a span of time that seemed endless, then Mandy sighed and gently attempted to disengage herself from Reilly's embrace. His arms tightened around her momentarily, but then he loosened his hold and freed her. She moved a step or two away and brushed her hair back nervously.

"So where do we go from here?" she asked with a catch in her throat.

"I don't know." He leaned his weight on one hip and tucked his hands into the back pockets of his jeans. "The way things stand right now, I shouldn't even be thinking about anything past tomorrow."

His statement reminded Mandy that their personal crisis wasn't the only one they were facing. She was just about to agree that they should wait to talk about their future, when he asked diffidently, "Where is it you want us to go?"

"After...after everything is over," she said, still refusing to accept the possibility that after the confrontation with Pennington, Reilly might not even be alive. "Afterward, are you planning to stay...in Black Rock?"

He shook his head slowly. "I can't. No matter what happens tomorrow, there's still a chance someone might come gunning for me. This is the first place they'll look."

"Will the witness protection program give you a new identity? A new life?"

"I won't be going into the program again."

Mandy wrinkled her brow. "Why not?" The answer came to her and she said, "You don't trust them anymore."

"No. I don't." He moved impatiently. "It probably isn't their fault that Pennington's men tracked me down, but I won't take that chance again."

She hesitated. They had settled nothing between them as yet, and she knew those emotional issues should be dealt with before asking the question uppermost in her mind. But time was short. If she didn't ask him now, she might not have another opportunity, and she wasn't about to let him leave without hearing his answer. "When you go," she said straight out. "Are you planning on taking me with you?"

His eyes narrowed a fraction. "I guess that depends on you."

Having screwed up her courage to ask the first question, the second wasn't quite as difficult. "Do you want me to go with you?"

"It would be safer for you."

"That's not what I asked." Her heart was pounding.

"Now that you know about—" she couldn't bring herself to say Cody's name "—about everything, do you *want* to take me with you this time?"

"*This* time?" He shifted the emphasis to the last two words of her question, denying it with a shake of his head. "I've *always* wanted you with me."

Reilly's low-voiced confession went straight to her heart, temporarily depriving Mandy of speech. His next words brought tears to her eyes.

"Then. Now. It makes no difference. I've always wanted you with me," he reiterated, "and I always will. I don't know what that says about me, about my pride, but—"

"Pride doesn't come into it," she said fiercely, making a valiant effort to hold back the tears. "Will pride sleep in your arms? Will pride guard your back? Will pride give you children to—" She almost couldn't finish. "To love and cherish and protect?"

He seemed taken aback at first, then he closed the distance between them, grasping her arms with a fine disregard for his strength. "You said—" He choked on the words. "You said this morning that you couldn't have children anymore."

She was confused for a few seconds, wondering what on earth he was referring to. Then she understood. Her voice was gentle as she explained, "I said I *would* never carry a child again. Not that I *couldn't.*"

His grip relaxed a little, but he was still tense. "But..."

A dozen different responses occurred to her, but Mandy went with her instincts. "I said something else this morning," she reminded him, capturing his right hand with both of hers and cradling it against her cheek. "I said I knew I would never love again. That implied I had a choice in the matter. What I should have said was, I *could* never love again. Not after loving you."

There was a fine tremor in his rigidly held muscles, and his voice wasn't quite steady. "You have a choice now."

She turned her head slightly to kiss his palm. A tremulous smile underscored the simple conviction in her tone as she said softly, "No. I have no choice at all. I never did."

He stood frozen for a moment, as if he were afraid to believe it, then he gathered her close. "Oh, God," he said, and for him it was a prayer.

He covered her face with frantic kisses, and when his lips eventually found hers, she kissed him back with the same intensity, the same yearning. Then she was swung off her feet into his strong arms. He carried her to the bed in the corner and laid her on it, following her down without giving her a chance to change her mind. Not that she would have. Not when he whispered her name again and again, his husky, urgent words sending shivers coursing through her body.

Somehow their clothes melted away and they were naked, skin to skin, in a glorious riot of sensations that reminded Mandy of the first time they'd made love, the first time she'd known the unique feel of a man's naked, muscled body hard against her own softness.

He cupped her breast with his hand, bending his head to taste and tease, and her whole body clenched, then shook, when he began to suckle. Her bones had liquified and the internal throbbing had grown unbearable when he finally lifted his head and positioned himself between her legs.

Yes, she thought at the first blunt probing. *Yes, yes, yes!*

Then he was inside her and she couldn't think at all, only feel. He took her higher with each thrust, pulling her knees up around his hips, allowing him deeper access to her body.

She cried out and arched like a bow when the first orgasm struck without warning, but Reilly gave her no respite. He held her in place and continued riding her with stroke after steady stroke, his lips drawn back in gritted determination not to let his control get away from him.

She wanted to rest for a minute, to catch her breath, but he wasn't having any of that. He nuzzled her cheek, then turned his attention to her ear, and she shuddered each time his tongue made forays into the delicate shell. All the while, his body kept up its rhythmic movement inside hers, until another shattering peak was reached.

He paused for a few seconds, corded muscles standing out in his neck and his body trembling against hers as he fought his own release, but he conquered it and soon picked up where he left off.

"No," she pleaded, while ripples of completion still pulsed through her. "Reilly, I can't."

"You can," he reassured her, capturing her lips. His tongue slid inside her mouth and out again, mimicking the hard-driving rhythm of his body.

She was helpless. Not against him but against her own desires. Her body responded instinctively to the man she loved: his musky male scent, his sweat-slick skin beneath her clinging hands, the dark flush on his cheekbones, the over-bright gleam in his golden brown eyes. Her body responded, and quickened once more.

"Come with me, Mandy," he panted between strokes, and somehow she knew he was referring to more than their lovemaking.

"I will," she promised, sliding her hands down, touching him where they were joined so intimately.

A groan rumbled out of him and he threw back his head, his hips hammering home one last time as her touch triggered his explosion. He filled her with his unsheathed essence—warm, lifegiving pulses—and Mandy's heart exulted fiercely just before she gave herself up to the culmination of their passion one last time.

She was vaguely conscious of Reilly collapsing against her, his breath rasping in his throat, even less aware when he shifted most of his weight off her. She smiled dreamily when he drew her into the shelter of his body and tugged the blankets over both of them, but she couldn't keep her eyes open. She curled trustingly against him, kissed the underside of his chin, which was the only part of his face she could reach without changing position, then sighed in deep contentment and fell asleep.

Reilly held Mandy close, watching her as she slept.

Maybe he would sleep, too, he thought, as soon as his heart stopped racing and the blood stopped churning hotly through his veins. Not now, though. Now he only wanted to hold the woman he loved and cherish this moment.

Eventually his pulse slowed somewhat, and he shifted, rolling onto his back, bringing Mandy to lie securely in the curve of his arm. He slipped his other arm beneath his head, and allowed himself the luxury of reliving what had just occurred.

Mine, he thought with a bone-deep satisfaction that cut through the waves of tiredness that had pulled at him ever since his adrenaline level had dropped. *She's really mine. Not Walker's. Mine.*

His arms tightened around Mandy in automatic response to the mention of Walker, as if he could create a physical barrier against his thoughts. After a moment he gave up the struggle. Hiding from the truth wasn't the answer.

Cautiously he examined the still-tender emotional wounds Mandy had inflicted on him with Walker's help. The wounds would never disappear completely, he realized, no matter what he did. He could cauterize them and carry the scars, or he could pretend they didn't exist. Either way he'd carry them for the rest of his life.

I can live with it, he decided. Given the alternative, there really was no other option.

Maybe someday he'd be able to put it all behind him. He'd made a start tonight. He'd just proved he could make love to Mandy without seeing the mental image of her in Walker's arms. And judging from her reaction to his love-making, both last night and tonight, there had been no room in her mind for thoughts of any other man.

He'd almost asked her afterward, a small, insecure part of him still needing confirmation that when she was in his arms she thought only of him. He'd been saved from what would have been a disastrous mistake when she fell asleep.

She loves me, he averred, angry with himself for needing reassurance like a child. *Walker means nothing to her.*

But a tiny niggling doubt remained, and he pulled her

closer. She stirred without waking, turning a little, and something fell against Reilly's chest. He reached down and picked it up. Mandy's locket was warm from contact with her skin, and the old-fashioned filigreed gold gleamed dully.

A frown marred his features. If Mandy had owned the locket before he'd left her, he'd never seen her wear it, and he wondered if Walker—

No! he decided after a tense moment. He wasn't going to think like that. *Mandy wouldn't wear another man's gift while making love with me.*

Mandy slept on, undisturbed, and the temptation was too great for Reilly. He fumbled with the locket, and finally managed to pry it open with one hand. Then he just lay there and stared at the contents.

His own face confronted him, his face as it had once been. He was smiling down at Mandy as if she were the center of his world, and she was looking up at him, her heart in her eyes. Even as small as the image was, he could clearly make out both their expressions. He didn't know how she'd come up with a photo of them, but the picture had obviously been cut out of a larger one, and in one of those rare instances, the unknown photographer had captured on film a poignant moment out of time for all eternity.

His last doubt melted away. He closed the locket with a tiny snap and reverently replaced it against her skin. And smiled.

When Mandy woke it was still dark outside, not yet morning, but she felt so well rested she knew there wasn't much likelihood of falling asleep again.

She stretched, easing away from Reilly so as not to disturb him. He must have somehow sensed her absence, though, because he murmured in his sleep and tightened his hold on her.

She smiled to herself as she snuggled back into his embrace, a secret little smile that nevertheless radiated some of the joy she felt this morning. It didn't matter that her body ached from last night's encounter. It was a good ache. A *delicious* ache. One she gladly accepted in return for the chance to sleep in Reilly's arms.

Actually, now that she thought about it, her body had already been sore, even before they started, from their previous round of lovemaking the other night. The physical part of making love was strenuous activity, requiring the use of certain muscles. When a woman wasn't used to it, her body protested afterward. But she wouldn't have stopped Reilly from making love to her last night even if it had been extremely painful.

It hadn't been painful. Not at all. The soreness had vanished after a few moments, blanked from her mind by rising passion. She blushed as she remembered how wild she'd been, how she'd clung to him, scoring his back with her fingernails as he'd driven her from peak to peak.

No pain could have withstood Reilly's sensual onslaught. He'd never made love to her quite like that before, holding his desire in check while seeing to it that hers raged out of control. He'd been relentless in his quest to take her places she'd never been before, almost as if he had something to prove.

Her smile faded. Maybe he *had* been proving something to her, or to himself. It might not even have been a conscious thing on his part, but she suspected there was more than a grain of truth to her supposition. She would never ask him, though. If there had been a demon of some sort riding him last night, she could only pray that the demon was now exorcised.

With a shake of her head Mandy banished those thoughts, and any others like them, for the time being. She had more important things to think about.

They might have made a baby last night.

She wouldn't let herself hope for that, of course, but she couldn't completely rule it out either. He hadn't worn a condom at all last night, nor the other night when he'd made love to her in front of the fireplace. Just as he hadn't worn one the first time they'd made love. She'd become pregnant that first time. Could it happen again?

The doctors had told her that as a result of the accident she might find it more difficult to conceive, but they had assured her it wasn't impossible. She hadn't cared at the time. She'd just lost Reilly's baby, and Reilly, too, so it might as well have been impossible as far as she was concerned.

Now she wanted that possibility with every fiber of her being. A baby. Reilly's baby. Not to replace the one she'd lost—for the rest of her days a part of her would mourn the tiny life snuffed out before it had a chance to draw breath—but a child to fill the emptiness in her arms and in her heart.

She knew that second chances didn't come to everyone, but God had granted her a second chance with Reilly. Maybe, just maybe, God in his mercy would smile on her once more.

Her eyes closed as she sent up a silent prayer. When she opened them again, Reilly was awake and watching her.

"Good morning," she said, suddenly and inexplicably shy.

"Is it?" His eyes twinkled at her. "Let's see." He leaned over and tilted her chin up for a lingering, heart-stopping kiss. Breathless seconds later he collapsed back against the pillow, clutching his heart theatrically like a bad actor in a third-rate script. "Oh, yeah. It's a good morning all right."

Mandy couldn't help it. She laughed.

"That's better." He raised his head and smiled down at her, turning on the Irish charm. "For a minute there I thought you were going all shy on me, darlin'."

"Shy?" She dismissed the possibility. "No way."

"'Course not. No reason to be shy with me, is there?"

"Nope."

Reilly slid his hands underneath her arms. "Then come here."

She clambered on top of him, savoring the warmth of

his skin over taut muscles that rippled and flexed as he moved beneath her. She rubbed her face against his chest and sighed with contentment.

She loved touching him without the barrier of clothes, had loved it ever since the first time on her front porch swing, when he'd unbuttoned his shirt and had granted her the freedom to explore. His body was so different from hers, and it was just as fascinating now as it was back then.

As Mandy continued her voyage of rediscovery, Reilly caressed her absently, letting his hands wander in aimless fashion over her body as if he were reacquainting himself with the glide of silky skin under his palms.

She reciprocated, tangling her fingers in the diamond-shaped thatch of hair on his chest, then tracing the line of hair as it bisected his body, finally coming to rest just above his now-throbbing manhood.

"Don't start something you can't finish," he warned.

"What makes you think I—" She gasped, partly in shock and partly in pain, when he slid his hand between her legs and brushed his long fingers over her swollen flesh.

Having made his point, he didn't linger. "You should have told me last night you were too sore to make love," he chided her.

"I wasn't, last night."

"Well, you are this morning," he said with finality, drawing her hand away and bringing it to his lips for a quick kiss before easing himself out from underneath her.

He rose from the bed and stood there for a moment in the early morning light, stretching. His muscles moved with easy grace beneath his skin as he arched his back, then twisted from side to side, shaking the kinks out.

Mandy watched him with loving eyes. If she'd seen him like this the night he returned, there'd have been no question of his identity. Plastic surgery had altered his face beyond recognition, but his body was unchanged. He was beautifully made: no muscle-bound weight lifter, but a man honed down to the essentials of muscle, bone, and sinew. The phrase, "a lean, mean, fighting machine," might have been coined to describe him, she thought with a touch of whimsy. The whimsical mood faded as she remembered what had made him this way, and she noted with a flick of pain each scar on his beautiful body that bespoke the harsh, dangerous life he'd led.

He turned to one side and she saw the still-raw wound on his arm, where he'd been injured while shielding her that night in the tunnel. She made a mental note to inspect it closely for infection later on, and rebandage it, even if Reilly protested. Maybe she couldn't protect him from every danger he faced, now and in the future, but she would at least protect him from what she could.

He turned once more, and a pattern of small, red, crescent-shaped marks interspersed with scratches on his back brought a blush to her cheeks and made her sit up abruptly.

Reilly swung around at the rustle of bedclothes. When his gaze took in her embarrassed expression and the sheet she clutched over her breasts, he raised a questioning eyebrow. She blurted out, "I branded you last night." The bald statement seemed to require more explanation. "Your back," she said. "I...I hope it doesn't hurt too much."

He sat on the edge of the bed and leaned over her, resting his weight on one arm. "You branded me a long time ago, Mandy. The first time I saw you." He rubbed the back of his hand against her cheek, then brushed his thumb over her bottom lip before adding, "It doesn't hurt any more now than it did then."

"I don't want it to hurt at all," she whispered, sliding her arms around him, stroking gentle fingers over the marks she'd left on him as if she could somehow heal him that way.

"It doesn't matter." His husky voice was very close to her ear. "Pain's a small price to pay for loving you."

The midday sun was high in the sky when the Learjet carrying David Pennington touched down at a private airstrip outside Chicago for refueling, then took off again. He glanced at his companion on this flight, the man he'd cho-

sen to accompany him on this critical mission. Carl Walsh
was a good man, and dedicated to the cause, but he was a
follower, not a leader. He would carry out any orders he
was given without question, but he couldn't be counted on
to come up with any original ideas. Not the best man to be
second-in-command of the militia, Pennington conceded,
but after the fiasco with Callahan, not a bad choice either.

Callahan. Just thinking of the man made Pennington's
hands clench the armrests until his fingers turned white.
He'd handpicked Callahan as his successor, promoting him
over other men with more seniority, so sure of his reading
of Callahan's character and abilities. Smart, dedicated,
deadly. And a loner. Ryan Callahan had seemed the perfect
choice to head up the militia's elite corps. The rank-and-
file members were good as a political power base, good for
intimidation and recruiting purposes, but Pennington had
always known his real power lay in the small, ultrasecret
corps of human "weapons," those men who could be
trusted to kill upon his command. Centurion had been one
of those men. Callahan, he'd thought, had been another.

That's what made Callahan's betrayal a personal thing.
That was the true reason why Pennington was handling this
execution himself, instead of delegating it again. Callahan
had signed his own death warrant with his testimony, but
death alone was not enough to satisfy Pennington's craving
for vengeance. Not anymore.

When Pennington had learned in prison that Callahan
was still alive, his first reaction had been fury. His second
had been suspicion. He'd trusted Centurion to carry out his
orders. Had he been betrayed again? But Centurion's explanation had been plausible, and the subsequent failure of
the other "weapons" Pennington had sent after Callahan
had added weight to Centurion's argument that Callahan
had the devil's own luck in sniffing out a trap.

But not this time, Pennington gloated, running over the
details of the plan in his mind and finding them flawless.
This time, Callahan, you're going down. I guarantee it.

Escape was impossible, the plan foolproof. After all,

there was more involved here than just Callahan's crimes against the militia or Centurion's previous failure to execute him. Centurion knew that his own life was hanging by a thread, but that threat was meaningless to a man like him. It was the other threat that ruled Centurion, and there was no way the man would let Callahan live now. Not with the woman at stake.

Chapter 14

"Walker will be here soon," Reilly said, running a fist-ful of soapy utensils under the water and stacking them helter-skelter on the drainboard. Breakfast, lunch, and an early dinner had come and gone all too quickly. Now he and Mandy stood side by side at the sink, their jeans-clad hips touching occasionally, doing the dishes together as they waited for dusk and the sheriff's arrival.

"I know." Mandy concentrated on the plate in her hand, scrubbing it much longer than necessary before handing it to him to rinse.

He caught a glimpse of her distraught face before she turned away, and he said, "We're going to have to talk about it pretty soon. We don't have much time left."

"I know," she repeated, a sharp edge to her tone this time.

"I don't want to wait until Walker gets here. I don't think you do, either."

"Why do you always call him 'Walker'?" she asked impatiently. "His name's Cody."

"Not to me it isn't." He knew she was trying to distract

him, and he sympathized with her. The possible outcome of his impending confrontation with Pennington tonight wasn't something he particularly wanted to discuss, especially now. But he had to make sure she knew what to do, just in case.

He glanced at his wristwatch. Depending on whether Walker arrived early or not, they had maybe a half hour left. He weighed the alternatives, then decided that if Mandy wanted to postpone the inevitable discussion for a few more minutes, it was all right with him.

"Cody's just as bad," she continued. "He never calls you by your first name either, not even when he's talking to me." She handed Reilly another plate to rinse. "It can't have anything to do with—" She stopped in midsentence, and when she picked up again there was a slight catch in her throat. "Because other men do it, too."

"It's a guy thing," he said flippantly, making an effort to keep the conversation light for her sake.

"What does that mean?"

He shrugged his shoulders. "I don't know that it means anything, really. I've never analyzed it before." He thought for a moment, running his thumb along the bottom of his mustache. "Maybe it's a macho thing. Staking your territorial boundaries. Establishing the pecking order. Something like that."

"Oh?" She gave him a dubious look.

"I guess last names are less personal, too." He thought about his buddies back in New York. Cops, most of them. Good friends, but other than his former partner, Josh, not what you'd call real close. And yeah, last names were the norm when they addressed each other, except for those who'd been tagged with embarrassing or descriptive nicknames.

"I don't know," he said, drawing his words out. "Maybe it's more than that." She'd started him thinking, and now he was caught up in answering the question to his own satisfaction. "Maybe it has to do with those emotional boundaries men are reluctant to cross with each other. It's different with a woman. A man can tell a woman things he'd never admit to another man.''

"That's not always true. Sometimes it's the other way around." Her eyes sought his to emphasize her point. "Sometimes men share secrets and keep women in the dark.''

Their gazes locked. "Yeah," he admitted. "You're right. But only when there's a damn good reason.''

They washed and rinsed in silence for a minute or so as Reilly continued turning the original question over in his mind. "Maybe there's another explanation," he said finally.

"For secrets?"

"No, the name thing. You know, a man's last name is linked to his identity, to who he is. I don't think women attach the same importance to it as a general rule."

"You mean because most women still take their husbands' names if they marry?''

"Yeah. But it's not just that." He squinted a little, struggling to put his thoughts into words. "A man's last name is as much a part of him as the shape of his eyes, the color of his skin. It's passed down to him from his father, and his father's father before him, and *his* father before that.''

He paused, smiling faintly, as a distant, vague memory came back to him. He couldn't have been more than three years old when it happened, but his dad's words had stayed with him all this time, waiting to be remembered. "He's a true Callahan, all right," Patrick had boasted, nearly bursting with pride as he showed off his son to his fellow construction workers. "Mark my words, boyos, my Ryan will do the name proud some day.''

His smile faded. *I tried, Da,* he thought, using the childhood name for his father that he hadn't used in over thirty-five years. *I tried to do the name proud.*

"Reilly?"

The strange name intruded on his consciousness, and for a fraction of a moment he wondered who that was. Then he remembered.

He glanced down at Mandy's worried face. "What is it?"

"That's what I was going to ask you," she said. "You were talking, and then all of sudden...it was like you weren't even there. Is something wrong?"

He shook his head. "No. Talking about fathers just triggered a memory of my own dad. That's all."

"You said you were very young when he died. You can't have many memories of him."

"No, I don't." But like his memories of Mandy, each one was precious. "At least I had a father once," he added. "Some of the kids I grew up with didn't even have that."

He took the pot she handed to him, thinking out loud as he rinsed. "You know," he mused, "it used to be that the worst insult you could give a man was to call him a bastard. Even though times have changed, even though out-of-wedlock children have become so commonplace it's almost fashionable these days, it's still a fighting word on streets and playgrounds everywhere."

Mandy had stiffened during his speech. Now she gave the washcloth a vicious wring and flung it over the faucet, saying in a tight little voice, "I don't quite see the connection."

He could have kicked himself. Mandy obviously thought he'd been reproaching her with a reference to their baby when he'd mentioned out-of-wedlock children. But that wasn't the case. Not consciously, anyway.

He caught her arm as she turned away from him. "We're not done yet."

"What do you mean?"

"I mean there are still things we have to discuss."

Fear replaced the flash of anger in her eyes, but Reilly knew it was fear *for* him, not fear of him.

"Not yet," she pleaded. "There's still time."

He checked his watch and saw there was even less time left than he'd thought. He shook his head and grasped her hand. "Come here."

He led her to the table and dragged out a chair, but instead of sitting her in it, he sat down himself and pulled her onto his lap. He pressed her head against his shoulder and wrapped his arms around her for a moment, drawing strength for what he had to say. Then he took a deep breath. "I know last night didn't resolve everything. I know there are a lot of things we still need to work out. But I want you to promise me something."

"What?" Her reply was muffled.

"Promise me first."

Her slight hesitation was barely noticeable. "I promise."

"If something happens to me tonight—"

"No!" Her hair flew back in a golden cloud as her head came up in vehement denial, blue eyes vivid in her pale face. "Nothing's going to happen to you."

"I'm not saying it will, but if something goes wrong—"

"I won't listen to this."

"You've got to!" He controlled her struggles for freedom. "Stop it, Mandy. You promised." The stricken expression in her eyes pierced his heart, but he couldn't afford to let her see how it affected him. "Please. I wouldn't ask if it wasn't important to me."

He counted his heartbeats in the silence that followed, making it all the way to seventeen before she answered.

"All right," she said in a toneless voice, averting her face from his. "What is it you want me to do?"

"O'Neill's a good Irish name," he began, "but if I die—" The shudder that coursed through her body forced him to halt for a second. Then he pressed on doggedly. "If I die, I want to be buried under my real name."

She blinked a couple of times, then nodded her assent, as if she didn't trust her voice.

Relieved to have the request over with, he said, "It's—"

"Ryan Callahan," she finished, still not looking at him. "I remember."

"Son of Patrick and Mary Callahan," he added softly, and she dutifully repeated the names after him, committing them to memory.

"And beloved husband of Amanda Callahan."

"Beloved hus—" She choked and broke off, burying her face against him, clutching his shirt with desperate hands.

He stroked the bright hair that tumbled around her face, tucking a few strands behind her ear, waiting until the tempest passed. Then he whispered, "I would have asked you to marry me a year ago, if I could have. You know that, don't you?"

He took the strangled sound that issued from her throat as a yes. "I would have bound you to me in every way I knew," he continued, the words pouring out of him unchecked, knowing this might be his last chance to say them to her. "But Mandy, in my heart I was already your husband before I ever came to your bed." His voice dropped a notch. "And you were my wife."

Her desperate grasp on his shirt increased and she pressed closer, her lips moving against his throat. He strained his ears and caught her faint words. "In my heart, too, Reilly. In my heart, too."

How was it possible to feel both pain and joy in the same instant? he wondered. Maybe someday, if he was lucky, he'd have the chance to pose that question to himself again when he had time to seek the answer. Right now, he only had time to extract the other promises he sought.

"Mandy, darlin'," he whispered above her ear, "can you hear me?" Receiving a tiny nod in response, he said, "There's another thing we have to discuss."

"What?"

"We haven't been very careful about…birth control."

She jerked at that, but he held tight. "Don't get me wrong," he said. "I want your babies, more than you know. More than *I* knew." He swallowed hard. How many times in the past few days had he imagined her with a baby in her arms, even before he'd learned of the one they'd lost?

"But Mandy," he continued, "I want my child to bear my name. I never understood before how much it means to me. How much it will mean to our child. That may be all the legacy I leave behind."

She quivered when he slid his hand around her slender waist and insinuated it between their bodies, rubbing the backs of his fingers against her flat stomach. "So I want you to promise me that if we made a baby..."

She trembled in his arms but her voice was steady. "I promise."

He let out the breath he hadn't been aware of holding, then said, "There's just one more thing I want you to promise, and then I'll be done."

She raised a grief-ravaged face to look at him. "No," she said fiercely. "No more promises until I get one from you."

Although there wasn't anything the least bit funny in their situation, a smile tugged at Reilly's heart. This was the side of Mandy he loved best—the fighter. Other characteristics appealed to a man's masculinity, his protective nature, but when you came right down to it, a man wanted a woman who would stand with him against the world.

"I guess that's fair," he said.

They gazed at each other for long seconds, and it was as if he could read her mind. *Promise you'll come back to me,* her eyes beseeched him, but she never voiced the request. She knew it was the one thing he couldn't guarantee.

Instead, she gripped his shoulders and said, "I want your word that you won't take any chances tonight."

He nodded, mentally inserting the word "unnecessary" between "any" and "chances" before he said, "Done."

Her eyes searched his for confirmation, then she relaxed her hold on him. "Okay," she said. "Okay."

She slipped her arms around him and laid her head against his shoulder once more, then sighed. After a moment she asked, "What's the third thing?"

Now it was his turn to grasp her shoulders, pushing her away a little, forcing her to look at him. "Promise me," he said, anguish creeping in as he remembered her bitter revelation from yesterday. "No matter what happens tonight, or in the future, promise me you won't ever..."

He couldn't frame the rest of his request, but she knew.

"I promise," she whispered, accepting that he had the right to demand she never again attempt to take her own life. "I didn't plan it the first time," she added. "It just…happened. I didn't really want to die." Her voice broke. "It just hurt so much losing you and…the baby…."

He pulled her close and they wrapped their arms around each other, giving and receiving comfort as they both grieved for what might have been.

They were still sitting there when Walker arrived ten minutes later.

"It's time," Walker said.

Reilly slid his .45 into its holster and shrugged into his jacket. "I'm ready."

"Wait!" Mandy darted to the cabinet where Reilly had stashed the nine-millimeter that morning. "Take your backup gun, too," she said. "You might need it."

He shook his head. "Keep it."

"But—"

"Don't worry, Mandy," Walker interjected. "You're forgetting that *I'm* O'Neill's backup this time."

She remained unconvinced, and Reilly said, "I want you to have it. And these, too." He shoved a hand in his pocket and pulled out a jangle of keys, which he handed to her. "If we're not back by—" He glanced at Walker.

"Midnight."

"Midnight," Reilly continued, "then don't wait for us. Take the gun and the ammo and whatever clothes and food you can carry in one bag, get in the truck and start driving. Forget Canada. You'd have to smuggle the gun past the border, and you can't afford to get caught doing it. So hit the interstate in whatever direction you want to go and don't look back. There's a lot of empty road between here and anywhere. Use it to your advantage.

"There are maps in the truck. After you've put at least five hundred miles behind you, pick a medium-sized city and lose yourself in it. Pay cash for everything, understand? Checks, cash machines and credit cards leave a paper trail.

But don't flash your money around—you want to blend into the background as much as possible.''

"But I don't have—''

"There's about two grand in my knapsack. That should cover the first few weeks, but when you run out there's more money hidden in the truck. You'll find twenty bucks and some change in the glove compartment, but that's just for cover. The glove compartment has a secret bottom— you'll need a screwdriver to pry it up. Both the driver's and passenger's sun visor are padded with small bills. Tens and twenties. A razor blade will slit the stitches so the visors will still be usable. The rest of the money is cached in a metal box under the tailgate. You won't recognize it for what it is. It's disguised as part of the trailer hitch, and you'll need to actually remove the hitch to get at it, so leave that for last. Got all that?''

She nodded. "How do I get in touch with you?''

He gave her a steady look. He didn't have to draw her a picture—if he and Walker weren't back by the time she left, odds were one or both of them would already be dead. If they weren't dead, they might be hunted men, and in that case neither of them would risk Mandy's life by coming back to this cabin or contacting her in any way. Still, long shots did pay off once in a while, and it wouldn't hurt to have a way to reach her as a last resort.

He thought for a moment. "Here's what you do. For the next two months, check the classified section in Friday's edition of *USA Today*. Most convenience stores carry it. If I'm alive, I'll put an ad in there. If not...''

"How will I know it's you?''

For just a moment he let his control slip. He reached out and cupped her cheek, imprinting the silky texture, the warmth, in his mind. And because he couldn't help it, he brushed his thumb over her parted lips in the way he knew she loved, before dropping his hand to his side. "You'll know,'' he promised with a husky catch in his voice. "I'll make sure.''

Walker cleared his throat, reminding Reilly that the other

man was a reluctant witness to this scene. He forced himself to turn away from Mandy, saying, "Let's do it."

"Right."

Walker was closest to the door, and consequently the first one through. Reilly was right behind him, but he paused in the doorway and glanced back. "If the worst happens, Mandy," he warned, "whatever you do, don't go back to Black Rock for any reason. And don't let *anyone* know where you are." He paused. "It's better to play dead than to *be* dead," he added softly. "I know."

Mandy roamed the cabin after the men left, unable to sit still for more than a minute at a time. "It wouldn't even help if I had a book to read," she muttered to herself. No book ever written could hold her attention now.

She hated waiting like this. If Reilly and Cody had given her a choice she'd have gone with them. Even if they'd made her wait in the truck, at least she'd have known what was happening. As it was, she was worrying herself sick.

She stopped pacing long enough to check her watch, and tried to gauge where the men were by now. In her mind's eye she saw Cody's rugged 4x4 gliding down the mountain road toward the highway, past the Little Creek turnoff, past the entrance to the J-Bar-J ranch.

They wouldn't be saying much, she figured. A terse comment here, a grunt or two there. Animosity still simmered beneath the surface—she'd be an idiot to think otherwise—but they were joined in a common cause for now. Their personal feelings towards each other had been set aside for the time being. What would happen afterwards was anybody's guess.

If there was an afterwards.

"No!" She swung around, furious with herself. "I'm not going to think like that. I'm not! Reilly's coming back. He has to!"

With nothing else to do, she started pacing again, then stopped in midstride and shook her head. "This is crazy! There has to be something I can do to keep busy."

But what? The bed was made, the dishes were washed, and she'd swept the ashes out of the fireplace and the dirt off the front steps this morning after breakfast. She'd scrubbed the entire cabin three days ago, the last time she'd been left here alone, and there'd hardly been enough time to get it dirty again.

She wrinkled her nose in distaste. The only thing that even remotely needed cleaning was the job she hated the most—the bathroom. True, she'd scrubbed it three days ago, but there was something about men and bathrooms, even one as rustic as this one, that just didn't mix.

Oh, well, she thought. *If I'm going to clean something, I might as well make it worthwhile.*

She dragged out the necessary cleaning supplies and set to with as much enthusiasm as she could muster. It wouldn't take her mind off Reilly, but at least it was something to pass the time, and would keep her from going stir crazy.

Fifteen minutes later she was almost done. She was running the broom under the big claw-footed tub, when it caught on something. She jerked, but it held fast.

"It figures," she said in disgust, then brushed her hair away from her face with the back of her arm and bent down to see what the problem was. It was too dark under there to see much, but it looked like the string binding the broom-straws had somehow gotten hooked on something sticking out of the floor. A loose nail head, maybe.

She manuevered the broom as best she could, trying to work the string loose, but the angle was too awkward. So she leaned over again, pushing the handle down, then lifting up and pulling. All of a sudden the broom popped free, catching her off balance, and she fell forward. She dropped the broom trying to break her fall with her hands, but she was only partly successful, and bumped her head hard enough against the wall to see stars. Something tugged against her neck, then snapped, and the broom handle clattered to the floor.

"Ow!" Mandy sagged weakly against the wall, then

turned and let herself slide down until she was sitting on the wooden floor. She pressed her palm against her temple, where a lump was already forming, and squeezed her eyes shut against the sharp pain. "Ow-w-w," she said again.

She cracked one eye open, found her vision not too blurred, and opened the other, then glanced around and down to see how difficult it was going to be to get up from here. That's when she saw the broken gold chain.

She caught her breath and felt around her throat, but there was nothing there. No chain. No locket.

She scrambled to her feet, the pain forgotten now. "Where is it?" she said frantically, her gaze darting here and there as she searched in vain for her great-great-grandmother's locket, the only family heirloom she had left. "It has to be here somewhere."

She dropped to her hands and knees and peered under the tub, but couldn't see anything. She groped around anyway, but came up with nothing. "Light," she said. "I need light."

Reilly had a flashlight, she remembered suddenly. She found it in his knapsack, the first place she checked.

Back in the bathroom, the flashlight's powerful beam illuminated every crack in the floor under the tub, but still no locket. She was almost sobbing now, from the throbbing pain in her head and from frustration, but she wasn't giving up. It *had* to be here.

"Think!" she demanded, forcing herself to calm down. After a moment, she positioned herself where she thought she'd been when the chain broke, then closed her eyes and tried to imagine where the locket, heavier than the chain, might have fallen. When she opened her eyes again and turned her head, she spotted a gleam of gold.

It was pure luck that she saw it at all, she realized, because it wasn't really visible. Only the direction of the flashlight and the tilt of her head had allowed her to pick up the reflection. The locket must have skittered across the floor when it hit, or maybe she'd knocked it when she fell, because it was lodged at an angle in a small crevice where the floorboards disappeared under the wall.

Mandy knelt and tried several times to work her fingers into the tiny space in order to pull the locket out. All she managed to do was push it further in. After the fourth unsuccessful attempt, she sat back on her heels, considering her options.

It wasn't just a matter of grabbing hold of the locket. She might have done that with a pair of needle-nose pliers, which she didn't have. But even if she had, there was the angle, too. The locket would have to be maneuvered around it, and it was almost a given that the locket would be dented or badly scratched in the process.

Guess there's nothing else to do, she thought after a moment. *I'll have to pry that board up somehow.* Then she remembered finding Cody's toolbox the other day when she was cleaning and went to retrieve it.

A hammer and a screwdriver weren't the ideal tools, she decided after emptying the toolbox, but the selection was limited. Reilly would know what to use without destroying the floorboard, but Reilly wasn't here. He was on his way to meet a man who'd already tried twice to kill him, and almost succeeded the last time.

Don't think of that! she admonished herself, but it wasn't easy dragging her mind back to the task at hand. Compared to what Reilly was doing, retrieving her locket seemed so trivial, but at least she had something to do.

She grabbed the hammer and screwdriver and went to work, thinking as she did so that Reilly probably had the tools she needed in the back of his truck. She had no intention of traipsing out there at this time of night, though. Not for something she wasn't even sure she'd find. She'd just have to make do with what she had, and hope that Cody wouldn't mind too much.

Four bent iron nails, two splinters, and a skinned knuckle later, she almost had the floorboard pried loose. It was a lot harder than she'd imagined, and a lot messier. She'd practically shredded one end of the board trying to get the screwdriver underneath it, and there was no way the board could be used again once she got her locket out. But she no longer cared at this point. All she wanted was to get it over with.

She slid her fingers under the board and pulled up. It creaked and groaned, iron nails screeching as they worked free from the joists, and she pulled harder. It gave way with a loud *crraaaack!* and the board came away from the wall. Mandy watched in stunned dismay as her locket slipped down, then vanished into the darkness below.

She tossed the floorboard aside and kicked it. All that work, for nothing. Nothing!

The heck with that, she thought. *I'm not giving up yet.*

She snatched up Reilly's flashlight and knelt on one side of the long, narrow hole, shining the beam toward the side where the locket had disappeared. She didn't see anything, so she moved the circle of light slowly back and forth, hoping to catch a glint of gold.

What she saw then almost made her drop the flashlight.

Chapter 15

As Walker's 4x4 toughed its way over the uneven road surface in the dark, Reilly leaned the back of his hand against the window and stared out at the blue-black shadows they passed. His thoughts, which should have been focused on the approaching confrontation with Pennington, were miles away in a little one-room cabin.

What was Mandy doing now? he wondered. Was she curled up in front of a crackling fire as she loved to do, watching the flames dance and sway? A half smile touched his lips as he pictured her that way, and there was a soft, yearning expression on his face that would have surprised him had he been aware of it.

He'd never known the simple pleasure of sharing a warm fire on a cold night until he'd met Mandy. He could still remember her astonishment when he'd confessed as much. It was inconceivable to her that anyone could reach thirty-eight years of age without experiencing it at least once.

His smile deepened. *I probably would have shocked her less if I'd told her I was a virgin,* he thought. Then the smile faded.

A virgin. She'd never volunteered the information, and he'd never asked, but he was fairly certain he'd been Mandy's first lover. There'd been no tangible proof, but he knew that was often the case with physically active women like Mandy, who'd been riding horses since she was five. Even if she hadn't, a good cop never relied on evidence alone. Sometimes you just had to go with your instincts.

Maybe it was the way her eyes had widened when he'd stripped off the last of his clothes that first night. Maybe it was the tiny gasp of surprise, barely heard and quickly repressed, when he'd settled between her legs and sought entry into her body. Maybe it was the way she hadn't seemed to know what to do with her hands until he'd shown her. Or maybe it was the wonder in her eyes as they'd climbed the mountain and soared together.

It wouldn't have mattered to him or to his love for her either way—he hadn't even thought of it before that night. If he had, he would never have expected a thirty-year-old woman in this day and age, especially one as lovely as Mandy was, to remain untouched. Besides, he wasn't a proponent of the double standard, and he could hardly claim she had been *his* first lover. But it was different with her.

Maybe that sounded like an old, worn-out line, but it was the truth. A truth every man should experience at least once in his lifetime.

The 4x4 hit a pothole, and Walker grunted his annoyance as he straightened out the wheels. Reilly glanced over at him. The greenish glow from the dashboard cast eerie shadows on the other man's face, emphasizing the sharp edges and bleak lines.

Something about him—his expression, the set of his jaw, something!—seemed strangely familiar. At first Reilly couldn't put his finger on it. Then his brows slid together in a frown.

That could be me over there. Before I came to Wyoming, before I met Mandy. Hard. Cynical. And very much alone. An emotion stirred within him, something he'd never imagined he could feel for Walker, but there it was all the same.

Pity.

The discovery rocked him. *Pity for the man who betrayed my trust?* he demanded of himself. *Pity for the man who made love to* my *woman?*

Confused, Reilly turned away and searched for an explanation that made sense. Anger he could understand, and possessive fury. Any man would feel the same, given the circumstances. But pity?

Then his own thoughts of a moment ago came back to him—*a truth every man should experience at least once in his lifetime*—and with a flash of intuition he knew. He *knew.*

Yeah, Walker had slept with Mandy, but he'd never shared what Reilly had shared with her. Walker had never known the precious, fragile unity of heart, mind, body and soul that transcended the physical act and transformed it into something rare and beautiful.

To possess Mandy's body without her love would be the cruelest trick fate could play on a man who loved her, Reilly realized. Hadn't he almost believed it was *his* fate only two nights ago? Hadn't the wonder and beauty of their lovemaking that night turned ugly and bitter when he'd doubted her love?

How much worse for Walker, who loved her, too. How much worse to know that the woman you'd loved all your life only came to you to forget another man, and left you with her love for that other man undimmed. No, pity wasn't such a strange emotion, after all.

"What in the world...?" Mandy steadied the flashlight and craned her neck for a better view of the wooden crates stacked neatly in the crawl space beneath the cabin. Black lettering and symbols were stencilled across the crates. Curious, she played the light over them trying to make out what they said, but it was a few seconds before their meaning sank in. *What's Cody doing with assault rifles and plastic explosives?* she wondered, drawing a complete blank.

Survivalists stockpiled weapons, she knew, along with

food, clothing, medical supplies and various tools and implements. Living in Wyoming, she'd come into contact with a few over the years. But Cody wasn't anything like *them.* Why would he—

She caught her breath. "No," she whispered, appalled at herself for even thinking something so disloyal to her oldest friend. "That's impossible."

Or was it? She sat up abruptly, scraping her forearm as she dragged the flashlight out of the hole in the floor. *Not Cody,* she kept insisting. *I don't believe it.* But her heart thudded in her chest and her pulse began to race.

There had to be another explanation, she told herself, trying to marshal her thoughts into some kind of order. But what could it be?

No other answer came to her, and the more she thought about it, the more possible it seemed. All the pieces started falling into place with frightening ease, making a horrible kind of sense. Cody showing up at the cabin out of the blue, when he was supposed to be working. Cody knowing so much about Pennington, and how the militia operated. She remembered now that she'd wondered about it at the time.

Cody had been in the marines, too, and hadn't Reilly said that Pennington recruited ex-military men? Even the knife Cody carried concealed in his boot, which was illegal as far as she knew, took on a sinister meaning now that she knew what was hidden beneath the cabin.

"Wait a minute," she said firmly. "This is *Cody* you're talking about. This is crazy. Just plain stupid." Her mind worked at a feverish pace trying to reassure herself. "You've known him all your life. He's not...he wouldn't...he *couldn't* do something like that."

Could he?

Her heart was beating so fast now she could hardly breathe, and she was shaking all over. Then a cold wave of terror swept through her.

If Cody was working for the militia, Reilly was walking into a trap.

* * *

A battered black pickup truck with stolen license plates waited at a private airstrip just north of the Wyoming-Montana border. The young driver, excited and scared by his first real mission for the militia, checked his watch nervously, then peered up through the windshield at the night sky. Eight o'clock, he'd been told, and it was past that now.

Impatiently he turned off the radio and rolled down his window, then heaved a sigh of relief when he heard a faraway sound like the whisper-soft drone of a jet engine. A quick scan of the sky, and he spotted the lights of an incoming plane circling for a landing. He jerked the keys out of the ignition and fumbled them under the seat, then jumped out of the truck and started jogging in the opposite direction.

He didn't know who was arriving, but his instructions had been clear: he was to stay with the truck and its dangerous cargo until the plane was sighted, then hightail it out of there. He was glad to obey.

Walker braked at the crossroad and shifted into neutral, waiting until a large semi rumbled past them before he turned onto the highway. The 4x4 picked up speed quickly.

"You're awfully quiet over there, O'Neill," he said. "You asleep?"

Reilly turned his head. "No. Just thinking."

"About Pennington? About the plan?" When Reilly didn't answer, he asked gruffly, "About Mandy?"

"Yeah."

"Me, too."

Reilly stiffened involuntarily, then forced his muscles to relax. *You can't control Walker's thoughts*, he reminded himself, *any more than he can. Any more than you can control your own.*

Walker said, "I didn't want to say anything in front of Mandy, didn't want to scare her, but I have a bad feeling about tonight."

Reilly's instincts had been telling him the same thing for

the past few hours, but he saw no reason to pass that information on to Walker just yet. "What makes you say that?"

"I don't know." Walker frowned. "Nothing I can pinpoint. I just have a hunch things aren't going to go exactly according to plan." His eyes slid in Reilly's direction for a second, then returned to the road. "You're a cop, so you should know what it's like. How many times have you played a hunch?"

"Too many to count," Reilly admitted.

"Same with me. I don't know *why* I'm uneasy, I just know I am, and my hunches are generally accurate." Air gusted out of his lungs. "One thing I do know for sure—Pennington doesn't quite trust me."

Reilly straightened in his seat. "How do you know?"

"He's cut me out of the loop."

"Because of last time? Or something new?"

"I'm not sure. But it could be a problem for us."

Reilly snorted. "Add it to the list. We'll deal with it."

"Yeah, but I'm thinking maybe we should change the plan."

"Kind of late to be doing that," Reilly said slowly. He glanced at the luminous dial on his watch. "When did you say his plane arrives?"

"Sometime after nine is all I know. He wouldn't tell me more, and he made his own arrangements to be picked up. But we should have plenty of time."

Mandy didn't waste a minute. She scrambled into shoes and a jacket, then grabbed Reilly's semiautomatic and the keys to his truck from the kitchen counter, where she'd left them earlier. She flung open the cabinet, banging it against the wall, and retrieved the spare clip and the box of ammo. She shoved everything but the gun into her jacket pockets, then checked that the safety was still on, and raced for the door.

She skimmed across the clearing on autopilot and skirted Reilly's traps the same way, distantly thankful she remembered where they were located. Then she pounded down the path to the truck, heedless of obstacles in her way. She tripped once, and stumbled, but caught herself before she went down, and pushed on.

Conscious thought was impossible. All her awareness was focused on two things: breathing and putting one foot in front of the other in mindless motion. But just below consciousness one phrase kept repeating itself in rhythm with her strides. *Not this time. Not this time. Not this time.*

Reilly nodded thoughtfully, making mental notes as Walker outlined his proposal. ''Sounds good,'' he said finally. ''Riskier, in one way, but—''

''But it gives us more options,'' Walker finished for him.

''Yeah.'' He assimilated the changes and made a decision. ''We'll do it.''

Neither man spoke for a few minutes after that, each keeping private counsel, then Reilly said, ''Hey, Walker.''

''Hey what?''

''About Mandy.''

There was a guarded pause, then the other man said, ''What about her?''

''If something happens to me—'' He broke off, then started again. ''Look, I know I said some harsh things to you, and I meant them. But if I don't make it this time and you do, take care of her.''

''You know I will.''

''I don't just mean look out for her.'' The words came harder than Reilly had expected, and he fought back a surge of possessiveness. ''I mean, take care of her, any way you can. Even if it means...the way you tried before.''

The truck spurted forward a little, then slowed back down to the speed limit.

''I don't believe you're saying this.'' Walker rubbed his chin, which sported a distinct bruise where Reilly had decked him yesterday morning.

''Yeah, well, I've done some thinking since then.'' His jaw tightened. ''I'm no saint, but it's different this time.

This time it's for keeps. If I die tonight, I won't be coming back." He shook his head. "I don't want her to be alone again." It hurt like hell just thinking of it, but Reilly played his trump card. "And you love her."

"But she doesn't love me," Walker stated flatly.

There wasn't any response Reilly could make that would help the situation, so he waited a bit, watching the other man's profile in the darkness, gauging his mood. Then said quietly, "I know what I'm asking."

"Do you?" Walker spared him a bitter glance.

"I think I can imagine."

"I doubt it."

The thrum of steel-belted tires over the smooth surface of the highway and the muted growl of the engine filled the silence that followed, until at last Reilly forced himself to say, "If I were dead, Mandy would eventually—"

Walker's harsh laugh cut Reilly off. "Is that what you really think?" He shook his head in disbelief. "I thought you were smarter than that, O'Neill."

"What's that supposed to mean?"

"Figure it out for yourself." But only a moment later he explained roughly, "Mandy loves *you*. I won't kid myself anymore that she'll ever feel any different."

A minute passed. Then another. And another. The tension inside the cab was so tangible Reilly thought he could almost feel it pressing against his chest.

Then, in a low voice, Walker said, "She cried. Did she tell you that?"

Puzzled, Reilly asked, "You mean when she lost the baby?"

"No. I mean when she and I—" Walker drew a deep breath and expelled it slowly. "Imagine," he said, raw emotion bleeding out of him with every word. "Imagine what it's like to sleep with the woman you love, knowing all the while she's pretending you're someone else." He drew another breath. "Imagine what it does to your heart, not to mention your ego, when she calls you by that other man's name at the moment when you—" He paused and swallowed. "Then imagine holding her afterwards, listening to her weep as if her heart were breaking all over again, and knowing there's not a damn thing you can do to make her pain go away." Tight-lipped, he shook his head. "When you can imagine living through that, then ask me to take care of Mandy for you."

The echoes of Walker's pain reverberated in his own soul, but still Reilly said, "I'm asking."

Walker shot him a narrow-eyed look as all-encompassing as it was brief. "Damn you, O'Neill," he said bitterly. His gaze returned to the highway stretching endlessly out in front of them.

He didn't say anything more, but he didn't have to for Reilly to know he'd do it. There wasn't a lot of privacy possible in the cab of a 4x4, but he turned away to give Walker as much as he could while the man got his emotions under control. It wasn't until they were entering the southbound interstate access ramp that he felt safe in saying, "Thanks."

"Don't thank me." Walker clipped his words. "I'm not doing it for you."

"I know, but that doesn't mean I don't appreciate it just the same. If our situations were reversed…"

"I still don't want your thanks."

"Why not?"

"Because…" Walker hunched one shoulder, as if something wasn't setting quite right with him. "I just don't, that's all."

Mandy downshifted into a turn, not even wincing at the slight grinding sound from the changing gears. She couldn't worry about that now. If she didn't get there in time to save Reilly, it wouldn't matter if she burned out the clutch and stripped every gear in the transmission.

She pressed down on the accelerator. Her legs were shorter than Reilly's, but she hadn't wasted time adjusting the seat before starting out, so she had to stretch to reach the pedal. The well-tuned engine responded, and the truck shot forward with a burst of speed.

She was going too fast on this winding mountain road. She knew that. Deep down inside, some part of her subconscious remembered the accident that had claimed her baby's life, and she was terrified. But she couldn't worry about that now, either. Reilly and Cody had a good forty-minute headstart on her. If Reilly was going to have any chance at all, she had to get to him as quickly as possible.

An S-curve warning sign loomed ahead, but she barely slowed, trusting heaven to watch out for her. The truck leaned precariously close to the edge and she held her breath for heart-stopping seconds, but it righted itself just in time for her to spin the wheel in the other direction. On the straightaway once more, she breathed again. Until that moment she hadn't realized she'd been praying all along. A wordless, voiceless prayer, but a prayer nevertheless.

God doesn't give us any more heartache than we can bear, Mandy remembered her mother saying more than once, when she was a little girl. She hadn't really understood. Heartache back then had been a fight with one of her friends or the loss of a cherished pet. She hadn't known that your whole world could turn dark, that despair could rob you of your will to live.

Her mother had been right, though. As a teenager, Mandy had mourned the deaths of her grandparents, one by one, and though she'd loved them and sorely missed them, their loss had been bearable. She'd grieved longer for her parents when their time came, but her grief had been tempered with the knowledge that they had gone together into eternity, as they would have wanted.

Even losing Reilly and the baby a year ago, losses she hadn't believed she could survive, had somehow been borne. Her faith had been deeply shaken, but not destroyed. Now that faith was the only thing holding her together.

God wouldn't have brought Reilly back to me if He was just going to take him again, she reassured herself. She rounded another curve, this time without slowing at all. *He*

*wouldn't give me hope, then smash it. He knows I couldn't
bear it this time.*

"I'm not asking for a miracle, God," she whispered, not
even aware that she had spoken aloud. "Just don't let me
be too late."

David Pennington slammed the battered tailgate shut.
"Perfect," he said, allowing himself a tiny smile of satisfaction. "Just perfect."

Carl Walsh stood to one side. Like his superior, he wore
the "uniform" of the New World Militia in the field: cam-
ouflage khakis. Unlike his superior, however, he wore a
troubled expression on his face instead of a smile. "I don't
like it, David. What if something goes wrong? How will
you stop it?"

Pennington meticulously peeled off the latex gloves he
wore and rolled them inside out, tucking them into his back
pocket. "You worry too much, Carl. Nothing's going to go
wrong this time. That's why I'm here. To make sure."

Walsh shook his head. "I still don't like it. Callahan's
too smart, and he's been on the run for a long time. A lot
of men turn feral that way. It doesn't make sense he hasn't
sniffed out this trap."

"Yes, Callahan's smart," Pennington said, "and yes,
he's survived on the run for a long time. But sometimes
that backfires. With that combination, sometimes a man
starts thinking he's invincible. He gets careless. Makes mistakes."

"Like you did with Callahan?" Walsh hadn't meant to
ask, but the question had just slipped out.

Pennington's eyes narrowed to slits, and his nostrils
flared, but he conceded coolly, "Yes, Carl. Like I did with
Callahan." Only the muscle twitching in his clenched jaw
betrayed his closely held anger. Then he smiled, but his
eyes remained deadly cold. "And like Callahan has done
with Centurion."

* * *

Reilly checked his watch again, then tamped down his impatience. It was always a mistake to let yourself worry about what couldn't be controlled, he reminded himself. He wanted this confrontation over with, wanted things settled one way or another, but watching the seconds tick by wouldn't make it happen any sooner.

He looked up when Walker flicked on the turn indicator and slowed for an upcoming exit.

He frowned. "This isn't the way to the reservoir." It wasn't a question exactly, but it demanded an answer.

"It's the old road around the mountain," Walker explained. "I told you about it, remember? It's the one Mandy—"

"I remember." Reilly didn't want to be reminded of Mandy's accident, but it was already too late. A nightmare image flashed before his mind's eye, one that wasn't a memory but was burned into his mind as if it were: Mandy lying pinned in the wreckage of her car for helpless hours as her life and their baby's life seeped away.

Pain made his voice harsh. "Why are we going this way?"

"It's shorter, and will get us there from the other side. I can almost guarantee Pennington will come by the main road, which means he has to go through town before he reaches us."

Suddenly Reilly knew that he couldn't ride on the road that had nearly been Mandy's death. Not tonight. He couldn't pass the numerous ravines and valleys that almost certainly lined the winding mountain road, without imagining her trapped and bleeding at the bottom of each one. And if he did that, by the time he reached the reservoir he'd be easy prey for Pennington.

"We have time," he said, shielding his unexpected weakness with a brusque tone. "Let's take the main road."

Walker turned speculative eyes on him, then shrugged. "Okay by me."

* * *

Mandy accelerated onto I-90, narrowly avoiding a collision with a cattle truck, whose driver blared his horn at her but refused to move to the left lane. She gripped the steering wheel, gunned the engine and passed him on the right shoulder, easily outdistancing the other vehicle.

She heaved a sigh of relief as she sped down the interstate, not because of her near miss but because the road's surface was made for speed. Reilly's truck had power to spare, but the shock absorbers weren't built to take the punishment she'd subjected them to coming down the mountain.

She pressed the accelerator to the floor and glanced at the speedometer once, then didn't bother again. If a state trooper caught her on his radar, he'd just have to chase her all the way to the site, because she wasn't stopping for anything.

As the reflecting mile markers whizzed by, she wondered how far she was behind Reilly and Cody. She had no way of knowing. Maybe she was already too—

"No!" she said fiercely, clinging to hope along with the steering wheel.

Her gaze slid to the gun, half-tucked beneath her right thigh to keep it from sliding off the seat, then back to the road. She didn't want to think about that, either, but it was better than the alternative.

There was a chance she was wrong about Cody. How much of one she didn't know, but still a chance. She wanted to be wrong. Prayed to be wrong. But if she wasn't...

She strained her eyes to see what lay ahead. The headlights didn't make much of a dent in the darkness, and at this speed she could easily hit some animal before she even saw it. A thought popped into her head and she made a sound of self-disgust, then clicked on the bright lights. *Should have thought of that sooner,* she reproached herself, but knew she was doing the best she could under the circumstances.

A few minutes later she spotted the sign for the old mountain road turnoff. Her eyes widened and her heart skipped a beat as she remembered the last time she'd driven that road. Then she pressed determined lips together and swung the wheel toward the exit.

Chapter 16

Reilly and Walker circled around and came in from the north on foot, skirting the reservoir's retaining wall and keeping to the cover of the trees for as long as they could while they worked their way toward the lights on the south end.

The rhythmic chugs of the turbine-powered water pumps resonated like a mighty heartbeat in the otherwise still night, and sent ripples skimming over the inky surface of the water. Pale moonlight glimmered off the ripples, turning the reservoir into an obsidian lake. But neither man spared a glance for its eerie beauty.

An eight-foot-high chain-link fence topped with three strands of barbed wire and arc lights surrounded the pumping station. Reilly stood guard with gun drawn, his eyes alert for any sign of movement in the well-lit enclosure or the darkness around it, while Walker snipped a hole in the fence just large enough for a man to crawl through. Once they were on the other side, Walker bent the edges of the chain-link fence back into place, so that only a close inspection would reveal it had been cut at all. Then the two men quickly headed for the concealing shadows behind the station.

Mandy wrenched the wheel to the left and stomped on the brakes with both feet. The truck swerved across the yellow dividing line and skidded to a halt on the far shoulder, kicking up a small cloud of dust and gravel in the process.

That was close, she thought, hitting the switch to kill the headlights. *And stupid. What was I thinking of?*

She hadn't been thinking at all, that was the problem. Otherwise she would have realized before now that she couldn't just drive all the way down to the reservoir. Not if she wanted to save Reilly.

At least she'd had the presence of mind to pull off the road on the sheltered side and turn the headlights off the minute she realized they could be spotted by anyone at the reservoir. They weren't the only lights on the mountain by any means—house and yard lights dotted the darkness—but they were the only ones moving, and could have been a dead giveaway.

Cody knows as well as I do how little traffic there is on this old road, especially at night. If he's in collusion with Pennington and the militia to set Reilly up, he'll be doubly suspicious of anything out of the ordinary right now. I know I would be.

She needed a plan, and not just to get down the mountain undetected. She also needed a way to get close to the pumping station without being seen. And if she managed to accomplish that, she still had to find a way to warn Reilly without getting him, or herself, killed.

The first step was easy, if she had the guts. Driving at night without headlights wasn't impossible, just extremely dangerous. Driving down a *mountain* at the same time, as fast as you dared, along a narrow, winding road that had already claimed you as a victim once before, well...it wasn't something you ought to try unless you were desperate.

Fear sent shivers through her body, but Mandy's hands were steady as she turned on the engine, shifted into gear, and pulled back onto the road. As the truck crawled blindly through the darkness, all she could think of was that if she was wrong about Cody she was taking a crazy chance for nothing. But if she was right, then *desperate* described her situation exactly.

"Don't forget this," Walker said in an undertone.

Reilly hesitated, then holstered his .45 and reluctantly accepted the electronic transmitter Walker held out to him. He hated wearing a wire, hated the restrictions it put on him. Every time he'd worn one he'd sworn it was the last time. And every time he'd been wrong.

This really is the last time, he vowed as he unbuttoned his shirt with one hand. *One way or another.*

It made no difference if they nailed Pennington the way Walker envisioned—the *legal* way, through the court system Reilly had tried once before—or if they had to take him down hard. Reilly was finished as an undercover cop. And if something went wrong tonight, then he would no longer be breaking, or making, vows of any kind.

Vows...marriage...Mandy. The word association was a natural progression that happened so fast he had no control over it, and for a moment a vision of Mandy as he'd last seen her flashed into his mind. *Don't think about her,* he warned himself as he fought off the memory. *Not now. Stay focused.*

His head came up sharply when he heard the plaintive cry of a night bird close by, and he saw Walker tilt his head to listen. His eyes caught Walker's for a moment, then he looked down again. Uncharacteristically clumsy, he fumbled with the transmitter, and muttered, "Give me a hand with this, will you?"

"I'm afraid I can't do that," Walker said softly, and Reilly heard the unmistakable click of a gun being cocked. He automatically reached for his .45, but before he could draw, found himself staring down the business end of Walker's service revolver.

Their eyes met again, but this time there was a coldness in Walker's expression that hadn't been there a moment ago.

Reilly shook his head in disbelief. "What the hell are you doing?"

"You won't be needing this," Walker said as he jerked Reilly's gun from its holster and tucked it into his waistband.

Reilly's eyes widened in growing comprehension, then narrowed. "You son of a bitch," he rasped. "You're with them." He dove at Walker without warning, and they both crashed to the ground, rolling over and over, struggling for possession of the sheriff's gun.

The fight lasted only a few seconds. Walker grunted and heaved himself on top, managing to free his gun arm at the same time, and clubbed Reilly across the temple with the butt of the revolver.

The blow dazed Reilly just enough so that by the time his head cleared, Walker had cuffed his arms behind his back and had dragged him, stumbling, to his feet.

"What are you waiting for?" Reilly's words were slurred together, but the meaning was plain. "You brought me here to kill me, didn't you? So just get it over with, damn you!"

"You don't get off that easily, Callahan."

Reilly froze at the chilling sound of that voice, a voice indelibly burned into his memory. Then two men stepped from the shadows behind Walker. One carried an Uzi submachine gun pointed directly at him. The other was David Pennington.

Mandy cut the engine and let the truck coast the last hundred yards to the foot of the knoll on which the reservoir's pumping station was situated. She'd already taken care of the inside dome light, so she didn't have to worry about betraying her presence that way, and she had grabbed the gun and was halfway out the door before the truck came to a complete stop. She hit the ground running, heading for the spillway.

Back when she'd been an adventurous ten-year-old and the reservoir had just been built, she and Cody had found a way to sneak into the station, circumventing the fence. No one had ever caught them, and it had always been their secret. Unless someone had discovered the design flaw in the security system and corrected it since then, she intended to get in the same way they had twenty-one years ago.

Mandy was short of breath by the time she reached the outlook near the spillway, and she paused for a moment. Her eyes scanned the top of the concrete structure where it abutted the fence surrounding the pumping station, and she exulted inside. *Yes!* she thought, relief mingling with other emotions when she saw there was still no obstruction blocking access to the enclosure from the top of the spillway. *Thank God they haven't changed it.*

Her gaze moved to the steady flow of water pouring through the sieve openings at the top of the spillway and gurgling down its face. Her elation dimmed when she realized that the water level in the reservoir must be unusually high, most likely caused by spring runoff from melting snow on the mountains. That was going to slow her down some, precious minutes she couldn't afford to waste.

She toed off her shoes, then tucked Reilly's gun in her hip pocket and pulled off her socks. Her feet would be cold, and she'd probably end up with some cuts and bruises by the time this was over, but she'd never made this climb in anything other than bare feet. Now wasn't the time to experiment, not with Reilly's life at stake.

She turned around and began her semicontrolled descent down the steep incline which led to the stream below much faster than she'd ever dared before—slip-sliding here, fingers and toes finding purchase there. When she finally reached the bottom, two fingernails on her right hand and three on her left had been torn off below the quick, and there was a nasty graze across the side of one foot from a painful encounter with a jagged rock. Her palms had been tender before she'd started out, with the blisters from the fire not completely healed. Now they didn't bear thinking about, but at least she was down in one piece.

The stream was bone-chillingly cold when Mandy waded into it, reaching above her knees at the midpoint, but the current wasn't as strong as she'd feared, and she made it across without too much of a struggle. As she splashed out of the water on the other side and picked her way along the stream's rocky bank, she had cause to be grateful for her numbed feet.

The spillway towered above her, seeming much higher from below than it did from above. She grasped the first of the bent iron bars embedded in the cement, which served as a ladder of sorts leading to the top. She took a calming breath, then ascended, hand over hand, making sure her bare feet were securely placed on each rung. In less than a minute she had climbed all the way up.

She walked across to where concrete met barbed wire. She didn't let herself look down, focusing on the far side instead. Once there, she squatted to determine exactly where she would put her hands to avoid the barbs, thankful that any noise she might make would be drowned out by the whine of the generators, then carefully climbed over and down.

She was in. She pulled Reilly's gun out, and crept around the corner of the nearest building.

"Did you really think I would let you get away with it?" Pennington gloated. "You could run to the ends of the earth, change your face a thousand times, but I would still track you down. You became a dead man the moment you betrayed me. It was only a matter of time."

"You never would have found me," Reilly sneered, "if not for this Judas here." He jerked his head toward Walker.

In retaliation, Walker moved behind him and yanked the cuffs upward until Reilly winced. "Let me finish him off now," Walker growled, but Pennington shook his head.

"Not yet." A smile of pure evil spread across his face. "You've underestimated me all along, Callahan. You thought you'd finished me before, but here I am. Free. And there you are." His smile widened. "Sure, Centurion made it easier to trap you, but I would have found you anyway."

"Yeah, right."

"Does the name Larry Brooks mean anything to you?" When Reilly's widening eyes revealed he recognized the name of one of the federal marshals who had worked on his case the first time around, Pennington gave a low laugh. "That's right. I even have followers inside the witness protection program. How do you think I found your partner's family?"

Reilly clenched his teeth against the rage that rose in him at the reminder, then faced Pennington squarely. "I guess your blood money *can* buy you almost anything you want—now. You can have people tortured and killed, and get away with it. Again, for now. But all you really have is money and the power it commands. Someday someone will find a way to bring you down for good, and when they do, all your loyal *followers* will desert you like rats from a sinking ship." His voice dripped contempt. "By yourself, you're nothing."

The smile was wiped from Pennington's face as if it had never been there, and he took a step toward Reilly. "Nothing? Is that what you call a man who holds the power of life and death over you? Nothing?"

"A man?" Reilly spat at Pennington's feet. "You're not a man. You're nothing but a worm who doesn't even believe in the cause he espouses, who uses it and the people who *do* believe for his own perverted purposes."

"That's enough!" Pennington backhanded Reilly across the mouth in sudden fury.

Even though he'd been deliberately goading the other man toward something like this, the blow staggered Reilly, and he would have fallen if Walker hadn't held him up. When he could stand unaided, he wrenched free from Walker and confronted his adversary. "Is that the best you can do, Pennington?'' he taunted. "Or don't you have the guts to kill me yourself?''

Pennington stepped back, rubbing his knuckles and breathing hard. "Just killing you isn't enough. I swore I would see you burn in hell, Callahan, and that's just what I'm going to do. Carl,'' he snapped. "Bring the truck around.''

The minute the man with the Uzi turned and faded into the shadows, Reilly said, "You're taking quite a chance killing me in front of witnesses, aren't you? You never used to be so careless.'' A smile of derision played over his lips. "Or maybe you trust these men implicitly.'' Reilly paused, letting suspicion take its toll before adding softly, "Just like you trusted me.''

"Shut your mouth.''

Reilly ignored the warning. "But then, that was before you went to *prison*, wasn't it?'' He cocked his head. "How did you like prison, Pennington? How did you like being locked up with the rest of the scum? Make any new…friends?''

Pennington lost it completely. "Shut up!'' he raged, the cords standing out in his neck. "Just shut up!''

"Or what?'' Reilly put every ounce of scorn he could muster into harsh laughter. "You'll kill me?'' He laughed again. "You miserable piece of sh—''

"Put a bullet in his head if he opens his mouth again,'' Pennington ordered Walker.

Reilly half turned, his eyes meeting Walker's, who nodded and raised his gun.

"No, Cody! No!''

Reilly pivoted toward the direction Mandy's voice had come from, not quite believing he'd really heard it. "What the hell?''

A shot split the night, slamming into Walker, spinning him around and sending him sprawling. The revolver flew from his hand and skittered out of reach when he went down. Reilly frantically thumbed the button that released the catch on his fake handcuffs, then dove for Walker's gun, coming up with it just as another shot rang out. This one ricocheted off the wall behind Pennington, barely missing him. Pennington drew his own weapon and ducked behind one of the pipelines, firing in Mandy's direction as he went.

Raw fear surged through Reilly as he realized that Mandy was Pennington's target. He didn't know how she'd come to be there, or why, but unless he did something to distract Pennington, she might not make it out alive.

But he couldn't ignore the rapidly spreading splotch of dark color staining Walker's left shoulder, either. It didn't look good for his temporary partner. The man was already unconscious or in shock, and that shoulder needed medical attention—fast. Barring that, someone needed to stop the bleeding at least, or *he* wasn't going to make it out alive.

Half expecting to be brought down by gunfire from either Pennington or his henchman, Reilly grabbed Walker by the collar and quickly dragged him around the corner of the building to relative safety. The movement jolted Walker into painful consciousness, but he clamped his jaw shut until they'd reached the shadows.

"Forget me," Walker gasped, clutching at Reilly's arm to stop him as he ripped open the man's shirt to see how badly he'd been injured. "Mandy's out there."

"You think I don't know that?" Reilly muttered, swiftly stripping off his own jacket and wadding it up, then pressing it hard against the wound. Walker's body arched in agony, every muscle taut, then his eyes rolled back in his head and he sagged into unconsciousness again.

Reilly yanked Walker's belt off and hurriedly strapped it as tight as he could around the bunched jacket and Walker's shoulder in a makeshift pressure bandage. It might not do the trick, but he had no more time to waste.

He took his .45 from Walker, preferring the familiar weight and feel of the semiautomatic that seemed to be a natural extension of his arm over the sheriff's equally powerful revolver. He kept the other gun nevertheless, caching it in his jeans at the small of his back, just in case. Then he went after Pennington.

There had been no more gunshots after the first exchange, but Reilly wasn't stupid enough to think Pennington had given up. He stole around the other side of the building toward Mandy's last known position. She wasn't there.

Damn it, Mandy, he cursed internally, his brain teeming with questions while his body automatically continued searching for Pennington. *Why didn't you do what you were supposed to do? Why didn't you just stay the hell away from here?* Cursing her was better than imagining her bleeding to death the same way he'd left Walker.

But she *had* come, for some reason known only to her, and she'd obviously misinterpreted what was going down. The alterations they'd made to the plan on the way here in order to allay any suspicions Pennington had about Centurion must have been more convincing than they'd realized, if they'd managed to convince Mandy, too. But damn it all, the basic plan hadn't changed, and she'd been there when they'd mapped it out. What was going on?

Reilly's lips compressed into a grim line. His Mandy had a lot of explaining to do when this was over. If any of them were still alive when this was over, that was.

The generators and hydraulic pumps hummed and throbbed, providing Reilly with the audile cover he needed as he stalked his prey from building to building. That it also gave Pennington the same advantage was something he refused to worry about. He just wished he knew where Mandy was; she seemed to have disappeared. She *couldn't* be dead—somehow he'd know it if she was. But if Pennington found her before he found Pennington...

Reilly glanced at his watch and cursed again. Where the hell were the reinforcements Walker had arranged for? Yes, Pennington had surprised them both by showing up earlier than expected, but the backup team should have been here by now to assist with Pennington's arrest. And there was Walker to consider, too, damn it. The wound had looked

pretty bad, and there was no telling how much blood he'd
lost by now. Walker didn't have a prayer if those reinforcements didn't show up soon.

Or maybe the reverse is true, Reilly thought. *Maybe
we're all better off if they* don't *show up. If Pennington has
one federal marshal in his pocket, maybe he has others,
too.*

Cold resolution filled him, and he instantly shifted from
Plan A to Plan B. *Arresting* Pennington was no longer an
option.

Mandy clutched Reilly's gun and scrunched down even
more, trying to squeeze herself further into the small niche
between Pump #2's generator and the pump housing, which
she'd long ago discovered made a great hiding place. But
she wasn't a ten-year-old anymore, and she didn't quite fit.
Still, Reilly was probably better off with her out of the way,
and this was better than nothing, even though the noise was
horrendous close up. If she didn't move she might escape
detection while she figured out what to do next.

I could have planned this better, she thought, *if only I'd
had more time. But at least Reilly got away. At least he
has a fighting chance now.*

She had to keep reminding herself of that. She had to.
Otherwise, the nightmare memory of the instant when the
bullet she'd fired ripped into Cody's body would over-
whelm her.

Shooting him hadn't even been a conscious decision.
She'd known as soon as she heard the voices that she was
too late to warn Reilly. So she had crept as close to the
four men as she'd dared, waiting for an opportunity to rescue him somehow. But when the man with the machine
gun had left and Pennington had ordered Cody to shoot
Reilly, time had run out. She'd acted on instinct, shouting
something—she wasn't sure what—and stepping away
from the building for a better shot. Her hands unexpectedly
steady, her vision clear, she'd sighted down the barrel of

the gun Reilly claimed had never let him down. Then pulled the trigger.

Only afterward, when she saw Cody fall, had she realized what she'd done. Only then had her eyes blurred as memories of Cody flashed through her mind: exploring with her when they were children; warning her dates that they'd better not mess with her or else; holding her as she cried at her parents' funeral. He'd been her friend forever, and she'd killed him.

And then she'd taken aim at Pennington, with true murderous intent. *He* was to blame. *He* had turned her friend into an enemy, forcing her to take a human life. *He* had tried to kill the man she loved, again and again. And *he* was responsible for the loss of her baby. Not Reilly. *Pennington.*

God forgive her, but at that moment she'd hated David Pennington with a ferocity, a *savagery* that stunned her to remember. In her mind he'd been evil incarnate, and she'd been more than willing to be his judge, jury and executioner. She'd wanted to kill him. Had meant to kill him. But her tears had blinded her just enough to throw off her aim and allow him to escape.

Now, as she crouched here, muscles burning from lack of movement, ears straining to hear something over the deafening sounds of water being pumped right next to her, she finally understood Reilly. Finally understood how easily the thin veneer of civilization could be stripped away, leaving nothing but primal instinct and emotion.

I won't let them hurt you. I'll kill them all before I'll let them touch you, Reilly had said once, and she'd been appalled at the time. She'd thought she understood what he meant by that statement later, the night Cody unexpectedly showed up at the cabin, but she hadn't really. Hadn't even come close.

I'm sorry, Reilly, she apologized in her mind, wondering if she'd ever have the chance to apologize for real. *I didn't understand before.*

A slight movement at the corner of her eye caught her
attention, and she froze. Too late she realized she was
wedged in too tightly, that she'd trapped herself with her
gun hand on the inside. Then a backlit shadow loomed over
her.

Chapter 17

"Callahan!"

The triumphant voice rang out loud and clear, and Reilly flattened himself against the nearest wall, .45 at the ready, waiting to see what Pennington was up to.

"I have the woman, Callahan."

Only years of training kept the sudden roaring sound in Reilly's head from erupting to the heavens in an outcry of anguished rage.

"Come out where I can see you," Pennington continued, "unless you don't care what happens to her."

The threat sliced through the mindless terror and helpless fury that held Reilly in their sway. He breathed deeply a couple of times, forcing everything from his mind but the need for control, knowing they were all dead unless he managed it. His eyes squeezed shut for a second. *Don't let it get to you,* he commanded himself. *Deal with it.* But it was the hardest thing he'd ever done.

He edged over to the corner of the building, almost surprised that his muscles obeyed because his body seemed to be functioning separately from his mind. Then he peered around. "Let me see her," he yelled. "I'll come out when I know she's okay."

"No Reilly! Don't—" Mandy's attempted warning ended on a cry of pain, and the sound twisted through Reilly's gut.

"Let me see her, Pennington, or it's no deal," he insisted.

Mandy suddenly appeared from behind a building on the other side of the compound, and though Pennington was too smart to show himself as a target, Reilly could see one of the man's hands curled around Mandy's neck, with the other holding a gun pressed against her head.

"Let her go, Pennington," Reilly called out, even though he knew it was useless. "I'm the one you want."

Pennington's mocking laughter ripped through the air. "Not a chance, Callahan. Now come out with your hands up."

Reilly started to comply, then paused. Knowing it probably wouldn't make a difference, he pulled Walker's revolver out from behind his back and tucked his own .45 in its place. Pennington was sure to make Reilly dispose of whatever weapon he carried, and he'd rather give up the revolver. Switching guns was no more than a tiny advantage, but sometimes that was the difference between life and death.

"Five seconds, Callahan!" Pennington's voice had lost its mocking tone and had taken on a nervous edge. "Five seconds, or—"

Reilly stepped out into the light, hands raised.

"Walk toward me," came the order, and Reilly complied, although he remained on the alert for any possibility. After ten paces, Pennington said, "That's far enough."

Reilly stopped. He was close enough to see the despair on Mandy's face, close enough to see the desperate pleading in her eyes. *Go back,* they seemed to say, and it was almost as if she'd spoken the words aloud. *I love you, so please go back.* And for the first time in his life he knew, really *knew* that he was loved the way he'd always yearned to be.

A peaceful calm descended on him, and for a few precious seconds the world around them faded away, leaving only Mandy and him. Heart spoke to heart, soul to soul. And when they were done Reilly knew that no matter what lay beyond this life, somehow, some way, they'd be together. Forever.

"Put the gun on the ground!"

Pennington's sharp command intruded on their silent communion. Reilly's eyes held Mandy's for one more second, then he obeyed, squatting down and placing the revolver at his feet.

"Now move back," Pennington said when Reilly stood up again, and he did just that, slowly easing himself away from the gun until the other man said, "Stop!"

Pushing Mandy before him, the gun now pressed against her spine, Pennington inched out from behind the building. Reilly automatically calculated the distance and the angle of the shot he would have to make to take the man out without endangering Mandy, and metaphorically shook his head. Pennington's height and build were only slightly above average for a man, and Mandy was tall for a woman—she made an effective shield for him. Reilly wasn't about to risk a shot. Not yet.

Pennington halted when they reached the revolver, and Reilly's flare of hope died almost before it was born when the man forced Mandy down with him to retrieve the gun. Pennington obviously wasn't taking any chances, even though Reilly was supposed to be unarmed, and Reilly would have approved his caution if they weren't adversaries.

"It's too bad you can't appreciate the poetic justice of this situation," Pennington said, gloating again. "All this time I waited, because I wanted my revenge to be perfect. If I'd known about your weakness earlier, I could have put you in hell a long time ago."

Although Reilly knew exactly what Pennington was talking about, he refused to rise to the bait.

"All I had to do was kill her," Pennington continued, bringing his gun up to stroke Mandy's cheek with it. "Isn't that right, Callahan?"

Above the noise of the pumps and the generators, and the blood pounding in his ears, Reilly now heard the sound of an engine laboring up the incline to the front gate.

Pennington must have heard it, too, because satisfaction was evident in his voice when he spoke again. "I thought I was going to have to forego the full measure of my revenge," he said, "but there's Carl, just in time." He relaxed his guard a fraction and took a step back, pulling Mandy with him.

The move shifted his position behind her slightly, and Reilly's eyes noted it, but it wasn't enough. *Come on, you son of a bitch,* he urged, easing his weight onto the balls of his feet and imperceptibly lowering his arms. *Just another few inches to your right. That's all I need.*

"Carl's not as knowledgeable as you are, Callahan," Pennington continued, "nor as good with weapons. But he is more—shall we say—*reliable?* than you ever were."

Headlights swung over the compound as the truck made the final turn toward the gate, and the engine revved.

"That's the difference between us," Pennington added, the ice-cold smile back in place. "I learn from my mistakes. You don't." And he leveled his gun at Reilly.

Everything happened in the space of a heartbeat as Reilly dove for cover, his .45 already drawn. Mandy tore away from Pennington's grasp and threw herself to the right, knocking his arm up just as he fired. The truck burst through the closed gate, tearing out sections of the chain-link fence as it roared into the compound. A flash of silver flew out of the shadows, quicker than the eye could follow. And Reilly squeezed the trigger.

Pennington's body arched backward a split second before the bullet found its target, spinning him around and slamming him into the wall. He dropped the gun and staggered a step or two, clawing at his chest, where a dark stain was rapidly spreading over the front of his khaki shirt. His expression of utter surprise gave way to blankness and he dropped to his knees, then toppled forward, a knife handle protruding from his back.

Gun in hand, Reilly sprinted toward Mandy, pulling her to her feet. "Run!" he shouted, pushing her behind him, shielding her from the barrage of gunfire he expected to explode from the truck any second.

Instead, half a dozen men, faces blackened and with guns drawn, swarmed out of the back. "Federal marshals," barked the nearest man, flashing a badge when Reilly drew a bead on him.

"It's okay, Callahan," called another, the driver of the truck. "We're the good guys."

Reilly's eyes widened as he recognized Trace McKinnon beneath the camouflaging paint, but he didn't lower his guard just yet. "What took you so long?"

"We picked up Walsh ten minutes ago," McKinnon explained. "And there was the little matter of defusing the nasty surprise Pennington had cooked up for you. Is that him over there?"

"It's him, all right," confirmed a third man, kicking Pennington's weapons out of reach, then kneeling beside him and feeling for a pulse that was no longer there. "He's dead."

Reilly blinked. The man kneeling beside Pennington needed no artificial blacking to cloak his face for night maneuvers, and Reilly recognized him, too. But Nick D'Arcy didn't handle field assignments anymore. What the hell was he doing here?

Reilly asked the question out loud, not bothering to hide his suspicion, and without even looking up D'Arcy said, "After Walker called, I decided I wasn't trusting this assignment to anyone else, and it's a damn good thing, too."

D'Arcy slipped a thin rubber glove over one hand, grasped the haft of the knife buried in Pennington's back, and pulled. The knife's six-inch blade slid out of the body with a sickening sound, accompanied by a small gush of blood, and Mandy gasped.

That was when Reilly realized she hadn't run when he'd told her to. He turned and swept an arm around her, pressing her face against his shoulder. Over her head, his eyes flew from the familiar-looking knife in D'Arcy's hand to the direction it had come from earlier. Walker stood there, half in shadow, clinging to the corner of the building, his face paper-white.

"McKinnon!" Reilly yelled, quickly locating the man and jerking his head toward Walker. McKinnon reached Walker's side just in time to catch him as he fell.

Events moved swiftly after that. D'Arcy radioed instructions, then briefed Reilly while McKinnon and Mandy did what they could for Walker. It seemed no time at all before a medevac chopper was landing on the other side of the fence, then lifting off for Sheridan carrying Walker, in stable condition, and Pennington's body.

When the chopper banked hard and whirled off into the darkness, Mandy's weary eyes followed it for a moment. Then she turned back toward Reilly. "Hold me," she pleaded. He held out his arms and she walked into his embrace.

She clung to him in silence for several minutes, and he was content to just stand there holding her. Both were oblivious to the bustle around them as the marshals continued their thorough search of each of the buildings in the enclosure.

When Mandy finally raised her head, her expression held joy and wonder in equal parts. "You're alive," she breathed, touching his face as if she still couldn't quite believe it. "I was so afraid I was going to have to watch you die again, but you're alive."

"Yeah," he said, with a husky catch in his throat. "Thanks to you and Walker."

Her face clouded up with remorse. "Thank God I didn't kill Cody," she said. "I thought for sure I had."

Another voice broke in on their conversation. "It would

take more than a bullet in the shoulder to kill Cody Walker," Nick D'Arcy said. "He's one tough SOB." The way he said it, the crude appellation was a token of admiration and respect.

"Listen," he continued. "We've just about wrapped things up here, but we'll need official statements from both of you." He noted Mandy's weariness and Reilly's protective stance, then amended, "I guess it won't hurt to wait until tomorrow. I've got a command post set up in Sheridan. Here's the address," he said, scribbling furiously on a pad of paper, then tearing off the sheet and handing it to Reilly. "I'll expect both of you there by ten."

Mandy waited until D'Arcy had rejoined his men, then looked up at Reilly. "You know," she said, brushing her wind-tangled hair away from her face with complete disregard for her appearance. "You still haven't explained what happened here."

Reilly snorted. "That's just what I was going to ask you. I know Walker and I weren't playing the scene the way we planned last night, but what made you shoot him?"

"When I saw him raise his gun, I thought he was going to kill you."

"I figured that out already. But why? And while we're on the subject, how about explaining what you were doing here in the first place."

"All those guns," she said obscurely. "And plastic explosives. I had to warn you."

"You want to run that by me again?"

Mandy sighed. "I found guns and plastic explosives underneath Cody's cabin earlier. I wasn't sure what to believe, but all I could think of was that he must be a member of the New World Militia. All the pieces seemed to fit. And if he was leading you into a trap…"

"Oh, hell," Reilly said without heat, rubbing a hand over his face.

"What? What is it?"

He looked down at her. "You're not going to like this."

"Just tell me, whatever it is."

He took a deep breath. "Walker's been working under-cover for the past four years, ever since he was first recruited by the militia," he said, then waited for the explosion.

"What?" Mandy's astonishment soon turned to narrow-eyed displeasure, and she leaned back a little to glare at him.

"That was the other reason why I moved to Black Rock in the first place," he added quickly, hoping to distract her. "It was D'Arcy's idea. He figured if Pennington tracked me out here, at the very least Walker would hear about it and be able to warn me in time to escape. It was a bonus that Pennington assigned Walker the job of getting rid of me last year."

Her glare became even more pronounced. "Why didn't you tell me?"

Reilly winced. "It wasn't my secret to tell—it was Walker's."

"Don't give me that," she said, treating his weak defense with the disdain it deserved. "That's the last time—the *last* time, you hear?—that you keep a secret from me. I want your word on it."

Reilly pulled her closer, then bent and surprised her with a kiss. "I'll have them put it into our wedding vows," he assured her.

"I mean it," she declared. "I want your promise and I want it—" She stopped abruptly, the lines of her face softening in vulnerability. "What did you just say?"

Her reaction was better than he'd hoped for, and he smiled down at her. "I said I'll have them put it into our wedding vows."

"We're getting married." She seemed dazed by the realization, and her voice trembled a little. "Yes," she said softly, her eyes shining now as if lit from within. "We're getting married."

Then her inner glow dimmed, and as he watched, a somber, almost wistful expression crept over her face. "But—"

she started, then cut off the rest, appearing to be wrestling with some inner dilemma for a moment.

"Mandy?"

She shrugged off whatever was bothering her. "Yes," she repeated. "Of course."

Her quick smile might have fooled someone who didn't know her, but not Reilly. He lifted her chin so she had to look him in the eye. "What's wrong, darlin'?"

She shook her head. "It's nothing."

Reilly thought he understood, and could have kicked himself. "I'm sorry, Mandy. That wasn't very romantic, was it?" He shifted self-consciously and gave a rueful laugh. "My only excuse is that I've never asked anyone to marry me before, and it just sort of…slipped out that way."

She cupped his cheek, her eyes glistening all of a sudden. "It was romantic," she insisted. "You have nothing to apologize for." She blinked away the tears, then added, "As a matter of fact, it's the other way around."

"What is?"

"I'm the one who owes you an apology. I promised myself earlier I'd do it the first chance I had. If I had the chance. But I think I'm too tired to apologize properly."

"Apologize? What for?"

A couple of marshals passed them, and Mandy glanced around. Others were headed their way, and she shook her head again. "Not here."

"Where, then? Walker's cabin?"

"No, not yet." She looked off into the distance for a moment, as if she could see beyond the darkness, and breathed deeply. Then, with a wistfulness that pierced what few defenses he had left, she said, "Take me home, Reilly."

"Mandy, no." He didn't want her to see what he'd seen the other day, didn't want her to be reminded of everything she'd lost. Not tonight. "It's late. You're worn out. And there's nothing there anymore."

"I know." Her expression held understanding. "I know it's late, and we're both tired, and it's a long drive back and we have to get up early tomorrow. I know all of that. But I still want to go home, even if it's just for a few minutes." Her eyes beseeched him. "Please, Reilly. Please take me home."

Reilly surveyed the charred ruins of Mandy's house in the pale light of a half-hidden moon. There was an almost ghostly quality about it, with the few timbers still standing reflecting what moonlight there was with the silvery-gray luminescence of a black pearl.

With all his heart he wished he hadn't brought her here. Just knowing about the destruction was bad enough. Seeing it was worse. It was a sad end for the house that had sheltered her and her family for almost a hundred years, and he wondered what was going through her mind as she stood there, lost in thought. She hadn't said a word since their arrival, and her silence weighed heavy on him.

"We were lucky to get out alive," he said eventually, unable to bear the silence any longer.

"No," Mandy answered softly. "Not lucky. Blessed." She turned toward him. "And not just that night, but tonight, too. And every day in between. When I think what could have happened, losing my home seems a relatively small price to pay."

He held out his hand, needing the physical contact with her, and she twined her fingers with his. "So you don't blame me anymore?"

"No, I don't blame you for anything anymore," she said, squeezing his hand reassuringly. Her eyes, though rimmed with the signs of fatigue, were clear and unshadowed. "That's what I wanted to apologize for. I judged you harshly in the past, and I'm sorry. I didn't understand. But now I do."

Reilly suspected there was a lot she wasn't telling him, but decided further explanations could wait for another time, when she wasn't so worn out.

"Come on," he said, putting his arm around her and

leading her unresistingly toward his truck. "What you need right now is sleep. And so do I."

At the last minute Mandy turned her head for one more view of the wreckage, then tore her eyes away. With false brightness, she said, "I guess there's one good thing about being burned out of house and home—I don't have anything left to pack."

Reilly frowned. "Pack?" His tired brain wasn't functioning properly anymore. "Where are you going?"

She threw him a puzzled look. "What do you mean, where am I going? I'm going wherever *you're* going." When he continued staring at her blankly, she explained patiently, "You said you couldn't stay in Black Rock, so I just wanted to come back home one last time before we moved on. I didn't know if I'd have the chance later."

The light dawned for him. "Is that why you were upset tonight when I mentioned marriage? Because you thought you'd have to leave Black Rock?" He relaxed and shook his head. "We're not going anywhere."

"But yesterday you said—"

"Yesterday Pennington was still alive, and I didn't know who had betrayed me to him." He leaned against the fender and drew her next to him. "About the only thing I knew for sure was that it *wasn't* Walker—he didn't know I was returning here for you. Only D'Arcy and McKinnon knew that, and if either one of them had been the traitor, Black Rock wouldn't be safe for us."

"How do you know it wasn't them?"

"Walker convinced me. He pointed out that D'Arcy and McKinnon knew he was working undercover, knew he'd helped me set up my escape a year ago. But Pennington never knew that, because if he had, the militia would have tried to kill Walker, too. He also reminded me that both men have known where I was ever since then, but Pennington never tracked me down until now.

"We tested them anyway, just to be on the safe side," he added, running the back of one finger along the delicate curve of her cheek, "because we weren't taking chances with your life. They both passed with flying colors."

"So who was it? Do you know?"

He nodded. "D'Arcy told me tonight while you and McKinnon were working on Walker. They traced the leak to some wet-behind-the-ears law clerk in the Justice Department who shot his mouth off to the wrong person. Can you believe it?" He made a sound of mild disgust over the stupidity that had almost cost them their lives.

"How did this law clerk find out about you?"

"Remember when I told you the list of suspects had expanded once I found out Pennington was getting a new trial?" he asked. Mandy nodded. "Well, it turns out I was right. The prosecution team panicked, thinking they had no case without me, so D'Arcy was forced to admit I was still alive. It was all supposed to be kept under wraps until I was back in protective custody, but as I said, this kid let it slip. D'Arcy couldn't reach me, but he knew where I was headed, so he sent a couple of his most trusted men to bring me in. One was McKinnon. The other was Larry Brooks."

"Brooks? But wasn't that the man Pennington said—"

"Yeah." He shook his head over the irony of it. "Brooks was Pennington's man on the inside, the one who betrayed my whereabouts the last time. He had no idea I was still alive until D'Arcy sent him after me. And from what D'Arcy tells me, it's a good bet Brooks was involved in the attack on us the other night."

Reilly's expression turned grim. "Brooks and McKinnon were watching your house in shifts," he said, "waiting for me to show up. McKinnon found him after the fire, bound, gagged, and supposedly unconscious, but there were a couple of things that made McKinnon suspicious, and he reported them to D'Arcy. They've been watching Brooks closely ever since, and he finally slipped up tonight."

Mandy sighed and sagged against Reilly in relief, resting her head against his shoulder. "So it's finally over."

"Yeah." He stroked her hair absently. "Brooks and Walsh are both in custody, and D'Arcy's fairly confident

Brooks, at least, will break under questioning and name names. Even if he doesn't, without Pennington's money and power backing them, it's not very likely the militia will come after me again. So it's really over.''

She sighed again, and the movement made him even more aware of her breasts pressing against his chest through the barriers of their clothing. His pulse speeded up, despite his exhaustion, and his body reacted in other ways, too. But he wasn't surprised.

Guess I'd have to be six feet under not *to react to her,* Reilly told himself, and his arms tightened around Mandy as he remembered just how close he'd come to that fate tonight. And what would have been far worse, how close he'd come to losing her.

''So what happens now?'' she asked after a moment.

He remembered her asking a similar question yesterday, and his response. But everything had changed since then, and he no longer had a ready answer.

Reilly gazed out over the top of her head toward the burned-out shell that had been Mandy's home, and his, too, for a brief span of time. There was an ache in the region of his heart that he'd refused to recognize before, but now the emotions he'd denied for so long rushed toward him, and he didn't have the strength to resist.

Mandy had been so proud of this house, not because it belonged to her, but for the heritage it symbolized. She'd recounted its history to him bit by bit over the months he'd known her, often by firelight, and he had vivid memories of watching the play of light and shadow over her emotive face. A natural storyteller, she'd delighted in bringing to life for him the generations of men and women who had lived here, each one leaving something of him or herself behind for the generations yet to come.

The lonely, rootless orphan inside the man without a name had listened intently, and remembered. And yearned to belong.

This house had stood steadfast as the mountain on which it was built through local uprisings and world wars and everything in between. It had survived blizzards, droughts, forest fires and landslides. But it hadn't survived the advent of one Ryan Patrick Callahan.

That was the Irish in him talking, Reilly acknowledged, that sort of fatalistic whimsy his father had indulged in on occasion. Strange he should think of that now.

Cool night air surged into his lungs as he breathed deeply. The crisp, clean scent he associated with the mountains was overlaid with faint traces of wood smoke and ashes, and both mingled with the soft, warm fragrance of lilacs and woman that was Mandy's alone, imprinting themselves on his memory. In that moment a lifetime of inchoate dreams and longings coalesced at last, and the answer he'd been searching for suddenly came to him.

"I know what I want to happen," he said with conviction, and Mandy raised sleepy eyes to his. She blinked at him curiously, as if he'd taken so long to answer she'd forgotten the question she'd asked, and he added, "But it's your decision."

She blinked again, then smiled, a slow, breathtaking process that raised his physical awareness of her several notches, and tugged at his defenseless heart.

"No," she said. "It's your decision, whatever it is. As long as we're together, nothing else matters to me."

"This might," he insisted.

"Then tell me."

"I'd like to take a crack at rebuilding that house over there," he said. "If you'll let me." Her eyes widened, but she said nothing. "I know how much it meant to you," he explained. "It meant a lot to me, too, more than you know. More than *I* knew."

He paused, wishing he were better at expressing his feelings, hoping that somehow she understood what he wanted to say but had no words for.

"I can't replace the heirlooms you lost," he continued, "but you still have the memories, the stories to pass on to the next generation. And once we rebuild, we can start fresh. Together we can create memories and heirlooms of our own to leave to our children, and their children after them." Emotion spilled out of his heart, roughening his next words. "Will you do that with me, Mandy? Will you?"

Lovingly she traced the contours of his face, subtly reminding him of everything he'd gone through to reach this moment with her. "You know I will," she said simply. "But is this what you really want? Don't say it just because you think it's what I want."

He threaded his fingers through her hair and tilted her face up for a lingering kiss. "It's what I've always wanted," he confessed. "A place to call home. I just didn't know it until I met you." The admission shattered the last barricade inside him, and the words finally broke free. "I've been running all my life, Mandy," he whispered, "searching for someplace to belong. But my running days are over. No place I go will ever be home unless you're there. So I'm staying right here. With you."

Epilogue

"Reiiil-lyyyy!" Mandy's distant voice, carrying a hint of exasperation, trickled through the closed workshop door. "Ryyyy-aaaan!"

Ryan Callahan shaved another wooden curl off the maple plank destined to become a part of a bunk bed, then put the plane down and straightened, wiping the sweat from his brow with his forearm. He glanced over at the towheaded boy perched on a sawhorse watching him, then at the toddler picking wood shavings out of the sawdust.

"Your mother's calling you, boys," he said. He checked his watch. "It's bath time. Better go on up to the house."

"Oh, Da, do we have to?" objected four-year-old Reilly, hopping down from the sawhorse. "I don't wanna take a bath." He rubbed his faintly grimy arms on his shirt. "See? I'm not dirty." And little Ryan, who loved baths but who adored his big brother even more and tried to copy everything he did, echoed, "Not duhdy."

"You know the rules," Ryan firmly reminded his sons. "Now scoot."

They trotted off and Ryan put away his tools, then made

his way toward the house, the sight of which never failed to fill him with satisfaction.

Rebuilding hadn't been easy, especially since he'd insisted on doing the bulk of the work himself. But he'd finished before the first snows came, and his pride in his accomplishment had been unequalled. Until his children had come along, that was.

Lord, was there anything in the whole world comparable to the thrill of watching your child being born, knowing that you'd played a part, however small, in creating that tiny life? If there was, Ryan had never found it, unless you counted the far different thrill of the creation process— making love to Mandy. His wife.

His wife. Going on for five years now, he realized, with a surprised shake of his head. Five years. Who could have foreseen back then that things would turn out as well as they had?

The New World Militia had fallen apart after Pennington's death, just as he'd predicted, helped along by the plea-bargained testimony of Walsh and Brooks regarding the militia's secret activities, including illegal drug trafficking. The authorities were still keeping a watchful eye on certain individuals, and Ryan still packed a gun—he was too much of a cop to ever relax his vigilance that much, and life was doubly precious to a man who had so many hostages to fortune—but he was breathing easier these days.

Cody Walker had completely recovered from his wounds, and shortly thereafter had resigned as sheriff to take a job with the Drug Enforcement Administration. Before he'd left, though, Walker had recommended Ryan as his replacement, a position Ryan still held.

Mandy still owned the Book Nook, although she'd shifted to part-time work once their second child had made his debut into the world.

Ryan smiled to himself. Five years, two children, and another on the way. A girl this time, he hoped. A miniature version of Mandy....

* * *

This was the best time of day, Ryan thought much later, as he walked into the bedroom after his shower and found Mandy undressing there. He came up behind her and slid his arms around her expanded waistline, caressing the warm skin over the slight outward curve caused by her pregnancy. The thought of his child growing safe and secure inside her was as miraculous to him this third time around as it had been the first, and his contentment deepened.

"Did you check on the boys?" he asked.

"Sound asleep, both of them."

"That's good." He nuzzled her ear the way he knew she loved and she shivered.

"Mmm." She tilted her head to give him better access, but sighed wistfully. "They're both growing so fast. Reilly's off the charts and little Ryan can hardly be called little. I looked at him tonight and I realized he's not a baby anymore."

"No, he's not." Ryan placed a hand over her stomach. "But in four months you'll be glad for that."

Mandy smiled and turned within the circle of his arms. "You always know the right thing to say."

"Miracles do happen, then."

She chuckled, a rich, contented sound that affected him deep inside, as it always did. His arms tightened around her and his tone shifted from lighthearted teasing to intense emotion held sternly in check.

"You're *my* miracle, Mandy. You know that, don't you? I probably don't say it enough, but—"

"Often enough for me."

"No one has ever loved me the way you do, and I don't ever want to lose you, or your love." He rested his forehead against hers. In a hushed voice, as if he were revealing a well-kept secret, he said, "For the longest time I was afraid to believe I could have it all."

Mandy cradled his face in her hands and kissed him. "Do you believe now?" she whispered, placing his hand over the child she carried in her womb, and reminding him at the same time of the two who slept so peacefully just down the hall. All three created from their love. "Do you believe enough now?"

"Oh, yeah," he said, pushing the words past the unexpected constriction in his throat. He saw his future spread out before him—laughter and love, and children growing up, and growing old together, and starting all over again with grandchildren—on and on in the endless kaleidoscope of life. "Oh, yeah," Ryan repeated, wrapping both arms around Mandy. "I believe."

And he smiled.

* * * * *

Daniel MacGregor is at it again...

New York Times bestselling author

NORA ROBERTS

introduces us to a new generation of MacGregors
as the lovable patriarch of the illustrious MacGregor
clan plays matchmaker again, this time to his three
gorgeous granddaughters in

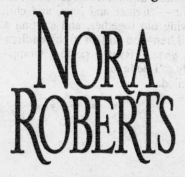

From Silhouette Books

Don't miss this brand-new continuation of Nora Roberts's
enormously popular *MacGregor* miniseries.

Available November 1997 at your favorite retail outlet.

Take 4 bestselling love stories FREE

Plus get a FREE surprise gift!

Special Limited-time Offer

Mail to Silhouette Reader Service™

3010 Walden Avenue
P.O. Box 1867
Buffalo, N.Y. 14240-1867

YES! Please send me 4 free Silhouette Intimate Moments® novels and my free surprise gift. Then send me 6 brand-new novels every month, which I will receive months before they appear in bookstores. Bill me at the low price of $3.34 each plus 25¢ delivery and applicable sales tax, if any.* That's the complete price and a savings of over 10% off the cover prices—quite a bargain! I understand that accepting the books and gift places me under no obligation ever to buy any books. I can always return a shipment and cancel at any time. Even if I never buy another book from Silhouette, the 4 free books and the surprise gift are mine to keep forever.

245 BPA A3UW

Name	(PLEASE PRINT)	
Address		Apt. No.
City	State	Zip

This offer is limited to one order per household and not valid to present Silhouette Intimate Moments® subscribers. *Terms and prices are subject to change without notice. Sales tax applicable in N.Y.

UMOM-696 ©1990 Harlequin Enterprises Limited

SILHOUETTE WOMEN KNOW ROMANCE WHEN THEY SEE IT.

And they'll see it on **ROMANCE CLASSICS**, the new 24-hour TV channel devoted to romantic movies and original programs like the special **Romantically Speaking—Harlequin™ Goes Prime Time**.

Romantically Speaking—Harlequin™ Goes Prime Time introduces you to many of your favorite romance authors in a program developed exclusively for Harlequin® and Silhouette® readers.

Watch for **Romantically Speaking—Harlequin™ Goes Prime Time** beginning in the summer of 1997.

If you're not receiving ROMANCE CLASSICS, call your local cable operator or satellite provider and ask for it today!

Escape to the network of your dreams.

See Ingrid Bergman and Gregory Peck in *Spellbound* on Romance Classics.

Share in the joy of yuletide romance with brand-new
stories by two of the genre's most beloved writers

DIANA PALMER

and

JOAN JOHNSTON

in

LONE STAR CHRISTMAS

Diana Palmer and Joan Johnston share their favorite
Christmas anecdotes and personal stories in this
special hardbound edition.

Diana Palmer delivers an irresistible spin-off of her
LONG, TALL TEXANS series and Joan Johnston crafts an
unforgettable new chapter to **HAWK'S WAY** in this wonderful
keepsake edition celebrating the holiday season. So
perfect for gift giving, you'll want one for yourself...and
one to give to a special friend!

Available in November at your favorite retail outlet!

Only from

Silhouette®